PRAISE FOR CARRIE STUART PARKS

"Danger and drama abide in this tale that takes a walk on the perilous side. With a flair for the macabre, the story will linger in your head long after the last page."

—Steve Berry, *New York Times* and #1 Internationally bestselling author, for *Relative Silence*

"*Relative Silence* is one of the most engrossing suspense novels I've read in a long time. Pitch perfect pacing and characterization along with Parks' knowledgeable hand with forensics kept me on the edge of my seat. If you enjoy suspense with a light touch of romance, you must read this one!"

—Colleen Coble, *USA TODAY* bestselling author of *One Little Lie* and the Lavender Tide series

"The perfect beach read! *Relative Silence* is an expert mix of family drama and slow-burning thriller, leavened with Parks' trademark humor. You'll be pulling for Piper and Tucker as the story builds toward a hurricane-force climax."

—Rick Acker, bestselling author

"With skill and her ever-present wit, Carrie Stuart Parks has arranged puzzle pieces and woven story threads into an engaging and quick-moving read with tantalizing questions, quirky characters, and . . . oh yes, some well-placed fictional curve balls along the way. Enjoy!"

—Frank Peretti, bestselling author, for *Relative Silence*

"What a great book! Carrie Stuart Parks has done it again. *Relative Silence* offers us characters we care about, a convoluted and clever plot, and hours of reading pleasure. Highly recommended."

—Gayle Roper, author of *Lost and Found* and *Hide and Seek*

"*Relative Silence* has all the bells and whistles. A relatable character in Piper Boone, a plot that keeps moving forward, and a surprising finish. It was hard to put down. A completely satisfying read. I highly recommend it!"

—Nancy Mehl, bestselling, award-winning author

"What a compelling story! I rarely read a book all in one sitting, but Parks' combination of intriguing plot, vivid setting, and characters you can't help but root for kept me turning the pages right through the very-satisfying ending. I highly recommend this excellent read!"

—Marlo Schalesky, award-winning author of *Women of the Bible Speak Out*, for *Relative Silence*

"Parks has it all in *Relative Silence*—mystery, romance, and a subtle message about God."

—Richard L. Mabry, MD, award-winning, bestselling author of *Critical Decision*

"I love Carrie Stuart Parks's skill in writing characters with hysterical humor, unwitting courage, and page-turning mystery. I hope my readers won't abandon me completely when they learn about her!"

—Terri Blackstock, *USA TODAY* bestselling author of the If I Run series

"[An] appealing inspirational thriller."

—*Publishers Weekly*, for *Fragments of Fear*

"Without fail, Parks delivers stories that reel me in and keep me turning the pages until I'm done and craving more. *Fragments of Fear* is sure to make you a Carrie Stuart Parks addict as well!" #CSPaddictandproudofit

—Lynette Eason, bestselling, award-winning author

"*Fragments of Fear* is a romantic suspense roller-coaster ride not to be missed. Parks has mastered the art of drawing in the reader and gripping our imaginations in a way that keeps us turning the pages."

—Kimberly Rose Johnson, award-winning author

"Parks skillfully blends a lovely yet treacherous locale into the very dark deeds of its human inhabitants. Readers will want to see more of the mysterious and sympathetic Murphy."

—*Publishers Weekly*, for *Formula of Deception*

"The sinister tone of this fast-paced story line creates an almost unbearable tension that will keep readers glued to the page. Acclaimed author Parks draws on her career as a forensic artist to imbue her stories with a true-to-life accuracy that will fascinate readers of CSI-type fiction."

—*Library Journal*, for *Formula of Deception*

"Parks (herself a well-known forensic artist) is a seasoned writer of inspirational 'edge-of-your-seat' suspense and mystery. Her latest title is a carefully researched and thoughtfully executed novel that will leave readers begging for more. Fans of Dee Henderson, DiAnn Mills, and Brandilyn Collins will flock to this suspenseful series."

—*Library Journal*, starred review, for *Portrait of Vengeance*

"Parks has created an intriguing female sleuth with depth, courage, and grit. The well-developed characters are complemented by a unique setting."

—*Publishers Weekly*, starred review,
for *Portrait of Vengeance*

"Rich characters, a forensic artist's eye for detail, and plot twists—Carrie Stuart Parks hits all the right notes!"

—Mary Burton, *New York Times* bestselling
author, for *Portrait of Vengeance*

"The compelling crimes, inscrutable community, and resilient heroine propel Parks's latest thrill-packed installment in the chronicles of no-nonsense Gwen Marcey."

—*Publishers Weekly*, for *When Death Draws Near*

"Besides having a resourceful and likable heroine, the book also features that rarest of characters: a villain you don't see coming, but whom you hate with relish. Moreover, you think said villain's crazy plans for world domination just might work. *A Cry from the Dust* will keep you hoping, praying and guessing till the end."

—*Book Page*

"Renowned forensic and fine artist Parks's action-packed and compelling tale of suspense is haunting in its intensity. Well researched and written in an almost journalistic style, this emotionally charged story is recommended for fans of Ted Dekker, Mary Higgins Clark, and historical suspense."

—*Library Journal*, starred review, for *A Cry from the Dust*

"Parks, in her debut novel, has clearly done her research and never disappoints when it comes to crisp dialogue, characterization, or surprising twists and turns."

—*Publishers Weekly*, for *A Cry from the Dust*

"A unique novel of forensics and fanaticism. A good story on timely subjects well told. For me, these are the ingredients of a successful novel today and Carrie Stuart Parks has done just that."

—Carter Cornick, FBI Counterterrorism and Forensic Science Research (Ret.), for *A Cry from the Dust*

Relative Silence

Also by Carrie Stuart Parks

Fragments of Fear

Formula of Deception

The Gwen Marcey Novels

A Cry from the Dust

The Bones Will Speak

When Death Draws Near

Portrait of Vengeance

RELATIVE SILENCE

CARRIE STUART PARKS

THOMAS NELSON
Since 1798

Relative Silence

Published in Nashville, Tennessee, by Thomas Nelson. Thomas Nelson is a registered trademark of HarperCollins Christian Publishing, Inc.

Interior design by Phoebe Wetherbee

Thomas Nelson titles may be purchased in bulk for educational, business, fund-raising, or sales promotional use. For information, please email SpecialMarkets@ThomasNelson.com.

Publisher's Note: This novel is a work of fiction. Names, characters, places, and incidents are either products of the author's imagination or used fictitiously. All characters are fictional, and any similarity to people living or dead is purely coincidental.

Library of Congress Cataloging-in-Publication Data

Names: Parks, Carrie Stuart, author.
Title: Relative silence / Carrie Stuart Parks.
Description: Nashville, Tennessee : Thomas Nelson, [2020] | Summary: "FBI-certified forensic artist Carrie Stuart Parks combines her knowledge of art and forensics in this case of family secrets and deception"-- Provided by publisher.
Identifiers: LCCN 2020001260 (print) | LCCN 2020001261 (ebook) | ISBN 9780785226185 (trade paperback) | ISBN 9780785226208 (epub) | ISBN 9780785226215
Subjects: GSAFD: Suspense fiction.
Classification: LCC PS3616.A75535 R45 2020 (print) | LCC PS3616.A75535 (ebook) | DDC 813/.6--dc23
LC record available at https://lccn.loc.gov/2020001260
LC ebook record available at https://lccn.loc.gov/2020001261

Printed in the United States of America

20 21 22 23 24 LSC 5 4 3 2 1

To Frank, who launched me on this journey
and inspired me to continue.

PROLOGUE

CURLEW ISLAND, SOUTH CAROLINA
FIFTEEN YEARS AGO

The piercing scream ripped up my spine. I dropped the spatula and spun.

My almost-three-year-old daughter, Dove, stood at the door to the kitchen and held out her favorite toy, a tattered stuffed bunny she'd named Piggy. Piggy's ear was hanging by a thread with stuffing protruding from the opening.

"Mommy," she sobbed. "P-P-Piggy's hurt."

I turned off the blender. I'd told Mildred, the housekeeper, I was going to make dessert and was elbow-deep in half-whipped meringue for the banana pudding now cooling next to me.

"Come here, Dove, and let Mommy see."

Still crying, Dove launched herself at me.

I lifted her and checked my watch. No one was at the family's Curlew Island home at the moment except my husband, Ashlee. He'd said he would look after Dove while I did some cooking. Yet here she was with a damaged toy and in need of comfort, while he, as usual, was absent.

"Sweetheart, Mommy will have to fix Piggy in a little bit. Where's Daddy?"

She shook her head. Her sobbing settled into hiccups and loud sniffles.

Shifting her to my hip, I caught sight of movement in the foyer. "Ashlee?"

The front door clicked shut.

Still holding Dove, I charged through the house and opened the front door. Ashlee was just climbing into a golf cart, the only transportation on the island. "Just where did you think you were going? You're supposed to be watching Dove."

"Don't give me a hard time, Piper." His face was pale with beads of sweat on his forehead. "I have an errand to run on the mainland. Mildred can watch Dove."

"Mildred's getting groceries and I'm cooking. Take Dove with you. You don't spend nearly enough time with your only child."

"Look, Piper, this is important and I don't—"

"So's your daughter. Or maybe we should all go to the mainland together if something is that important. Better yet, you finish dessert and I'll get to play with Dove." I was heartily tired of Ashlee's constant racing off to "something important." His work as head of marketing at the family business, Boone Industries, was stressful and kept him busy, but this was getting ridiculous.

He took out a handkerchief and swabbed his sweaty brow. "N-no. I'll take her."

Dove had relaxed against my shoulder. "She's overdue for her nap, and the boat always puts her fast asleep. Just be sure to put her life jacket on. There are snacks on the boat if she gets hungry."

Ashlee opened his mouth, then shut it. A vein pounded in his forehead.

"Dove, sweetie," I said. "Go for a boat ride with your daddy. I'll take care of Piggy, okay?"

She nodded under my chin and allowed me to hand her over to Ashlee.

"Will you be long?"

"As long as I need to be." Without another word he got into the cart and drove toward the dock. The late October day was pleasantly warm, and although Dove wore a white T-shirt and short skirt, she could always crawl under a blanket in the saloon if the boat ride was too cool.

I took poor Piggy back into the kitchen and placed her on the end of the counter, hoping the meringue was salvageable. I topped the banana pudding, stuck the dessert into the oven, set the timer, and moved to Dove's room to change the sheets. Finishing just as the pudding was ready, I placed it on the counter to cool.

After washing the dishes and cleaning the kitchen, I still had laundry to do. How could I be washing more clothes than we'd packed?

Once a year the entire family would gather on the private island for a stockholders' meeting and retreat, joining the year-round staff. I'd like to say that seeing my family together in this beautiful paradise was a special treat. Unfortunately, I was closer to the housekeeper than to my own mother. At least the beach was sandy, the ocean refreshing, and the house spectacular and spacious. Dove, of course, was perfect. And Ashlee? Back to the laundry.

After shifting a load from the washer to the dryer, I made

my way past the workout and sewing room toward the kitchen. Could a rabbit ear be repaired on a sewing machine? Ha! I didn't even know how to thread a bobbin. I found Mildred in the kitchen, checking a store receipt. "I didn't know you'd returned. Do you need help with the groceries?"

"Already done."

"Then I timed my offer perfectly. Do *you* know how to thread a bobbin?"

"Have you been out in the sun too long?"

"It's a rabbit-ear question."

"Next time wear a hat."

I grinned at the older woman. "To thread a bobbin?"

"You are the oddest child," she muttered, then nodded at my banana pudding. "But you do make the most beautiful desserts." We busied ourselves preparing dinner. The stockholders' meeting was tomorrow, and the remaining members of the family would arrive tonight.

"Strange," Mildred said after the pot roast had been placed in the oven.

"What?"

"I'd have thought everyone would be here by now."

I glanced at my watch. Ashlee and Dove had been gone for five hours. Dove would be starving. "I'm sure—"

The phone rang.

"That's probably them now." I picked up the receiver. "Boone residence."

"Piper!" It was my older brother, Tern. "Oh, Piper, I'm . . . I'm at the hospital. It's Ashlee."

I squeezed the receiver tighter. "What's going on? Is Dove okay?"

Tern groaned.

I reached for Mildred. She took my hand, then put her arm around me to keep my knees from buckling. "Tern? Tern!"

Tern didn't answer. A male voice took over. "Mrs. Piper Yates? This is Officer Stan Gragg of the Marion Inlet Police. There's been an incident involving your husband. He was attacked on the dock and your family's yacht was stolen. He'll be fine, but we're having the doctor check him out—"

"What about my daughter, Dove?" I tried to keep my voice under control, but the words came out shrill.

"We believe she was still on the boat. I'm afraid she's missing."

CHAPTER 1

MARION INLET, SOUTH CAROLINA
PRESENT DAY

I couldn't breathe. A man's weight across my body crushed me to the sidewalk. The grit of the cement and shattered glass dug into my cheek. My ears rang with the *craack, craack* of gunfire and the screams of the wounded. A thousand bees stung my ankle. I kept my eyes tightly shut. If I opened them, I knew I'd see the sightless gaze of my friend Ami, stretched out beside me. Even with my eyes closed, I could still see Ami's face. *I should be the one lying dead.*

I tried to cover my ears.

"Don't move." The man's voice whispered in my ear, his breath stirring my hair.

I froze.

A final *craack!*

The man jerked. The shooting stopped. Like the eye of a hurricane, silence. Then the screaming resumed. In the distance, a siren, then a second.

The man didn't move.

My shoulder felt warm. Something wet slithered around my neck.

In spite of the man's warning, I inched my hand upward and touched my shoulder. I opened my eyes and looked at my fingers. Blood.

Adrenaline shot through my body. I was boxed in, closed off. My claustrophobia took over, shoving aside my fear of the gunman. I shoved upward, shifting the man sideways.

He groaned.

Sliding from underneath him, I had a chance to see who'd knocked me from my chair and covered me with his body when the gunman opened fire. He was about my age—midthirties—dressed in a light-tan cotton sports jacket and bloody jeans. His gray-white skin contrasted sharply with his shaggy black hair. He opened his eyes briefly, revealing ultramarine-blue irises, before closing them again. Blood streamed from a gash on his forehead. More blood pooled around his right leg.

I was breathing with fast, hiccupping breaths. I wanted to put my hands over my ears to block the screaming, but they were covered in blood. *Maybe this is a movie.* Patriot Games. *Harrison Ford . . . No. Movies don't smell.*

What year was Patriot Games *made?* I couldn't remember.

The distant sirens grew overwhelming, then stopped. Police officers, guns drawn, swarmed the overturned chairs and tables of the outdoor café. Swiftly they checked the motionless dead, the sobbing survivors, the wailing injured.

"Help! Here! Over here!" I waved my arm to get someone's attention. Sliding closer, I lifted my protector's head onto my lap, smearing his cheeks with blood. Wait. Was his head supposed to be below his heart? "Please help me!" A female officer raced over. "He's shot." I cradled his head in my lap. "Hurry. Please hurry and get help."

The officer spoke into the mic on her shoulder. "Dispatch? Where are those ambulances?"

The reply was a jumble of words and static.

"Okay, ma'am," the officer said to me. "Stay calm. The ambulances are on their way. I need you to put your hand on your husband's leg and apply pressure to slow the bleeding—"

Her mic squawked again. "Ten-four," she said. "I'll be right back."

"He's not my—" The officer raced off before I could finish. "Husband," I whispered. I pressed a trembling hand on the man's injury. *Please, God, don't let him die like this.*

He moaned but didn't open his eyes.

Another officer, this time male, came over. "Are you injured? You're covered in blood."

"It's his. At least I think it's his." Was I hurt? I didn't like this movie. It was filmed all shiny. Everyone moved in slow motion.

"Did you see the gunman?"

"Briefly."

He nodded, then waved his hand to get someone's attention. An EMT appeared and crouched beside me. "Are you okay?" His voice was distant and slow. "Laady, aarre yoouu ooookaaaaaayy?"

"Y-yes, I think so. He's . . ." My vision narrowed. Blackness lapped around my brain. "Lunch . . . we were having lun—"

The blackness took over.

I opened my eyes. Above me was a green canvas umbrella. Did I have an umbrella in my bedroom? I didn't think so.

What a strange dream.

My bed was hard. And gritty. And smelled of fried fish mixed with . . . the pungent stench of body fluids.

Turning my head, I blinked to make sense of what I was seeing. Overturned tables, chairs, a purse. Golden brown with the letter *C* forming a pattern. Coach purse. My purse. Spattered by a shattered bowl of creamy shrimp and grits.

Not my bed. Not a dream. Not a movie.

Sound finally registered. Talking, more sirens. Yelled directions.

I slowly pushed up to a sitting position. Uniformed officers were corralling witnesses, and EMTs were treating the wounded. Next to me was a pool of blood. The man—Harrison Ford? No, he was an actor. The man who'd saved me was gone.

When I looked the other way, Ami came into focus. Her eyes were open, looking beyond me. Beyond this life. A pool of her blood had reached the puddle from the man's injury.

All my senses had returned, but I still felt . . . detached. Should I make a list? Write down what happened and make everything neat and tidy? I'd been having lunch. At a café. A gunman opened fire. That's right. And my friend . . .

I reached over and took Ami's hand. The warmth had already left it. She wore coral nail polish and an engagement ring. Did we talk about her engagement?

A giant lump in my throat made it difficult to swallow. *She's so still.* Just a few minutes ago she was animatedly talking to me, like Téa Leoni in *Spanglish*. 2004. *See, I remembered the year that movie was made.* Why couldn't I remember *Patriot Games*?

Why was I obsessing over movies now? And lists?

Movies and lists are safe.

My eyes burned, but no tears appeared. I hadn't cried in more than fifteen years. "I'm so very sorry, m'friend. I . . ." I shook my head and placed Ami's hand gently on the sidewalk.

The shooting. The blood. My dead friend. It was all real.

Looking away from her, I spotted the man being placed into an ambulance. He saved my life and I didn't even know his name.

I started to get to my feet. An EMT raced over and gently placed her hand on my shoulder, easing me back down. "Easy there. It won't be much longer. We're just getting the badly wounded off first—"

"I'm fine," I lied. "Harrison Ford—"

"What?"

You're not in a movie. I pointed. "Um, that man, the one being put into the ambulance—who is he?"

The woman looked in the direction I was pointing. "I don't know." She called to the EMTs loading the man. "Hey, guys, what hospital are you going to?"

"Mercy."

The EMT glanced at me. "Got that?"

"Thanks. Look, I'm not shot. I need to thank that man and make sure he's going to be okay, then tell my family I'm not hurt." I tried to stand again. "I promised I'd—"

"Sorry, honey." This time the EMT pushed me down. "But you're not going anywhere right now. You passed out. We don't know if you sustained a head injury. You have a lot of blood on you, and your ankle is cut. And that officer"—she jerked her head—"said you're a potential eyewitness. He said you can't leave."

"Please. I'm not injured—"

"We'll decide that." The EMT signaled the officer. "She's awake. We'll be moving her soon."

The officer came over and squatted beside me. He looked to be in his early forties, lean and athletic. His name tag identified him as S. Gragg. "Miss Piper Boone? I'm Lieutenant Stan Gragg. I understand you may have seen the shooter." His voice was soft and soothing.

"You know my name."

"Yes, ma'am. Marion Inlet is a small town. Hard not to. And"—he looked away—"I was on the department here . . . before."

"Oh. I'm sorry. I didn't recognize you."

"Long time ago."

"Yes. Mr. . . . Lieutenant Gragg, I have to cover her face. It's not right, her just lying there." I started to take off my jacket.

The officer stopped me. "Now, Miss Boone, I know it doesn't seem respectful to your friend, but this is a crime scene and we have to secure and preserve it until the crime-scene folks can process it." He glanced over my shoulder. "Looks like your ride is here."

"Really, you're making a big fuss. All those other people—"

"Just being cautious." He stood and stepped away.

An EMT took his place. I grabbed my heavy, oversized purse and clutched it while they arranged for my transport to the hospital.

The nearest medical center was normally a twenty-minute drive, but the ambulance cut the time in half. I was raced into a small room, placed on the examination table, questioned about my injuries, and prodded. They cleaned and bandaged my ankle. The last of the feeling of detachment left with the scrubbing of my ankle cut. That hurt.

During one of the lulls when the doctor or nurse wasn't tending to me, I pulled a notebook and pen from my purse and started a list.

Look up the year Patriot Games *was made.*

I stared at that a moment. That didn't matter. It was a movie, and it had a bombing, not a café shooting. I drew a line through it.

Call family and tell them I'm okay.
Contact Ami's parents and offer condolences.

- *Take food to the house.*
- *Order flowers.*
- *Offer to help with funeral arrangements.*

Retrieve car.

Lieutenant Gragg entered. "How are you doing?"

"A few bumps—nothing really." I looked down at my list.

"Are you writing down what happened for me? Your statement?"

"Oh. No. Making notes on what I need to do. You know. With Ami and all." Heat rushed to my face. "Writing things down keeps me . . . sane."

"And Ami is . . . ?"

"Oh, sorry, Ami Churchill. The woman I was having lunch with."

"I see. Maybe before you forget anything you could tell me what happened."

I nodded. "Okay." The blood had dried on my jeans, blouse, and jacket. I breathed through my mouth to not take in the metallic odor. *I just want to get out of these clothes.* I bit my lip at the uncharitable thought. The blood was from the man who saved my life.

Lieutenant Gragg took out a small notepad and pen, checked the time, jotted something down, then looked at me.

"So let's start at the beginning. Your full name is Piper Boone?"

"Sandpiper Boone."

He raised his eyebrows.

"Mother is an ornithologist, a bird-watcher. She named her children after birds."

"So that's why your brother, the senator, is Tern?"

"Yes. My sisters are Sparrow and Raven. I'm just happy Mother didn't name me Albatross or Plover." I smiled, then immediately looked down and tightened my lips. How could I make a joke when all those people were shot and Ami was still dead on the street? The police officer was taking the time to interview me when he had so much else to do, and all I could do was try to be funny. Unsuccessfully.

He quietly handed me a tissue. "Take your time."

I took the tissue and crumpled it in my hand. "I'd agreed to meet Ami for lunch. I hadn't seen her in years—since high school. Out of the blue, she called me up and asked to have lunch . . . I'm sorry, I'm not very organized in my thoughts right now." The detached feeling was returning.

"And you were eating lunch?"

"Lunch. Yes. I mean no. We were finished. We were just talking and having a last glass of iced tea."

"You were sitting facing the street?" he asked.

"No. I had my back to the street. Ami was facing me."

Lieutenant Gragg paused and looked up from his writing. "You indicated you saw the shooter. If your back was to the street, how did you see him?"

"I . . . um . . . looked around when I smelled something . . . a homeless man. I caught a glimpse of the shooter then, but he wasn't doing anything at that time. Later I could see his reflection in the window of the café. He'd moved behind me across the street and was watching the café. Something about him was . . . disturbing. I was about to mention him to Ami when he raised a rifle." I started to tremble but dug my fingernails into my palms until it hurt. "Before I could say or do anything, the man at the next table grabbed me, threw me to the ground, and covered me with his body. Ami"—I took a deep breath—"Ami must have been one of the first people shot. She fell next to us as soon as the shooting started."

"What happened next? What did the man do?"

"He saved my life."

"Yes, but physically, what was going on around you?"

"I don't know. I closed my eyes. I heard *pop, pop, pop*, screaming, the scraping of metal chairs and tables on the pavement, crashing dishes." I took a shaky breath.

"Would you know the shooter again if you saw him?"

"I believe so, yes, if that would help you."

A nurse entered. "Almost done? We need the room."

"Almost." The lieutenant gave her a quick smile.

She gave a curt nod and left.

"You said Ami was facing the street. Did she notice the man as well?"

"No. She was trying on my straw hat and was asking me if it looked good on her."

"Piper! Thank the Lord you're not hurt!" My brother, Tern, pushed into the room, followed by my mother, Caroline.

Mother stopped as soon as she spotted me. "Oh, Piper! You're covered in blood! How badly are you hurt?"

"Okay, folks." Lieutenant Gragg put his arm out to stop Tern. "We're almost done here. She's going to be fine. I need you to wait outside—"

"Do you know who you're talking to?" Tern's face was white. "That's my little sister."

"Yes, Senator Boone." Lieutenant Gragg gently took Tern's arm and turned him toward the door. "We're taking good care of her."

"Not as good as her family. We're here to take her home and get the best possible care for her."

"You will be able to, but we need to arrange for a forensic artist to meet with her as soon as possible—"

"Please, everyone, I'm fine. I have a slight graze on my ankle. That's all." I gripped the table. *It's Ami who needs family right now. And those other poor people.* I looked down and allowed my hair to partially cover my face until I could get some modicum of control over my expression. "Could I call you about the artist?"

"Absolutely, Miss Boone."

A strong arm wrapped around me and pulled me to my feet. I recognized the cherry-vanilla aroma of Tern's pipe tobacco. "Come on, little sis," he whispered. "Everything else can wait. You need to get home."

"Tern!" my mother said. "She can't go out in public looking like that."

"She'll have to." Tern propelled me from the room, down the hall, through a set of doors, and into a chaotic nightmare.

CHAPTER 2

"Senator Boone!" *Click, click, click.*

"Senator, look this way!" *Click, click.*

The press was everywhere, yelling to get my brother's attention, jamming microphones in my face, snapping digitals. "What do you have to say about today's shooting?"

I kept my head down and wished I still had my hat to help conceal my face. Around me were milling legs and shoes—oxfords, pumps, cross-trainers, and one pair of Chloé Rylee cutout open-toed boots. Beyond cute. I glanced up at the boot wearer. A porcelain-complexioned redhead swiftly took my photo. *Rats.*

"Now that your own sister was shot, does this change your stance on gun control?"

"My sister wasn't shot—"

"She's covered in blood!"

"Now then, ladies and gentlemen." Tern gave my arm a squeeze. "Please stand back and let my little sister and mother through, then I'll give you a statement."

The legs moved away. The press, particularly the female members, would be ecstatic for the chance to interview my strikingly handsome brother. And Tern knew how to use his good looks and charisma to charm even the most acerbic critic.

Tern ushered Mother and me into the back seat of the family's silver Lexus LX, placed my purse on the floor, then bent down to talk to us. "I'm having Joel drive you home. I'll put in an appearance at the children's hospital fund raiser, then leave as soon as I can." He shut the door.

Joel Christianson was the driver, handyman, and all-purpose help at the family estate on Curlew Island. He gave Tern a sketchy salute, put the car in gear, and slowly pulled out of the hospital parking lot. We drove up Highway 17 in silence. I rested my head against the car window. The blood, *his* blood, had stiffened on my jacket and blouse. *Why did he risk his life saving me? I'm not worth the effort.* I pulled out the list I'd started and added:

Find out man's name.
Figure out how to thank him.

Joel took the exit to the picturesque hamlet of Marion Inlet. When my grandparents moved here, the town was little more than a fishing village. A row of white storefronts and historic homes faced the main street, and a fishing fleet anchored in the small harbor. In 1989, Hurricane Hugo made landfall just south of Marion Inlet, uprooting ancient trees and tossing the shrimping boats around the town as if they were children's toys. The locals rebuilt and now the town was booming again.

Curlew Island, located less than a mile from the mainland, was almost entirely owned by the Boone family. It provided a seasonal home for vacations, retreats, and the annual family stockholders' meeting in October. Normally the only permanent inhabitants were Joel and his wife, Mildred, the housekeeper. For the past year, I'd called the island home.

I'd often said I was dying to leave. Today I'd almost gotten my wish. I shook my head at the grim thought.

"What is it, Piper?" my mother asked.

"I suspect it's what's called gallows humor."

"You always did have a strange sense of humor." Mother patted me on the leg.

This from a woman who named me after a bird known for eating critters it plucked from the mud. "Mmmm."

Mother brushed a stray lock of hair behind her ear. "Once we get to the house, you can take a shower and get cleaned up. I'm sure you'll want to get out of those bloody clothes." She gave a tiny shudder. "I'll get Mildred to make you a pot of chamomile tea. She can add a spoonful of raw honey. Very calming. I'll look up some organic pain medication so you can throw away those pills the doctor gave you." She tapped her finger on her lips. "No. Don't throw them away. That's not safe. I'll research how to dispose of them." She gave me a slight smile.

I stared out the window, ignoring the twinges of pain from my scrapes and rapidly forming bruises, and tried not to think about Ami lying next to me at the outdoor café. *Nineteen ninety-two. That was the year* Patriot Games *was released.*

The SUV pulled in front of a small elevated house. The entire ground floor was open and served as a garage. The house was the original family home but had served as overflow guest quarters since my parents constructed the far larger house on Curlew Island. A day cruiser was tied up to the private dock waiting to transport the family to the island. Smaller boats, also owned by the family, were tied along one side.

I tapped the driver on the shoulder. "Joel, can you see that Mother gets to Curlew safely? I need to take the car."

"Where are you going?" Mother asked.

"Ami"—I gulped some air—"was one of the victims murdered today. I need to talk to her parents—"

"The police will take care of that."

"Shouldn't they hear about it from me? I was the reason she was at the restaurant." I held up the list. "If not for me, she'd be alive. Now I need to make things right."

Mother patted my hand. "Really, Piper, you don't know these people. You don't know what they want or need right now. You need to let the family grieve in peace."

"But I could tell them what happened—"

"What happened was that you were both in the wrong place at the wrong time. Now, I'm going out for my afternoon meditating session. I think you should join me. Let nature help you heal."

Joel opened the door beside Mother and helped her out. I remained in the SUV.

"Come along, Piper." Mother headed for the boat.

"I need to get my car. It's still parked near the restaurant. I'll have Joel drive me over."

Mother stopped, turned, and looked at me. Her gaze flickered over to Joel. The message was clear. *Don't make a scene in front of the help.*

I sighed and looked down. A weight settled across my shoulders.

"Give me your keys," Joel whispered. "I'll retrieve the car in a bit."

Opening my purse, I handed him my key chain, then slipped from the SUV and slowly followed Mother. *I wish it had been me killed today.*

Tucker Landry opened his eyes. A nurse sitting behind a counter directly in front of him stood and walked over. "How are you doing?"

"Where am I?"

"Mercy Hospital. You got out of surgery and you're in recovery. Do you have any pain?"

"No. What happened?"

"Do you remember getting shot?"

Tucker closed his eyes. Flashes of memory slid across his mind. Lunch at an outdoor café. A beautiful woman at the next table. The thunderous staccato of gunfire. "Yes."

"The doctor will be by to talk to you soon."

"When can I get out of here?"

She patted his hand. "Don't be in such a rush. You lost a lot of blood."

A woman in green scrubs with her hair tucked into a surgical cap appeared next to him. "Welcome to the land of the living, Mr. Landry. I'm Dr. Rice. You are one lucky man."

"I don't feel lucky."

"You are. The bullet that just grazed your head and struck you in the leg was a .223. Nasty business. A different angle and you'd be dead." She tilted his head slightly upward and checked his forehead. "This will heal fine with just these butterfly bandages. They come off on their own in about ten days. Your leg injury will take longer. No broken bones, but I want you to keep weight off it so it has time to heal. You'll be on crutches, which you'll need to use even if you feel better." She folded her arms. "I'd usually comment about the scar you'll end up with, but I noticed you have quite a few all over your body."

He could hear the question in her comment. "I do, yes."

She waited another moment as if hoping he'd elaborate, then continued. "Now you need to rest and heal. I'll be back when you're settled in your room." She walked away before Tucker could ask her any questions.

Settled in my room? How long was he supposed to be in here? He had work to do.

I sat in the boat's aft holding my long hair to keep it from whipping across my face and watched the small town of Marion Inlet recede.

I'd looked forward to having lunch with Ami. Now I was thinking about funeral plans and memorial wreaths. And blood. *Think about something else.* I could join Mother in meditation, but while she sat on a comfortable mat, I had to sit on the ground. All I ever got out of it was leg cramps, bug bites, and dirty pants. Maybe I could do a movie marathon. Lock myself in my room and not come out for a week. Would a week be enough to erase everything? What about the man who saved my life? Would he be around in a week?

After Silva, the boat captain, tied up on the island dock, I headed straight to the house and my room, not willing to wait for one of the golf carts used as transportation.

The two-story, elevated, low-country home had been designed to preserve the existing natural environment. A series of dunes separated the front of the house from the sandy beach. Except for a small partially enclosed foyer leading to the living quarters on the second floor, the space beneath the house was surrounded by lattice.

Unlike the rest of the house, my bedroom didn't have an indifferent, model-home look. Stacks of books covered most of the surfaces, and the built-in shelves sagged under the weight of more books and journals. I'd taken down the bird prints found on all the other bedroom walls and replaced them with a framed photograph of my father from a magazine piece about his art. Two movie posters flanked it. Next to a flat-screen television was a media storage unit holding my collection of classic movies. A half-packed suitcase sat open on a cedar chest, where it had rested for the last six months.

I dropped my oversized purse onto a nautical-themed chair and dashed into the bathroom. I stared at my face in the mirror. *Does it show?* Everything else did. Every passing thought was clearly written on my features and reflected in my complexion. *Does the presence of death etch into the face?* A tightness around the mouth? Eyes narrowed, or worse, turning cold?

After peeling off my bloody clothes, I stuffed them into a plastic garbage bag, then jammed the bag into the trash container. I'd never wear that outfit again. I didn't even want to see it in my closet. My thick watch band on my left arm was clean, but the wide leather bracelet I wore on my right arm was crusted in blood. Sliding it off, I tried not to stare at the parallel raised white scars across my wrist. In the shower, I scrubbed my skin until it turned red. I washed my hair twice. The pink-tinged water eventually drained clear. My conservation-conscious mother would say I was using too much water, but today I didn't care.

Maybe today is my wake-up call. Once the stockholders'

meeting was over, in three days, I'd leave for good. Nothing held me to Curlew Island. *Well, okay, free room and board. And a small rock cairn at the north end of the island.*

I just needed to pack the last of my things in the suitcase and arrange for my books, journals, and movie collection to be shipped to . . . *Where?*

I stopped scouring my hands and leaned against the cool marble tiles.

Maybe back to Atlanta? I could see if any jobs had opened up.

Oh yeah. Who'd want to hire a washed-up, has-been editor from a now-defunct publishing house? Yet another failure in my mess of a life.

Maybe I should look at someplace new, where no one knew me. *It's this stupid indecision that keeps my suitcase half packed.* Leaving here was not a destination, only a decision.

When I stepped from the shower wrapped in towels, Mildred was waiting for me. The older woman was slightly plump but solid, plain-faced but with a radiant smile that transformed it. She wore her long gray hair in a tight bun, and oversized tortoiseshell glasses mostly hid her hazel eyes. A floral print apron covered her blue-checked cotton housedress.

"Child, I just thank the stars you weren't killed today."

"Thank you, Mildred—" The words caught in my throat.

"Let me look at you." She lifted my chin and inspected my face. "It was bad, wasn't it?"

I didn't have to answer. I could keep nothing from Mildred. My face would show it all, and she knew how to read it.

She patted my cheek and let go. "Be strong."

"How did you hear about it?" I finally asked. "Is it on the news?"

"Probably, but I wasn't watching the news. Tern called after putting you and your mother in the car. He said you'd had a close call. Your mother sent some tea." She glanced toward the Wedgwood tea set resting on a tray on the dresser.

"That's so thoughtful of both of you. Thank you." I made a point of pouring a cup and taking a sip. I didn't care much for tea but didn't want to appear ungrateful. "I wouldn't be here now if not for the man who saved my life."

Mildred raised her eyebrows.

That's one of the things I love about this woman—her quiet strength and serenity. And her intelligence. I gave Mildred a quick hug. "I think I'll take a walk along the beach."

Her gaze darted to my wrist.

"I'm okay. I . . . I need to be alone."

"You sound like Marlene Dietrich."

"Greta Garbo," I said automatically. "*Grand Hotel*, 1932."

"The same year Jesse Owens won four gold medals in the Berlin Olympics?"

"That was 1936 . . . Wait a minute! You knew that answer."

"Just testing you."

"Well then, 'You want to know something, Leslie? If I live to be ninety, I will never figure you out.' *Giant*, 1956. I just have to substitute 'Mildred' for 'Leslie.'"

"Same year your mother was born. Good year all around." Mildred patted my cheek. "You'll be fine." She hesitated a moment. "Ashlee's here."

Ashlee. My ex-husband of fourteen years. When we divorced, he'd stayed on at Boone Industries as head of sales. The only non–family member to have a financial interest in the company, he held on to the stocks he'd received when we married and once a year was present at the shareholders' meeting. Although our divorce was amiable, or at least as civil as such things can be, I did my best to avoid him.

"Duly noted."

"I've put him in his usual room at the far end of the house."

"Perfect." Ashlee's usual room was my sister Raven's old bedroom. As she hadn't shown up for any meetings in years, Ashlee took over the space.

"He did mention he had something to tell you." Mildred pursed her lips.

My stomach churned. Somehow I knew it wouldn't be good. "I see."

"And you got a call from Four Paws Rescue."

"Let me guess. A blind hamster? An elderly goat?"

"A goose." Her lips puckered in disapproval.

"A goose? Who keeps a goose for a pet? Don't answer that. What's wrong with the goose?"

"It needs medical attention. The owners kept it in a dog crate in the house. Walked it daily. Then they lost the lease on their home and had to surrender their pet."

Four Paws Rescue was another reason the free rent came in handy. My income from the family business always seemed to be needed elsewhere. "How much?"

"They think two hundred would cover the vet and first month's care."

I nodded. "Make me—"

"A note to send a check. Already done. Now, what else can I do to help you?"

Find me a job that pays well enough to live on and support all my two- and four-legged projects? "Nothing. No . . . wait. Could you call Mercy Hospital and see if they'll release the name of the man who saved my life? Black hair. Blue eyes. About my age or a bit older."

"I can try. You know how such things can be."

"Thank you, Mildred. If that doesn't work, I'll ask Lieutenant Gragg to find out."

Mildred turned to leave, then turned back. "Gragg? Why does that name sound familiar?"

"He said he was on the department . . . before."

"I see. Oh, before I forget. You also got a call from Joyce." Joyce Mueller was our sole neighbor on the island. She kept a seasonal home on the northern end. "I posted it on the bulletin board in the kitchen, then figured you probably wouldn't check for messages."

"Did she call because she heard—"

"No. She called last night. She wanted to talk to you."

"Did she say what about?"

"No. But there was something in her voice . . ."

I raised my eyebrows. "Like . . . ?"

"If I didn't know better, I'd say she sounded scared."

CHAPTER 3

An orderly and several nurses rolled Tucker into a private room overlooking several palmettos. They fussed with his IV drip, some kind of leg-compression boots, oxygen, and a host of other tubes and attachments to his body. He had enough morphine pumped into him to feel no pain, but his vision bounced annoyingly whenever he blinked.

A police officer entered and approached his bed.

"Hi, Tucker. The nurse said I could speak with you for a few moments. I'm Lieutenant Stan Gragg. I'm so sorry for your injury."

"Thanks."

"I'm the lead investigator on the shooting. We're trying to get an identification on the sniper. Did you see him?"

"Yes."

The lieutenant straightened and pulled out a small notebook and recorder. "Mind if I record this? I don't write that quickly."

"That's fine."

The officer placed the recorder on the bedside table. "Would you describe what happened? Please don't leave anything out, even if you think it's unimportant. Start from a point before the incident. What you were doing, how you were feeling, that sort of thing."

Tucker thought for a moment. "I arrived at the restaurant at about one and was seated at an outside table next to the street. The lunch crowd was finishing up and several tables were open. The waiter took my order and brought me a tea. I had a book to read, but I decided to people watch."

"People watch?"

"You know, observing the people at the different tables, the folks passing on the street, the waitstaff working at the restaurant."

"I see."

Tucker paused. "Are you sure you want me to report everything, even things that have nothing to do with the shooting?"

"Yes." The lieutenant looked up from his writing. "Sometimes a memory of one thing will trigger a memory of another. And something you saw that you think is unimportant may be important to us."

He nodded. "Just before the shooting, a homeless man wandered up the street. You could smell him before he got close. The people seated nearest the street turned away as he approached."

"Was he begging?"

"Not really." Tucker pictured the scene. "He just shuffled along. That's when I noticed the two women at the next table."

Lieutenant Gragg looked up from his writing. "And you noticed them because . . . ?"

Should I tell him I could hardly take my eyes off one of the women?

"Um, well, they were attractive. Hard, really, to ignore them." His face burned.

Lieutenant Gragg nodded. "Tell me about them."

"They were about the same age, maybe late twenties to midthirties. Both had long, light-brown hair, but one was wearing a hat."

"The one with the hat . . . ?"

"Was facing the street. The other had her back to the street. She didn't see the homeless man, but as he approached, she turned and looked. I'm sure the smell attracted her attention. She reached in her purse, pulled out some money, and signaled the waiter. She gave the waiter the money and nodded to the homeless man. The waiter went over to the man and motioned for him to go to the back of the restaurant."

"What did you think the waiter was going to do?"

"I think the waiter told the man he'd get a meal if he went to the back door." Tucker looked down and frowned.

"What?"

He slowly nodded. "That might be," he said quietly, then looked up. "The waiter seemed to know the woman and wasn't surprised by the gesture."

"So?"

"So I think she must have eaten there often, and buying a homeless man a meal or other similar acts of kindness wasn't unusual."

Lieutenant Gragg nodded. "Good observation."

"Anyway, I didn't want to look like I was gawking." *Which I was.* "So I looked across the street. That's when I saw the shooter. He was staring at the two women."

"Could you tell which one?"

"No. But . . ." *Don't get involved. Just the facts.* "No."

"What happened next?"

"The man lifted a rifle. I didn't think. I just grabbed one of the women and threw her on the ground. Is she . . . ?"

"Slight cut, a few scrapes and bruises, but otherwise okay."

"How bad was it?"

Gragg seemed to know what he was asking. "Two dead. The woman in the hat and another woman. A third is in critical condition."

Tucker let out a deep sigh.

"What did the shooter look like?" Gragg asked.

Tucker thought for a moment. "Um, Caucasian, medium height. Unkempt brown hair. Mustache and goatee. Forties. Jeans and green T-shirt. Average."

"Would you know him again if you saw him?"

"Yes."

"Would you be willing to work with our composite artist to get a sketch of him?"

"No."

Lieutenant Gragg raised his eyebrows. "Oh?"

Tucker shifted as far as his IV lines allowed. "I'm sorry. That came out wrong. You don't need to bring in a composite artist. I'm a forensic artist. I was down here working. I can do my own sketch."

"Well. That's a first. What department are you working for?"

"No department. I work for a company called Clan Firinn. I'm here about the *Hunley*."

"The old submarine?"

Tucker nodded.

"What do you do?"

"Uh, research. Clarifying the faces of the dead sailors found with the sub. Going with a two-dimensional image this time."

"Sounds like a grim business."

Tucker shrugged. "No more than yours."

"Clan Fur . . . ?"

"F-i-r-i-n-n."

"Private company?"

"Yes. Which reminds me, I'll need to update them. My cell is in the pocket of my jacket. If you could find that for me?"

Lieutenant Gragg glanced around the room, then opened the door to a small locker, pulled out a plastic bag, and opened it. "Phew. You'll need a change of clothing before you leave." He reached in and pulled out a phone, then handed it to Tucker.

"Thanks." He slipped the phone under his blanket. "Now, if you'd bring me some drawing paper, pencil, and eraser, I can start on that composite sketch. As soon as my eyes stop going crazy from the morphine, that is."

A nurse bustled into the room. "Not today you won't. Lieutenant, he needs his rest and you've overstayed your visit. Doctor's orders. No more visitors today."

"I'm running an investigation and he's a witness—"

"He'll be an exhausted witness and you'll be a dead investigator if you don't get out of here." The woman pointed to the door.

"I'll be back." Lieutenant Gragg turned to leave, then paused. "Would you be willing to work with the other witness? Piper Boone? She was the one I believe you took a bullet saving."

Tucker tried not to smile. Actually meet the woman he'd yanked from the crosshairs of the killer? "Absolutely."

Gragg left. Tucker's smile disappeared as he looked out the

window. *So, the beautiful woman has a name. Piper Boone.* And the waiter hadn't been surprised when she gave him money for the homeless man. He must have been familiar with her charity. That meant she must dine at that restaurant often. A pattern the shooter could have learned, especially if he wanted to know where she'd be at a particular time.

After covering the scars on my wrist with a wide, studded bracelet my brother had made for me, I dressed in beige slacks, a coral long-sleeved T-shirt, and mesh water shoes. I left my hair loose to dry.

I still felt itchy and raw. Maybe watch a movie? I picked up *John Wick*. Keanu Reeves was walking forward, an intense look on his face, carrying a gun. The quote on the cover said, "A wild and bloody ride."

I dropped it.

My room seemed too small. I grabbed my latest journal out of my purse and stuffed it into a beach bag along with a blanket. I started for the kitchen, then stopped. I picked up the teapot and emptied it into the bathroom sink along with the half-empty cup. I slung the beach bag over my shoulder, lifted the tea service, and resumed my stroll.

With no cell phone service, the only communication with the mainland was via a two-way radio or satellite phone, both located in the kitchen. Mildred was snapping green beans into a colander. She looked up, her gaze going from the tea service to my covered wrist. "How are you feeling?"

I placed the tray on the counter, turned, and gave her my best attempt at a smile. “Mmm. Mother’s tea hit the spot. That doesn’t look like we’re going to have greasy hamburgers for dinner?”

“Hardly. Your mother requested broiled cod, organic green beans, and carrot juice red curry.”

“I really liked it better when I was the only one you were cooking for.”

Mildred stopped snapping beans and frowned at me. “But I never made you greasy hamburgers. Your mother only has me prepare food from the organic farmer’s market and oversees . . .”

“Minor details.”

“Hmm. How about you bake something for dessert?” she asked casually.

“No.” I made a point of loosening my fists. “Did you find out the name of my knight in shining armor?”

Mildred sniffed. “No. They said they could ring his room if I had his name. We went round and round, but I couldn’t get them to budge.”

“Thanks anyway.” I tried calling Lieutenant Gragg, then Joyce, but only got voice mail and an answering machine. After leaving brief messages, I aimed for the beach.

A large, glassed-in porch on the back of the house gave a panoramic view of the ocean. Along one wall, a row of hooks held jackets and rain hats, with an open pail of flip-flops underneath. I snagged my favorite pale-yellow windbreaker in case the breeze was chilly.

An open deck filled with white wicker patio furniture overlooked the empty pool directly below. When I was younger, my father had installed a slide from this level. When Joel emptied the pool for the winter, he’d remove the slide and place a chain across the opening. As we grew up, we simply stopped filling the pool. Mother claimed it used up too much fresh water and the chemicals could be harmful to the island. On the left side of the deck, a wooden path crossed the dunes to the beach.

I strolled down the path until it ended between two sand fences. Each step lifted a bit of the weight dragging me down.

Near a grassy dune, I spread the blanket and sat facing the sea. I loved the restless ebb and flow of the waves, the slap and hiss as the water crashed on the sand, and the ocean colors ranging from emerald to turquoise.

I hated its cold indifference. And what it had stolen from me.

Pulling out a pen and my journal, I opened it, then stared at the blank page. *What shall I say about today?*

Dear Dove,

I wrote to my daughter every day.

I lost a friend today. A classmate. She just called up one day and said we should get together. We hadn't seen each other in years, but it was like we'd just been apart for a day. Friends are like that, aren't they? At least good ones.

I tapped the pen against the journal for a moment, then slipped Dove's photo from the front of the journal. She smiled at me while clutching her favorite bunny. I returned the photo, then wrote again.

If I were to make a list—now, don't you go and chide me on that—but if I wrote down all the people I consider friends, none of them would be recent. Acquaintances maybe. When I worked, I had colleagues. Maybe I just don't try now. Or maybe I don't care anymore.

I stopped writing and stared at a line of white-topped breakers. Bottlenose dolphins surfaced, then dipped under the waves in an undulating parade. A light breeze fluttered the nearby grasses and brought the scent of salt. My ankle throbbed a bit as the pain medication wore off.

I reread what I'd written. It sounded so gloomy. Dove wouldn't like a somber entry any more than she'd liked overcast and dreary days.

Sorry about the whine fest. We added a new friend to the Four Paws Rescue. A goose. Now isn't that fun? Maybe I could swing by and visit the newest member. I've never met a pet goose before. There's a man I need to find and thank for—saving my life? No—his kindness today.

Kindness? Not the right word, but I couldn't think of a better one. I closed my journal, tucked it into the beach bag, took off my shoes, and headed for the water. Before I could reach it, Mildred called to me from the end of the walk.

"Piper? That policeman called and gave me the name you wanted. Did you want to call the hospital?"

I reversed direction and trotted toward the house, scooping up my bag, shoes, and blanket as I passed. "Thank you," I said to Mildred as I got closer. "Did Joyce return my call?"

"Not yet." We walked to the house, pausing at an outdoor faucet to wash our sandy feet and shoes. As soon as I turned on the water, Nana, the resident Newfoundland dog, joined us.

Over the years a succession of Newfies had lived on the island, all named Nana, regardless of sex, in honor of the Newfoundland in the children's story *Peter Pan*. This Nana was an imposing, 165-pound brown male, looking more like a grizzly than a dog.

"Hi, Nana. Don't drool on me." I moved the dog's water container, a large bucket, under the faucet. Nana inspected the filling bucket for a moment before lapping up great quantities of water. I stepped away to keep from getting soaked when he lifted his head. "Mildred, don't you think calling is too impersonal for a man who saved my life? I should drive to the hospital and see him in person."

"Piper—"

"Take him something . . . maybe flowers? Balloons? Of course, a released balloon would become litter that could kill or injure animals. Stuffed toys seem rather juvenile for a man."

"Piper—"

"That all seemed so trivial—"

"Piper? Are you listening?" Mildred frowned at me.

"Sure. Um, what?"

"That policeman, Lieutenant Gragg." She pulled a slip of paper from her apron pocket. "He said the man's name is Tucker Landry and he's going to be fine. He's out of surgery but weak. He's an artist, apparently, and is willing to work with you to draw the shooter. The lieutenant wants to schedule the composite drawing for tomorrow."

"Why not today?"

"Apparently Mr. Landry is not allowed visitors today."

I moved the bucket over, rinsed my feet, then turned the water off. "In that case I guess I'll . . ." Call Ami's family? Finish packing? Watch a movie? Make some plans? Set some goals?

Write another list? "Um, I'll visit Joyce and find out what she wanted to talk to me about."

"I'd try calling first. She may have headed for the mainland. Or I can give her a ring."

"Thanks, Mildred, but I don't want to slow you down. You have too much to do for the shareholders' meeting. I'll try calling, but I think I want to head over even if she doesn't answer."

She nodded and looked behind me toward the ocean. "That's strange."

I turned to see what she was looking at. A marine patrol boat was racing north at high speed.

My stomach knotted. "I need to get going." I tugged on my water shoes and strolled toward the path leading to the other side of the island and Joyce's house. The sight of the marine patrol flying past brought too many memories. None of them good.

CHAPTER 4

Nana followed me as I strolled toward Joyce's end of the island. The crushed-shell path meandered down the center of the island through a thick maritime forest filled with chirping birds. This feathered population, both in the forest and near the water, kept my mother busy. She'd had several permanent bird-watching blinds constructed here, though she had several portable blinds.

Joyce shared my mother's passion and the two of them had become close friends over the years, often taking birding cruises together. I'd never found their hobby particularly interesting, as the only birds I enjoyed were fried chicken, Thanksgiving turkey, and now apparently a rescued goose. I hadn't spent much time with Joyce Mueller. *Strange that she would want to talk to me.*

In keeping with Mother's environmental philosophy, Mildred had placed eco-friendly, nonpoisonous traps along the path to live capture any lizards, geckos, or snakes. Once a trap had captured a critter, Mildred would show it to Mother, who would determine if it was indigenous to the island or needed to be taken back to the mainland. I thought of it as their own form of Four Paws Rescue, though none of their critters had paws.

Joyce's winter home sat on the highest point of the island and overlooked the ocean on three sides. A wide porch circled the small dwelling, and a Kowa spotting scope was aimed at the shoreline. An open birding journal, field guide, and camera sat on a nearby table.

"Joyce? It's me, Piper. Joyce?"

Except for Nana's loud panting beside me, the house was silent. I tapped on the screen door. "Joyce? Hello?" The door beyond was open, and I could see the living room and kitchen. "Joyce?"

She's probably birding. I stepped over to the table and peered at the journal. It was filled with handwritten notes, colored-pencil sketches, and references to the field guide.

Glancing around one last time, I turned to head home. I stopped. *If Joyce is birding, why doesn't she have her camera and journal with her?*

"Joyce? Are you okay? Joyce?" *Maybe she fell.* I entered the house and checked it out. The simple layout had a combined living-dining-kitchen area, a bedroom, and a bathroom. The air smelled of lemon furniture wax. The bedroom had thick cement walls and ceiling and resembled a nun's cell at a convent, albeit a spacious convent with designer furniture. Rumor had it that this original structure had been part of a Civil War–era coastal defense bunker. A journal my father owned claimed a shipwreck occurred here. I'd researched both stories but hadn't been able to find any record of either claim. My sisters, brother, and I had spent some of our youth climbing to Joyce's roof and watching the ocean. Indoors, the thick walls provided a welcome relief from the hot and humid summer heat.

No Joyce.

Back outside, I strolled around the house, looking for any

sign of the woman. Nana contented himself by investigating an interesting thicket of shrubs.

"Joyce? Jooyyyyce!" A well-used trail took me to a slight bluff overlooking the ocean. Below was the small dock where Joyce usually tied up her boat. The boat was missing. "Well, that explains it," I muttered. "As Mildred mentioned, she headed into town."

To my left, on the leeward side of the island, was a small spit of rock and sand extending into the ocean. A stone cairn marked the edge of the natural seawall. Some driftwood had caught on the edge of the monument, knocking a few stones down. *I'll need to fix that.*

As I returned to Joyce's house, I rubbed at the prickling I felt at the base of my neck. Maybe she'd called to tell me about the damage, and Mildred was mistaken about the fear in her voice. No. Joyce would just leave a message.

Once again I went to the porch and looked at the open journal. If Joyce suddenly needed to head to the mainland, would she leave her journal open and out? Wouldn't she have put it in the house so an unexpected squall wouldn't ruin it?

My unease grew. I entered the house, this time staring around the room for any sign of . . . something. Nana pushed in behind me. "Nana, no, out." The dog ignored me and aimed for the kitchen. I followed. The Newfie sat in front of a wall of shelves holding books and seashells. "Nana, come."

Nana's attention was riveted on the shelves. I moved closer. The backing on the shelving unit was vertical beadboard, painted white. A thin black line ran up one side. I pushed slightly on the paneling and it sprang open, revealing a small pantry with a washer and dryer, cleaning tools, and a box of dog biscuits on the top shelf.

"It would appear that you visit here often."

A long rope of saliva dangled from Nana's jowls. He stared at the dog cookies as if he could get one by sheer force of will. A Newfoundland mind-meld. *Feed the dog. Feed the dog.*

I grabbed a biscuit, handed it to the dog, then closed the panel. Nana took his treasure outside, opening the screen door with practiced ease.

The kitchen table held apples in a copper colander. A couple of dishes were drying on the dish rack next to the sink.

The closet in the bedroom held the fuse box for the house and Joyce's neatly hung clothing—mostly cotton plaid blouses and khaki slacks. A dark-green field vest hung next to a windbreaker jacket. Her shoes were lined up underneath—a pair of water shoes, black pumps, and brown hiking boots. I didn't even know what I was looking for at this point.

The phone rang.

I jumped.

The phone jangled again.

Racing to the living room, I hesitated over the small black handset resting on the desk next to an old oil lamp. Like the Boone residence, Joyce had a satellite phone.

It stopped ringing. I turned to leave, and the phone rang again. "Hello?"

"Oh, I think I got the wrong number," a youngish female voice answered. "I'm sorry—"

"Who were you calling?"

"Joyce Mueller."

"This is Joyce's phone—"

"Who are *you*?"

"I'm a neighbor . . . well, technically I should use a definite article and say I'm *the* neighbor, as she only has one set. My name is Piper Boone. I came over to talk to her but can't find her. Now it's your turn. Who are you?"

"Hannah. Hannah Mueller. Joyce is my grandmother."

Wow. I hadn't even known she was married, let alone had children and grandchildren. "I'm not sure where she is right now, but I can take a message."

"Strange. Grandma wanted me to call about now so we could finalize my visit."

"Her boat is missing, as is her purse and car keys. Maybe she forgot the call and went to town on some errands." The comment sounded lame even to me.

"Maybe. I guess if you just leave a note that I called."

I found a piece of paper and a pencil and jotted the message. "What's your phone number in case I hear anything?" I wrote down Hannah's number, then disconnected. After one last look around the house, I started walking home. The sun was setting, and inky-blue shadows covered the path. Katydids crackled from the overhead palms and palmettos. Every few steps I'd stop and listen for footsteps, then check the dense foliage around me. I couldn't shake the feeling that something bad had happened to Joyce. And that I was being watched.

Tucker needed to call his boss. He had to check in daily to give his progress reports. Getting the job at Clan Firinn had been a lifesaver. Literally. He didn't want to mess this one up. He waited until the endless parade of nurses left him alone, then pulled out his cell, which he'd hidden under his blanket. He dialed.

A smooth male voice answered. "Clan Firinn. How may I direct your call?"

"Tucker Landry checking in."

The phone clicked and a second male voice answered. "Tucker. This is Scott. What's your status?"

"I was involved in a shooting incident unrelated to my work. I'm in the hospital."

"I heard about the shooting. Do you need a caraid?"

"A counselor? Negative. I'll stay in touch." He disconnected, placed his phone out of sight behind his pillow, and finally let the drugs whisk him off to sleep.

A screened-in porch on the side of the house led directly to my bedroom, and I was able to slip into the house unnoticed. Voices from the living room told me my family had gathered. I locked the door leading to the rest of the house, retrieved my journal, and opened it to today's entry. My last line was, *There's a man I need to find and thank for his kindness today.*

I continued to write.

> *I found out today Joyce Mueller has a granddaughter. And Joyce is missing. At least I think she's missing. See? I don't even know enough about her to know how often she leaves for the mainland.*

Someone knocked on my door. The house had a room-to-room intercom system, but we never used it. Voices always came out weird sounding and echoey.

Reluctantly I closed my journal and answered. Mildred had one hand raised to knock again. I couldn't decipher her expression. "What's wrong?"

"An officer from the marine patrol is here and wants to see everyone. She's in the living room."

My stomach knotted. "Did she say why she's here? Is it about the shooting today? I'm supposed to see—"

"No." Without explaining any further, Mildred turned and left.

The voices in the living room ceased as I entered. Seated around the room were Ashlee, my mother, and Tern. Mildred and Joel were standing near the kitchen with a young brown-haired woman. I hadn't seen her before, but Mildred routinely hired extra help for the annual meeting. A female police officer with Asian features stood in the center of the room. Her gleaming black hair was pulled back off her flawless tawny skin. She wore dark olive-green slacks, a white polo shirt, and a holstered pistol. I vaguely recognized her from seeing her around Marion Inlet.

"Miss Piper," the officer said, "hey, I'm Officer Chou, marine patrol. How y'all doin'?"

I nodded a greeting.

"Yeah, I know." She smiled at my expression. "Lookin' like I do, it just dudden add up I'd talk like this. Anyhow, we found an empty boat a couple hours ago and towed it into the marina at Marion Inlet. It's registered to a Dr. Joyce Mueller from over here on Curlew Island."

I felt the blood drain from my face. *Dear Lord, not again.*

"We tried callin' Dr. Mueller but haven't been able to get ahold of her. We called here and spoke with your housekeeper,

Miss Mildred, who said you were at Joyce's house earlier this evenin'."

"I was. I couldn't find her."

"There's a chance her boat could've simply gotten loose from her dock, but since no one's been able to locate her, I'm followin' up with a welfare check. I've spoken with all but you."

All eyes shifted to me. I really wanted to bolt from the room. "Joyce called and left a message that she wanted to talk to me. When I got there, I noticed the missing boat and assumed she'd gone to the mainland."

"Why'd you assume that?"

"I didn't see her purse or car keys."

"Did you notice anythin' . . . out of place or . . . ?"

I shrugged. "I've seldom visited her, but to me the house looked fine. She did leave her birding journal open on the porch."

"Joyce is an avid bird-watcher, as am I." My mother folded her hands in her lap. She appeared relaxed, but her lips were pressed together in a thin line. "That's just not like her."

"I'm wonderin' if you'd go with me to Dr. Mueller's place," the officer said to me.

"I can take you." Joel stepped forward. "Piper's had a rough day. If anything has happened to Joyce, I can help. She was always a good neighbor."

"I should go." My mother stood and smoothed her cream linen slacks. "Joyce is my friend and I've been to her home many times. I'd notice anything missing."

"I'll go." Tern stood also. "As Joel said, Piper's had a long and terrifying day. She was at the restaurant when the shooter opened fire. It's a miracle she wasn't killed."

Officer Chou looked at each of them as they spoke, then

back at me. "Thank y'all, but Miss Piper here was the last one at the house. I'd like for her to take me over."

I nodded. "I'll get my jacket." I headed for the line of coats hung on the porch and tried not to think, but Joel's words echoed in my brain. *"She was always a good neighbor." Why did he refer to Joyce in the past tense?*

CHAPTER 5

With me driving, Detective Chou and I took one of the electric carts. The headlights provided the only illumination on the white crushed-shell path. The night was moonless and still, the island strangely quiet.

"Why did you want me to go with you?" I asked after a few moments.

"I just had a feelin'."

"A feeling?" I glanced at the officer.

Chou pursed her lips, then gave a brief nod as if coming to a conclusion. "Have ya ever heard the words 'separation of church and state'?"

I lifted one shoulder. "Of course. It's paraphrased from Thomas Jefferson referring to the First Amendment, which requires the government's neutrality on religion."

Chou glanced at me. "Ya must have a thing for history."

"That too."

"Well, the boss thinks it ain't fittin' to talk 'bout what I believe, so I wouldn't be able to tell ya that the Holy Spirit gives me a nudge now and again."

"I'd like to think that's true."

"But?"

"I used to be a believer. At least I thought I believed. Now? I guess I can't figure out why a loving God would allow suffering." *Or let an innocent child die.*

"Lots of folks have trouble with that, yes indeed. Well, the boss would not be happy with me if I said I'd pray for ya, so I won't say that, but if ya need to talk sometime, here." She reached into her pocket and pulled out a business card. "Sometimes talkin' can help."

"Thanks." I took it and stuck it into my jacket pocket.

"So now on to business. How well do you know Dr. Mueller?"

"Not well. She's my mother's age and close to her. She spends time in Wisconsin somewhere when she's not on the island. Um, I just found out today that she has a granddaughter. I didn't even know she was married, let alone had children or grandchildren."

"How did ya find out?"

I told her about the phone call as we pulled up in front of the dark house. The windows reflected the headlights' harsh glare. I stopped the cart and turned it off. Darkness enveloped us. The air smelled of fresh earth. Chou pulled a flashlight from her duty belt.

"So what are we looking for?" I stepped reluctantly from the cart.

"Ideas." The detective flashed the light across the house's facade, stepped up on the porch, and shone the light through the screen door into the living room. "Inspiration. Clues. Evidence. All I have is an empty boat, which isn't against the law, and a missin' woman, again not against the law. This could be nothin'. But that's a big ocean and a small boat, so we're followin' through." She tapped on the door. "Hey, Dr. Mueller? Hello? Officer

Chou, marine patrol. Are you in there?" After waiting a moment, she reached into a pocket, pulled out some thin rubber gloves, and pulled them on. She handed a second pair to me. I held the gloves, rubbing them between my fingers before pulling them on. They somehow made Joyce's disappearance ominous and horribly real. Chou opened the door and fumbled for a switch. The room sprang to light.

Nothing had changed since my earlier visit, but the space seemed emptier. Chou stood in the center of the room and slowly turned in a circle, her gaze finally coming to rest on a set of shelves next to a built-in window seat. She strolled over and picked up a framed photograph. "Who's this?"

I moved next to her. "That's Joyce. Dr. Mueller."

The image showed Joyce a number of years ago when her short-cropped gray hair was more of a ginger color. She had a lean, rather horsey face and was wearing shorts, a green plaid shirt, a photographer's khaki vest, hiking boots, and a pair of binoculars. She was wearing the expensive watch Mother gave her one year for Christmas. A second photo in a smaller frame showed Joyce sitting in her bathrobe and slippers at a table covered in breakfast dishes in some tropical location.

"I think my mother took those photographs on a birding trip to Costa Rica. Maybe nineteen or so years ago. Her hair is gray now and she has her share of wrinkles."

Chou returned the frames to their exact place on the shelf. "No other family photos?"

I walked around the room, searching. "No. Funny. I never noticed that."

"But ya said a granddaughter called. Are ya sure it was her granddaughter?"

"That's what she said. She left a phone number."

The officer moved to the kitchen, repeating her slow circle. The colander of apples was still on the table. Without thinking I placed the apples in the refrigerator.

When Officer Chou looked at me, I shrugged. "Keeps them from going bad."

A bowl and coffee cup rested in a bamboo dish rack, but otherwise the room appeared immaculate. After completing her examination, she opened the cabinet under the sink and took out the trash container. "So Dr. Mueller woke up this mornin', probably had her bowl of oatmeal, drank two cups of coffee, and finished the crossword puzzle in last week's paper."

I stared at her. "You sound like Sherlock Holmes. The one played by Basil Rathbone, not Robert Downey Jr. How did you do that?"

Chou grinned, exposing perfect teeth. "Elementary, my dear Watson. Oatmeal." She held up the wrapper for a serving of instant oatmeal. "Coffee." She lifted two Keurig containers.

"And the crossword? How did you know she finished it this morning?"

"Paper—last week's—was on top of the breakfast items. Ya know, ya pay attention to detail. Ya mentioned the open journal. Tell me what *you* see."

I took a fast breath. "Oh, I don't think I see anything."

"Ya haven't looked."

"Is this another one of your feelings?"

Chou smiled slightly.

Moving into the bedroom, I followed Chou's example, turning around in the center of the room. The single bed was made with a gray-and-teal cotton bedspread. On a white dresser was a carved wooden seagull and a handblown glass bowl full of shells. The bedside table held a dark copper lamp, an alarm clock, a pair of reading glasses, and a book, *Vulture: The Private Life of an Unloved Bird* with a ribbon bookmark. I picked up the book and glanced at the inscription, then returned it.

"What do ya see so far?"

I waved at the room. "Joyce used the same interior decorator as my mother. I recognize some of the same objects. The furniture is expensive—in fact, all the decorations are. That lamp"—I pointed—"has a mica shade and costs over a thousand dollars. That matching floor lamp over by the chair was over two thousand." I lifted the bedspread and looked under the pillow, opened each dresser drawer and glanced inside, then stepped into the bathroom and checked behind the door. After a swift inspection of the closet, I peered under the bed, then stood.

"Well?" Chou asked.

"One more thing." I walked to the hidden laundry area and glanced into the washer and dryer. Both empty.

"Okay." I turned to Chou, who'd watched my every move. "I think we need to call Joyce's granddaughter immediately and let her know her grandma is missing. I think you need to haul Joyce's boat into wherever it is you process such things and look for signs of foul play. And I think you need to call for a search for Joyce."

"Why do ya say that?"

"The book beside her bed is from her granddaughter, Hannah, and was a birthday present, so there really is a granddaughter. A suitcase is under the bed, but I don't know how many suitcases she owns. I don't know all her outfits, but she seems to be very particular about hanging her clothes up or folding them neatly.

But as neat a housekeeper as she appears to be, I couldn't find her pajamas and robe, although I did find a pair of slippers. Of course, maybe she slept in the nude, but I don't think so."

"So far, so good." Chou nodded at me. "What do *you* think happened?"

I thought for a moment. "How about this scenario? I think Joyce got up at her usual time, 6:00 a.m. That's the time her alarm is set for. She had her breakfast of oatmeal and coffee, finished the crossword, then, still in her robe, went out on the porch to do some early bird-watching. She put on shoes, maybe in case she needed to move off the porch. Someone she knew—"

"Why do ya think it was someone she knew?"

"The house was unlocked, doors open, and she made no effort to dress, so it was someone she was comfortable with while dressed in her nightclothes. And it seems she's still wearing them, hence my thought of foul play. She'd never go beyond the house dressed like that."

"Outstandin', Piper! See, I told ya this was somethin' you'd be good at."

An odd emotion nudged me. I felt . . . like I'd finally done something right. "So . . . what next?"

"I'm fixin' to give the granddaughter a call, then get ahold of my department. Even though it looks that way, we can't conclude somethin' bad happened to her. My feelin'"—she gave me a tight-lipped smile—"is that we need to at least consider foul play a possibility. The department may send someone, but with the shootin', most of the staff's been called in to help Marion Inlet PD and are working overtime. They may choose to call in SLED—that'd be the South Carolina Law Enforcement Division. At any rate, we need to finish gettin' all the facts, then put the missin'-person machine into action." Chou pulled out her cell.

"That won't work here. You can use Joyce's phone." I lifted the handset.

Chou put her cell away. In short order, she'd called the local hospitals, jail, and coroner's office. "That avenue's been explored. No Joyce or Jane Doe." Finally, she lifted the paper with Hannah's phone number on it and gave it and the receiver to me. "Why don't ya place the call, then turn it over to me. That might be less frightenin' for the woman."

I dialed. The call was answered before the second ring. "Grandma?" I held the phone away from my ear so she could listen. "No, Hannah, it's me, Piper. We spoke earlier—"

"Did you find her?"

"I'm afraid not yet. Officer Chou is standing beside me and would like to talk to you."

Chou took the receiver, introduced herself, and told Hannah about the empty boat. Hannah gasped but said nothing. "Would your grandma have gone somewhere without telling anyone?"

"Not in this case." Hannah's voice trembled. "I was flying out to visit her. I have my flight to Charleston tomorrow. She was looking forward to . . . Something terrible has happened."

"We'll be doing all we can to find her. Now, a couple more questions. How many pairs of pajamas does your grandma own?"

A pause came before the answer. "One. One . . . when she goes on a trip. She travels light. Why?"

Chou gave me a thumbs-up and mouthed, *Good call.*

My face burned.

"Can ya email, fax, text, or phone me the names of her relatives and friends that I might contact?"

"She has all that on her laptop. I've never been there, so I don't know where she keeps it. The password is capital E-a-g-l-e-2–2–3."

"Do you see a laptop?" I asked Chou.

She quickly strolled through the house, returning to where I stood, and shook her head. The top of the desk next to me was empty except for a lamp, my note, and the phone. "That seems to be missin', Hannah."

"Oh. Well then. She keeps an address book in her purse . . . but I'm guessing that's missing also."

"Yes."

"I'll look around and see what I can find. I'm going to see if I can get an earlier flight tomorrow. I'll call you if I do. Could someone in your department pick me up? I don't have a driver's license."

Chou caught her lip with her teeth. "Oh man, we're so short-handed, but—"

"I'll pick her up."

"Are ya sure?"

I nodded.

"What's your flight information?" Chou asked.

"I'm on Delta 2425, arriving from Milwaukee at three."

"Okay," I said. "I have light-brown hair with sun streaks in it and will be wearing a cream-colored straw hat."

"I'll find you."

"How will I recognize you?"

"Don't worry, Piper, you won't be able to miss me."

CHAPTER 6

I returned Chou to the dock where her boat was tied up. The soft slap of the ocean against the dock kept time with our steps across its wooden surface. "How can I get hold of you?" Chou untied the front of her boat, handed the bow line to me, then unfastened the stern.

I recited my cell number. "I'll be at Mercy Hospital tomorrow to do a composite sketch, so the cell should work. Then I'll pick up Hannah. Where do you want me to take her?"

"Unless I call ya and say something's different, bring her to her grandma's place. We should be done by then, assumin' I can get someone to process her home for clues."

"You think there's a chance they won't consider this serious enough to investigate?"

"Let me share a little law-enforcement insight with ya. Almost every department is understaffed and underfunded. The workload's huge, and certain crimes get priority, like homicide. Missing persons, unless it's a child or an at-risk adult, ends up with whatever time is left."

I nodded. "I've had some experience with that."

"Oh!" Chou's face flushed. She reached over and squeezed my arm. "I didn't mean to be insensitive."

I patted her hand. "I somehow think that would be difficult for you."

She checked my expression, gave a short nod, and said, "Maybe you and Joyce's granddaughter can do some investigatin' on your own. I know I did some nudgin'."

"What do you mean?"

"I considered the tides and currents, then estimated where Joyce's boat might have been to have ended up where we found it. I suggested the department take a look. Who knows?" She shrugged. "At least it's somethin'."

The Boone home was silent when I returned, with only a few lamps left on in the living room. A narrow crack of light came from under the kitchen door. Entering, I found Mildred sitting at the table with a cup of tea, a book open in front of her. "I hope you didn't wait up for me."

"No . . . well, yes. Tucking all my charges in for the night. Would you like a cup of tea?"

"No, thank you." I was suddenly exhausted. After turning to leave, I paused and looked back at Mildred. "Do you ever get a feeling about something?"

"Feeling?"

"Never mind." I headed for bed.

I was at the outdoor café with my back to the street. Instead of my friend Ami, I was across the table from my daughter,

Dove. She grinned at me and my heart melted. I lifted my gaze to see the shooter. He was staring at Dove. He raised his rifle.

I leaped to my feet, spun, and threw out my arms to block the bullets.

One-two-three-four. The bullets struck me, searing through my body.

I screamed.

Jerking upright, I opened my mouth to scream again. *No.* Outside lights filtered into my bedroom. My bed was soaked with sweat. The clock said five.

I shoved away the crumpled bedding, trudged into the kitchen and made a pot of coffee, then took a steaming mug to the deck to watch the sunrise. I could still faintly feel the places where the nightmare bullets struck me. The sky turned coral, salmon, then finally brilliant yellow. I pulled out my journal.

Dear Dove,

There was a beautiful sunrise this morning. All it needed was for John Barry to write a score for it, something like he penned for Out of Africa. *One of those sweeping numbers with lots of violins.*

Tern sauntered in and sat with his morning brew.

"Pretty spectacular." He took a sip.

"Mmm."

He put his feet on the bottom of the deck railing. "I was concerned about you overdoing it last night by going to Joyce's house.

You had a terrible day. You should have let me go, or Joel, or even Mother."

"I was fine." I put away my journal.

"But the nightmares . . ." His gaze went to my wrist.

"Don't worry." I slipped my arm out of sight. "We didn't find much. Her computer may be missing. Officer Chou is going to try to get the crime lab to process her house this morning."

"They don't think she just decided to go into town and maybe had a boating accident?"

"Only if she went boating in her pajamas. I noticed they were missing."

"My kid sister is turning into a regular Nancy Drew." He grinned at me, then grew serious. "If you ever decide to go back to work, I could use a good researcher on my staff. I could even pay you enough to support your menagerie."

That would mean moving to Columbia. Was that the destination I'd been looking for? "I'll let you know." We watched Newfie Nana splashing along the shoreline for a few moments.

"Storm's brewing out there." Tern nodded toward the rising sun. "Tropical storm so far."

"It *is* the hurricane season." I drank some coffee.

"So it is. So it is."

"What's everyone doing?" I finally asked.

"I saw Mother hard at work in her office. Probably getting the last-minute details for the shareholders' meeting tomorrow. I didn't see Joel, but Mildred's got something delicious-smelling in the oven. The temporary gal is helping. The last I saw Ashlee he was in his jogging clothes, so I'm guessing he's doing his morning workout. And me . . ." He stood. "Well, I've got to put in a few hours for the office, get ready for the meeting, and somehow find time to interview two interns who want to work out here next summer when the sea turtles are hatching. Stay out of trouble." He ruffled my hair as he left.

Mildred brought me the phone. "Lieutenant Gragg."

I took the handset. "Yes, Lieutenant?"

"Are you still up for that composite drawing with Mr. Landry today?"

"Yes."

"Shall I pick you up?"

"Um. Let me check." I put my hand over the mouthpiece. "Mildred, did Joel get a chance to pick up my car?"

"Yes. It's parked in the usual spot under the house on the mainland, keys by the front door here."

I removed my hand. "I'd rather take my car, if you don't mind. I have an errand or two to run."

"Okay. I'll meet you at the hospital at ten, if that's all right with you."

As I handed the phone back to Mildred, it rang. I put the handset to my ear. "Hello?"

Mildred took my coffee cup, pointed to the house, and raised her eyebrow.

I mouthed, *Yes, please.* The older woman left to get a refill.

"Piper? This is Officer Chou. I just wanted to give y'all an update. The crime lab will be processin' Dr. Mueller's boat this mornin' and then the house later this afternoon. They don't want the granddaughter to be there until they finish. Just to be on the safe side, see if she can stay at a hotel tonight."

"That's not necessary. We have a guesthouse on the mainland. She can stay there, then come over to the island tomorrow morning."

"Perfect."

After I hung up, I watched a cargo ship disappear over the horizon, then I headed to the kitchen. I met Mildred returning with my fresh coffee. A young woman about my height but in her early twenties trailed behind.

Mildred handed me my coffee, then turned to the woman. "Piper, this is BettyJo. She'll be helping out while everyone's here." The young woman nodded shyly.

"Hi, BettyJo. Welcome to Curlew. Thank you for the coffee, Mildred."

"What's your agenda so I can plan the meals?" Mildred asked.

"I won't be here for lunch. I'll let you know about dinner."

Mildred left with BettyJo following. I wandered to my room to dress. *I want to look nice.* The thought made me pause. *I can't remember the last time I even cared how I looked.*

Tucker woke from a fitful sleep as the breakfast cart clattered down the hall. He drank the delivered coffee and orange juice but passed on the packaged cereal and peaches. After the dishes were whisked away, he leaned back against the pillows and tried to figure out his next move. He closed his eyes.

A light tap at the door was followed by a voice. "Tucker?"

Tucker straightened. "Scott?"

Scott Thomas, his counselor from Clan Firinn, entered. The man wore a rumpled navy jogging suit and red running shoes and carried a small suitcase. He ran a hand through his thick gray hair and smiled. His eyes were bloodshot. "Hey, Tuck. Looking good, considering."

"Hopefully better than you." Tucker grinned to show he was joking.

"I hate red-eyes."

"I hear ya." Tucker used the bed controls to raise the back of the bed higher. "So . . . to what do I owe the honor? Oh, and have a seat."

"Thanks, but I've been sitting too long." The older man set his suitcase next to the chair. "Anytime one of our folks hits a bump in the road—or in your case, rescues a damsel in distress"—he smiled—"we like to check in. I'll be swinging by the *Hunley*'s staff next to explain what happened, so you don't need to do that. You need to rest up and heal."

Tucker's throat tightened. Scott was yet another reminder of all the support the Clan had given him. "Thanks."

"Call in every day or so. Let us know how you're doing. And if you need someone to come alongside you, let us know."

This time Tucker couldn't answer. He simply nodded.

"You did an amazing thing, saving that woman. We think you're ready."

Tucker cleared his throat. "Ready?"

Scott reached into his pocket and took out three polished stones, then placed them on the side table. "Take these with you. Keep them on you."

Tucker picked one up. "Worry stones? Ammunition in case I encounter Goliath?"

Scott gave a half smile. "When the time comes, you'll know what they are and what to do with them." He picked up his suitcase, gave an encouraging nod, and left.

Tucker turned the stone over. It was reddish brown without

markings. He placed it next to the other two, lowered his bed, and closed his eyes. Maybe he could figure out . . .

A puff of air brought the scent of perfume—something citrusy.

He must have drifted off to sleep again. He opened his eyes. A woman was standing beside his bed. Her shoulder-length red hair was artfully tousled, her lips a slash of scarlet. She was lean to the point of boniness. "I hope I didn't wake you." She didn't seem like she was particularly worried about it.

"Who are you?"

"Bailey Norton, *Charleston Times*. I'm writing an article about the shooting. Did you know it was Sandpiper Boone, sister to Senator Tern Boone, when you risked your life to save her?"

"Excuse me?"

"And the Boone family has more money than they know what to do with?"

"What is that supposed to mean?"

She pulled out a notebook and pen. "Rumor has it that Senator Boone is on the fast lane to the political top—"

"I need you to leave." Tucker reached for the call button.

"What are you doing here?" Lieutenant Gragg stood at the door holding a container of coffee and a small white sack. "You're with the press?"

Bailey stuck out a hand to shake his. "Bailey Nor—"

"Out." Gragg gestured with the white sack. "The press conference is at two. This man is off-limits."

Bailey flipped her hair back, gave Tucker a rueful smile, and stalked out of the room.

"Thanks." Tucker took the proffered coffee.

"I'll talk to the hospital staff about visitors. How do you feel today?"

"Like someone shot me."

Gragg set the white bag on the table. "Scones. Great for the healing process. Are you ready to meet with Miss Boone?"

"I'm looking forward to it. Did you bring—"

Gragg produced a sketchpad and a pencil set.

Promptly at ten, Piper arrived balancing a box of chocolates, a stuffed rabbit, an immense purse, and a vase of flowers. Her face flushed at his expression.

"Hello. I . . . I didn't know what to bring."

"Miss Boone, meet Tucker Landry. Tucker, meet Piper Boone." The lieutenant moved toward the door. "I'd like to stay, but I have some follow-ups to tend to. My phone number is on the card on the table. Call me when you're done."

After the door closed, Piper busied herself placing the flowers and candy near the bed, then putting the bunny on a chair. She refused to meet his gaze, keeping her head down and using her long hair like a curtain.

"Do you mind if I call you Piper?"

"Not at all."

"Piper, have a seat."

The woman stopped fussing with the rabbit and sat in a chair against the wall, placing her purse beside her on the floor. She smoothed her cream-colored linen slacks, straightened her matching jacket, and folded her hands.

They both spoke at the same time.

"I don't know how—"

"I appreciate you—"

Tucker grinned. "'What we have here,'" he said in his best Southern drawl, "'is a failure to communicate.'"

"*Cool Hand Luke*, 1967." Piper smiled slightly.

He lowered his voice. "'Of all the gin joints in all the towns in all the world—'"

"'She walks into mine.' That was easy. *Casablanca*, 1942."

He thought for a minute. "'He's a Pooka.'"

"I should tell you that Jimmy Stewart is my all-time favorite actor. That's from *Harvey*, 1950. My turn. 'Last night I dreamt I went to Manderley again.'"

"*Rebecca*, but I don't know the year."

She grinned, causing deep dimples to appear on her cheeks. "Nineteen forty. I'm impressed." Her gaze darted to the monitor, which announced his increased heart rate. Her face flushed and she looked down.

So much for hiding my thoughts. "Um . . . well . . . besides being a bona fide movie buff, what else can you tell me about yourself? Do you have a job?"

"I'm . . . between jobs. I was an editor. Books. Novels."

"Did you want to be a writer?"

"Yes. No. I'm not good enough to be a writer."

Now came the question he wanted to ask first. "Are you married?" *Please be single.*

"Divorced."

"I'm sorry."

"I'm not." She looked up at him.

"Children?"

It was as if all her muscles loosened and her face sagged. The sparkle left her eyes and her shoulders dropped. "No." Her voice was barely a whisper.

Fool. Change the subject. Before he could speak again, she straightened in her chair. Her face returned to normal, though her lips were tight. "What about you, Mr. Landry? Tell me about yourself."

A woman entered wearing green scrubs under a white jacket. He recognized Dr. Rice from the day before. "Good morning and good news. We're releasing you today. We can arrange for home nursing to come in and change your dressing."

"Good. I'm itching to get back to work, and I have a flight to catch in a couple of days."

"Not so fast." The doctor frowned. "You're not in any condition to travel for at least a week. Where are you staying?"

"I have a hotel room."

The doctor folded her arms. "I don't think you realize the amount of press coverage this shooting has launched, with you at the center of the storm. You'll be hounded. Senator Boone just announced a $50,000 'reward'"–she made quote marks in the air—"for the man who tried to kill his sister."

"Oh no!" Piper put her hand over her mouth.

"You need to lay low for a bit while you recover," Dr. Rice said. "I'd recommend you get someone else to collect your things from the hotel. I'd bet the press has it staked out. I need you back here to take out those stitches in two weeks and recheck the wound."

"He can stay with me." Piper stood. "With my family," she amended quickly. "We can arrange for a nurse if needed."

The doctor smiled. "On Curlew Island? Now that's a plan." She looked at Tucker. "I think you just got an offer you can't refuse."

"*The Godfather*," Tucker and Piper said together.

Tucker smiled but shook his head, and immediately regretted it. *The pain meds must be wearing off.* "I couldn't put you out like that."

"You saved my life. You're hardly putting me out. And the house is huge. And private."

"Then it's settled. You should be set to go after lunch." Without waiting for Tucker's response, the doctor left.

The room was silent for a moment, with only the clicking of the machines still plugged into Tucker. He finally spoke. "I hope you know what you're doing."

I surprised myself when I offered to take Tucker to Curlew Island, but as soon as I said it, I knew it was the right decision. "I'll call and let Mildred know to expect another person for dinner. Maybe two if Hannah doesn't want to eat on the mainland. There's not much food in Joyce's house, so—"

"Wait! Whoa! Who's Mildred? And Joyce? And whoever else you just said? And have you forgotten we're here to do a composite drawing?" Tucker held up a sketchpad.

I slowly sank back into my chair. "No. I'm sorry."

"No, *I'm* sorry. Where were we before the doctor arrived?"

I looked out the window at the palmettos. "Um . . . you were about to tell me about yourself. I suspect that's part of your interview process."

"It is. You already know I'm a fan of old movies. I work for a company, a group, called Clan Firinn."

My expression must have asked the question.

"*Clan* means 'children' in Gaelic but can refer to people with a perceived kinship. *Firinn* is Scottish Gaelic for 'truth.' It's a group of law-enforcement and forensic experts based out of Spokane, Washington. We work on cases outside of traditional law-enforcement jurisdiction."

A thatch of his dark hair had caught in the square bandage on his forehead. I wanted to smooth it away. *Stop it. I'm not attracted to him. I'm grateful.* "Hmm. And you're a composite artist?"

"Forensic artist. I do more than just composites."

"Such as?"

"Skull reconstruction. Unknown remains. Age progression. Crime-scene reconstructions."

"You have a fascinating career."

He looked away from me. His heart monitor sped up, then returned to normal.

Something I said struck a nerve.

He smoothed the bedsheet and settled his sketchpad on his lap. "Well then. Shall we get started on the sketch?"

"Of course."

"I have to admit, this composite will be a first for me. I've never been both the artist and one of the witnesses." He smiled at me, then motioned around the hospital room. "And I'm a bit far from all my art supplies and materials, so I'll be doing this differently than I usually draw."

I smiled back. "I wouldn't know the difference."

He opened the sketchpad. "I'm going to start drawing what I remember, then show it to you to see what you'd like me to change. I'll do this several times. Okay?"

I nodded.

He bent over his sketchpad, pencil flying.

"Do you mind if I talk to you while you're drawing?"

Once again the monitor sped up, but all he said was, "Not at all."

"You mentioned you do skull reconstructions. Is that like the clay sculptures?"

"Yes, and drawings." He turned the artwork around so I could see it.

"Yes. That looks like him. Maybe a bit longer hair."

"Good." Returning the sketch to his lap, he continued to work.

"What is age progression?"

"Drawing the face of a known suspect and updating it." He didn't look up. "Missing-children age progression. That sort of thing."

Missing children? "What if . . ." The little hairs on my arms stood on end. "What if the child is . . . dead, and you want to know what she might have looked like, you know, now?"

Tucker's eyebrows drew downward. "Yes. I've done that."

Do I dare? Could I stand the pain? Maybe, but I have to know. "Could you do a drawing for me?"

His pencil stopped moving. Slowly he raised his head and looked at me.

"I need you to draw my daughter. She died fifteen years ago."

CHAPTER 7

Tucker placed his pencil on the bed and stared at Piper. The muscles of her face had again sagged. "I am so sorry. Could I ask what happened?"

She didn't move.

Me and my big mouth. He hated anyone asking about his past—why would he think she would be any different?

An array of emotions flickered across her face. Her gaze drifted toward her purse. Slowly she reached over and opened it. After lifting a leather journal from its depths, she opened it and pulled out a photograph. She stood, brought it to him, then walked to the window. "That's Dove. She drowned."

He looked at the image. Dove had been an exquisitely beautiful child, with large blue eyes, light-brown hair, and a slender build. "It was this same time of year. October. The whole family was on Curlew Island for the annual shareholders' meeting." She glanced at him. "Boone Industries. My brother, Tern, is the CEO, though Mother oversees the financials. Anyway, Mother, Tern, my ex-husband, and I are the stockholders. And my sister Raven, of course. My other sister, Sparrow, passed away years ago." She absently reached up and pulled out a yellow-colored necklace, held it in her hand for a moment, then tucked it back into her blouse.

"Your daughter's necklace?"

"Good guess. Yes. It's an amber teething necklace—a gift from my mother on her birth—I had it restrung."

"I'm sorry, I didn't mean to interrupt you. Your family meets once a year?"

"Ironic, isn't it? We meet on an island during hurricane season. Anyway, one day Ashlee—that's my ex—had an errand to run on the mainland, so he took Dove with him on the *Faire Taire*, the main boat we used. Dove loved to go out on the water . . ." With her finger on the windowpane, she traced the outline of a palm frond outside.

He made a point to loosen his white-knuckled grip on the photograph of Dove. Fortunately he hadn't bent it. *I know this kind of pain.* His mind returned to That Night. That's how he always thought of it. That Night. The night his old life ended. Followed by The Darkness.

"I said, are you okay?" Piper was staring at him. "You kind of zoned out there for a moment. Are your pain meds wearing off?"

"I'm sorry. No, I'm fine. Keep going."

"When Ashlee arrived on the mainland, while he was tying the boat to the dock, someone came from behind and smashed him over the head, then tied him up. He's lucky he wasn't killed. His attacker took the boat . . . with my daughter still in it. The boat was never seen again." She turned back to the window. "Dove's body washed up on the northern tip of Curlew, near Joyce's house, but Joyce was in Wisconsin. The family Newfoundland, Nana, found Dove's body and didn't leave her side." She took a deep breath. "We didn't hear Nana's barking. Not for almost a week.

Everyone was concentrating on the ocean and places where the boat could have docked on the mainland. Poor Nana was barely alive when we finally did . . . find them."

"How old was your daughter?"

"Almost three."

He wanted to ask more questions, but she was drooping as if she could barely stand.

"As you'll be my host for a bit," he said, "I'll do a portrait of her for you. I have my art equipment at my hotel room."

She straightened and cleared her throat. "I would like that a lot." She moved to his bedside and took back the photograph.

"Would you take another look at the composite sketch and see what you might want to change?"

She nodded, sat, and returned the photo to her purse.

Turning the sketch so she could see it, he watched her expression.

Her eyes opened wider and she paled slightly, then whispered, "That's him."

He nodded toward the business card Lieutenant Gragg had left on the table. "Do you want to give him a call?"

She checked her watch. "I have some time before I have to be at the airport. I'll drive the sketch over and see if there's anything new on Joyce."

"You mentioned this Joyce before. What's going on?"

Piper updated him on the missing doctor and her plan to pick up Hannah, the granddaughter. "I think something bad happened to Dr. Mueller. I'd like to help, but I don't know what I could do . . ."

"You know, a great number of criminal cases are solved with the help of civilians."

She looked down and allowed her hair to drape over her face. “I was always told to let the police handle it. That I would be in the way, maybe even . . . I don’t know . . . make it so the case couldn’t be solved.”

“Piper, look at me.”

She raised her head.

She looks so fragile. “The police, law enforcement in general, are slammed with cases, many of which go unsolved. You can be a squeaky wheel.”

“That’s pretty much what Officer Chou told me.”

“Well then, as long as you don’t get in their way . . .”

“Would it be a problem if I did?”

“I don’t know. I can make suggestions.” He clenched the sheet. *What am I saying? I can’t get involved with anyone. I have nothing to offer but a boatload of regrets, guilt, and shame.*

“I just feel bad about Joyce’s granddaughter, but honestly, how much could I, as a civilian, find out?”

“You never know until you try.”

“Would you help me?”

He slowly nodded.

I collected the composite and headed for the Marion Inlet Police Department. I’d have time to drop off the sketch, grab a bite of lunch, then return to the hospital to pick up Tucker. Joel agreed to collect his things from the hotel, drop off a change of clothes for Tucker, and transport everything else to Curlew. I would take Tucker with me to pick up Hannah from the airport.

As I pulled into the visitors’ parking area, I spotted Officer

Chou leaving. She had her head down and raced toward a nearby car.

"Officer Chou?" I stepped from my car. "Is everything okay?"

Chou paused midstride. She glanced at me. Her eyes were red-rimmed and her face pale. "Wave at me, then ignore me. Meet me in half an hour. Buddy's Diner."

I waved.

Officer Chou waved back, then got in her car and drove off.

Reaching into the car, I brought out the composite sketch. As I turned toward the police department, the blinds covering one window dropped back into place. Someone had been watching the exchange.

The lobby of the police department had two chairs. Bulletproof glass protected a uniformed officer in the reception area on my left. The stainless steel counter had an opening allowing for small items to be passed under the glass. The building smelled of cleaning products. I approached the officer and spoke into the intercom.

"I'm here to drop off a composite drawing for Lieutenant Gragg."

"May I have your name and some identification?"

"Sandpiper Boone." I pulled my wallet from my purse, extracted my driver's license, and passed it through the slot.

The officer examined my license, then picked up a phone and dialed. "Miss Sandpiper Boone here to see you." He paused. "Yes, sir." After hanging up he returned my license. "Lieutenant Gragg will be right out. Please have a seat, ma'am."

I eyed the stiff chairs lining the wall and opted to read the bulletin board near the front doors. Prominently displayed was a wanted poster featuring a blurry image of a man with a rifle—

obviously taken from a video surveillance camera some distance away. The poster said, "$50,000 Reward for Information Leading to the Identification and Conviction of the Marion Inlet Café Sniper."

"We've been swamped with calls since that came out." Lieutenant Gragg had come up behind me. "I'm surprised you didn't get swarmed by the press when you came over here. They've been camped outside since this happened."

I wanted to ask about Officer Chou. Instead I handed him the sketch. "I thought I'd save you some time."

"I appreciate it." He took the drawing and looked at it. "Mr. Landry is quite the artist. I have to admit, he's better than our own. Do you know when he's getting out of the hospital?"

"Today. He'll be staying on Curlew Island for a few days if you need to speak to him."

"Good plan."

"Anything new?" I indicated the flyer.

"Not yet. Lot of shoe leather and phone calls. We'll keep in touch." He nodded and left.

I moved toward the door. Outside a news van had arrived and parked, with several people bustling about. I found a tissue in my purse, placed it over my nose as if blowing it, and strolled to my car, ignoring the press. I tried not to run. My shoulders were stiff, waiting for an outcry of identification. None came. I risked a glance at the van.

Lieutenant Gragg had stepped from the building, drawing attention away from me. I was sure he'd done that on purpose, allowing me an escape window.

I relaxed and pulled out my car key.

"Miss Boone?"

Rats. I clenched my jaw and turned.

The striking redheaded reporter from outside the hospital shoved a mic attached to a recorder into my face. "How does it feel to be at the center of tragedy again? Do you think the Curlew Island curse has struck once more? Are you—"

"No comment." I unlocked the car door, jumped in and slammed it shut, then locked it. *Curlew Island curse?* I hadn't heard those words since Dove's passing. The reporter was obviously trolling for a story.

Buddy's Diner was a local favorite and very much off the tourists' radar. It featured inexpensive local dishes like shrimp and grits, fried green tomatoes, and chicken with waffles. I hadn't eaten there in several years, but nothing had changed. The tables and chairs were still mismatched, the menu was still stuffed into a sticky plastic holder, and two ceiling fans still rotated lazily overhead. It smelled of fried fish and mac and cheese.

Officer Chou sat in the back-corner booth. I joined her. "What's wrong?"

Chou clutched the red plastic glass of iced tea with both hands. "Let's just say if they weren't shorthanded, they would have put me on administrative leave."

"Good heavens, Officer Chou! Is Lieutenant Gragg doing this?"

"You can call me Mandy. No. He's with the police. This is the boss of marine patrol. I turned in the report on our welfare check for Dr. Mueller. I also told them about the research I did on the currents and tides. Apparently I did everythin' wrong. I shouldn't have brought ya along when we checked out the house. I shouldn't have touched anythin'. I shouldn't have used her phone to make the calls. I shouldn't have talked to the granddaughter."

She stopped and gulped some tea. "I was 'outside my level of expertise.'" She made quotes in the air. "They found nothing in Dr. Mueller's boat and don't intend to follow up at her home at this time. She needs to be missin' for forty-eight hours. They told me to back off." She studied me over another sip of tea.

"But what about the pajamas? The missing computer? The unlocked house?"

"They said I had no proof of anythin', just speculation, and they didn't have the manpower to look into every person who doesn't know how to tie up a boat." She glanced around the room, then leaned in closer and whispered, "Here's the strange part, the reason I wanted to talk to ya. They told me to stay away from anythin' to do with Curlew Island, and especially *you*."

A waitress appeared with a glass of water and placed it in front of me. "What can I bring you to drink?"

"Tea. Unsweetened." After the waitress left, I asked, "I wonder why I'm off-limits to you."

"I suspect it's not you so much as your senator brother. Everyone's stayin' away from politics these days."

"Any idea what's going on? Joyce is missing—there's no doubt about that."

"I'll be charitable and say the sniper attack yesterday has everyone on edge. The press wants to know when there'll be an arrest. Your brother puttin' up that reward has the phones ringin' like crazy. Another woman died from her injuries. That makes three dead."

A jolt shot through me. I hadn't followed up on Ami's family. I hadn't even called with condolences.

"What?" Mandy was staring at me. "Your face just went splotchy."

I gave her a rueful smile. "My face gives away my every thought. I just had a guilt attack about my friend Ami. She was one of the three who died."

The waitress reappeared. "Have you decided?"

I looked at Mandy. "Go ahead. My treat."

"In that case . . ." Mandy glanced at the menu. "I'll start with a bowl of she-crab soup, then a roasted beet salad and blackened grouper."

"You can eat all that?" I stared at Mandy.

"Yup. And enjoy every bite. Oh, and banana puddin' for dessert."

I suddenly lost my appetite. Pointing to the menu I said, "I'll have a salad. House dressing on the side. No tomatoes or onion. No croutons." I handed it to the waitress. After the woman left, Mandy asked, "On a diet? You're already too thin."

"Lost my appetite." I leaned forward. "So what now?"

"I kinda, sorta already done put somethin' into play." Mandy glanced around the room. The diner had filled, and the clink of silverware, dishes, and conversation rose considerably. "My brother has a fishin' boat. I asked him to fish near where I figured Joyce's boat may have been. He griped that the fishin' was terrible around there but agreed to go tomorrow. He has scuba gear so could look around if needed."

"Look around? For what?"

Mandy just lifted her eyebrows.

I knew.

CHAPTER 8

I finished eating my salad, then pulled out my list from the previous day.

Contact Ami's parents and offer condolences.

- *Bring food to the house.*
- *Order flowers.*
- *Offer to help with funeral arrangements.*

"I see you're a list maker as well." Mandy popped the last bite of grouper into her mouth.

"Yes, but I didn't follow up." I pulled out my cell, looked up Ami's parents' number, then dialed.

Ami's younger sister answered. "Churchill residence."

"Hi, this is Piper Boone, and I'm calling to offer my condolences—"

"You! You brought the Curlew Island curse, or should I call it the Baal Island curse, on my family! How dare you call here."

"I . . . I don't know what you're talking about."

"It's all over the internet." She started crying. "The news. Social media. Stay away from my family!" *Click.*

"What's wrong?" Mandy asked.

Instead of answering, I logged on to the diner's internet and typed in "Curlew Island curse." An article in the *Charleston Times* appeared, written by Bailey Norton.

Curlew Island Curse Strikes Again?

Could the recent shooting spree at a downtown café in picturesque Marion Inlet be the result of a curse? Sandpiper Boone, a resident of Curlew Island, was caught in the hail of bullets that left three dead and five injured.

According to legend, in 1801 a schooner ship bound for Charleston Harbor went aground on the island. Only one sailor lived to tell of the horrible fate of his fellow seamen. He declared the island cursed and named it Baal. For over 150 years, sailors and locals alike avoided the area, until William and Lucinda Boone purchased the land in 1958. They immediately changed the name from Baal to Curlew.

Their only child, Montgomery, sold an acre of land at the north end of the island to a doctor, then built the 7,000-square-foot house in 1999. Montgomery was the first to succumb to the alleged curse. An amateur but talented metal sculptor, he was electrocuted when welding in his studio in 2001. No one was on the island at the time.

Less than a year later, Caroline and Montgomery's 22-year-old daughter, Sparrow, died under mysterious circumstances. The family moved off the island but continued to use it as a retreat and vacation home. Tragedy struck again when three-year-old Dove, the daughter of Sandpiper Boone Yates, was abducted and later found dead. A third member of the Boone family, Raven, vowed she'd never set foot on the island again . . .

A photo of me, snapped the day before as I left the hospital, was next to the article. I snorted. "Total nonsense. Ridiculous."

"What is?"

I handed my cell to Mandy. The woman read the article, then handed it back. "Is any of that true?"

"Sparrow did die, but hardly under mysterious circumstances. She was thrown from one of the golf carts on the island and hit her head. Father's accident was just that. He'd been welding on his latest piece and apparently thought he'd turned off the electric power inside the welder case, but the power disconnect switch was faulty. And Dove . . . well, yes." I carefully folded the napkin in my lap and placed it on the table.

"That's three people in one family. I can see where someonc would start to think that way . . ."

"Two of them were accidents. As for Raven, I have no idea where they came up with that statement. Raven is estranged from the family, but she lives in Mount Pleasant." I sighed. "Tern is going to go ballistic."

"What about the ship? The legend?"

"I've heard about it, of course. At one time my dad had a journal, handwritten, that told about the shipwreck. I read it and asked him about it. He said it wasn't true."

"Who wrote the journal?"

"I don't remember."

"Do ya still have it?"

I shook my head. "You're like a bulldog with this legend thing."

Mandy grinned at me. "Aren't you?"

The waitress brought the bill and left it on the table. I checked the total and took out my wallet. "I suppose at one time or another, all of us kids—Sparrow, Raven, Tern, and I—scouted the island looking for treasure, or graves, or some evidence of the shipwreck. It was like a game to us." I pulled out a credit card. "The only man-made thing we ever found was the concrete building at the north end, which is now part of Joyce's house. Joyce loved the view and didn't want to tear down something that could be historical, so she added on to the structure. As for the journal, I think Raven asked for it when she moved out." I checked my watch. "Do you have to be back at work?"

"Not today. My shift ended with the dressin' down."

The waitress snagged the card and bill as she scurried past.

"Well." Mandy placed her napkin on the table. "Thanks for the great lunch. And the sympathetic ear."

"Glad to help."

The waitress returned with my receipt and card. "Have a nice day."

I signed, tucked my card into my wallet, and stood. Mandy joined me. The café had become packed and we had to weave between the diners. More than a few of them paused in eating to watch me move past. I ducked my head and let my hair cover my face. *Doggone that reporter.*

Once outside, Mandy paused. "Aren't ya pickin' up Dr. Mueller's granddaughter this afternoon?"

"Yes. And Tucker, the man who took a bullet for me. He

needed a place for some R & R." I caught Mandy's expression. "It's the least I could do."

Walking to my car, I pulled out the keys. Mandy, walking beside me, slowed, then stopped. "Piper, do ya think ya could get that journal from your sister? Mount Pleasant is on your way to the airport."

I jerked to a halt. "I don't really know if she has it, and anyway, I haven't had contact with Raven for something like sixteen or seventeen years. I doubt she'd want to see me now."

"Why? Why the silence, if ya don't mind me askin'?"

Around us the palms and palmetto fronds softly clacked in the breeze. The humidity was slight this time of year, and the air was pleasantly warm. "You know, after all this time, I really don't know. I don't even know if she stays in touch with other members of the family."

Mandy pursed her lips for a moment. "If this is a forgiveness thing, if she's somehow wronged ya, don't ya think it's time ya made up? Sixteen or seventeen years is a long time to hold a grudge. She's family."

"It's not like that. We were never close. She went her own way. I mean, the last gift I got from her was this key ring." I held up a key ring with a robin engraved on a medallion. "It came with a key on it."

"That could be a clue to—"

"No." I separated one of the keys. "The key's a blank. It opens nothing. Just to let me know I should put keys on it, I guess." How to explain my family? I stared sightlessly at the line of clouds forming in the east. "Have you ever had times in your life that seem like a blur? Like you were on a hamster wheel and the world was rushing by?"

"Yes."

"That whole time of my life was like that. I was supposed to marry well, have children, carry on the family name. I went to a private boarding school, got good grades, did everything I was supposed to. I was just nineteen when I married Ashlee, and we got pregnant right away. I was thrilled. Dove came along and she was my world. Then she was gone. I could barely function. I . . . really wanted to just curl up and die." I grasped my right wrist, making sure my bracelet covered the scars. "Nothing had meaning. I had a hole in my chest that wouldn't heal. My marriage disintegrated. I didn't care. No one called or came around anymore, because they didn't know what to say. I moved away, went back to college, got a job . . ." I sucked in some air and let it out slowly. *This is the first time I've been able to talk about Dove without feeling as if a knife were turning in my stomach.* I brought my gaze down to Mandy. "I'm sorry, that was too much information, and I'm diving into a pity party. But I think you're right. Maybe I will pay Raven a visit. That journalist had to have had a source for the legend. Maybe Raven is trying to stir up trouble for the family."

"Or reach out to ya. What did she want to say to ya with that blank key? Call me if ya find the journal."

"I will." I slid into my car, pulled out my cell, and dialed Mildred. "Do you know if Raven's moved from her condo in Mount Pleasant?"

Mildred was silent so long I thought the connection had dropped. "Hello?"

"As far as I know, she still owns the condo."

I could hear the question in her voice but decided to ignore it. "I'll be home for dinner and will be bringing a guest. He'll be staying with us for a bit."

"He?"

"Tucker Landry. The man who saved my life. He needs recovery time away from the press, and I offered him a room."

"I see. Not a problem for dinner, but where are you having him stay? All the rooms here are full."

All but one. I gripped the steering wheel in my suddenly sweaty hands. I knew what Mildred was asking. "Put him in the blue room."

"Are you sure?"

"Yes." The blue room. Formerly painted pink and white and filled with dolls, stuffed animals, and little girl's clothes. Even though it had been redecorated as a guest room, no one had slept there for fifteen years.

CHAPTER 9

"Okay, just about done." A nurse removed the IV line from Tucker's arm. "Do you have someone picking you up?"

"Yes. She'll be here soon."

Someone tapped on the door, then opened it. A tall, distinguished-looking man with short-cropped white hair entered. His posture reflected a military background. "Tucker Landry?"

"I'm Tucker."

"Mr. Landry, I'm Joel Christianson. I work for the Boone family. Piper called and had me pick up your things at your hotel to take to Curlew. She thought you might need a change of clothing." He held up Tucker's suitcase.

The nurse patted Tucker on the arm and left.

"She thinks of everything." Tucker moved his legs so the suitcase could be placed on the bed. "Thank you."

"Thank *you*, Mr. Landry, for saving her life. My wife, Mildred, and I think the world of that girl." He set the suitcase on the bed and opened it. Tucker's clothing had been precisely folded and carefully packed.

"Been with the Boones long?"

"Mildred has been with Piper's mother since Caroline was a child. Mildred's mother worked for Caroline's family. To my wife, Caroline's like a sister and the Boones are her family."

Tucker pulled out his loosest slacks and a golf shirt. "I hope I won't be a bother staying with the family," he said casually.

"Not at all. They all gather this time of year for the stockholders' meeting, so one more isn't a problem. They bring on extra staff to help. And you would be their honored guest."

"So the whole family gets together on the island only once a year?"

Joel straightened and stepped back. "Sort of. Piper's been living at the family compound for a while. Both Mrs. Boone and Tern come over fairly often as they live nearby. Ashlee comes once a year—"

"Piper's ex-husband is there now?"

"He is head of sales and a shareholder." His nose twitched as if smelling something bad. "I doubt you'll see much of him. He'll be on the computer or phone or working out."

Tucker closed the suitcase. "Sounds like you don't much care for Ashlee."

Joel rubbed his hand across his mouth, then shrugged. "Ancient history." He picked up the suitcase and headed for the door.

"Does this have something to do with Dove?"

Joel stopped. "You know about Dove?"

"Piper told me."

"Well. That's new. She never talks about her. Ever." He studied Tucker for a moment. "What's your angle here? What were you doing in Marion Inlet yesterday?"

It was none of this man's business, but alienating the family help wouldn't be the best course of action. "I've been working at the *H. L. Hunley*, updating some facial reconstructions. I thought I'd take a day to see the area."

"The *Hunley*?"

"The world's first successful combat submarine, launched in 1864—"

"Yes, yes, I know all that." Joel shifted the suitcase to his other hand. "Retired navy myself." His features relaxed. "I've been to the museum in Charleston a number of times. Fascinating history. The *Hunley* was discovered by NUMA, the National Underwater and Marine Agency."

"That's right. You know your history."

"NUMA. Wasn't that started by the author fellow?"

Tucker nodded. "Clive Cussler. The remains of the sailors were still on board after 131 years. A casting of the men's skulls was used to create three-dimensional facial reconstructions. I'm reviewing the reconstructions to confirm the correctness of the work and possibly create a two-dimensional painting."

"You'll find Piper to be a history fanatic, so be prepared." Joel looked as if he wanted to say more but instead said, "We are . . . The whole family is grateful to you, so thank you again." A curt nod of his head and he left.

Tucker picked up his cell, logged on to the hospital's internet, and typed in Piper's name. Thousands of hits about the shooting showed up. He narrowed the search by typing in "Dove." Still a huge number of hits. One newspaper article written by Bailey Norton, the woman who'd barged into his room earlier that morning, jumped out at him. "Curlew Island Curse Strikes Again?"

He was going to recover on a cursed island? What else could go wrong?

I walked into Tucker's hospital room as the man was practicing walking with a pair of crutches. He didn't notice me at first. I waited quietly by the door, watching him. Though the crutches were awkward, he moved with a practiced grace, as if he'd had to use them before.

I revised my estimation of his age, adding a few more years. A sprinkling of gray lightly frosted his temples. The day's growth of beard and mustache gave him a craggy look.

He pivoted and spotted me. His eyes opened slightly and a soft smile appeared on his lips.

The heat started in my neck and rushed to my face. Rats! I ducked, letting my hair swing forward, and inspected the bathroom doorknob. A sideways peek told me he wasn't buying my fascination with the hardware. I cleared my throat. "Um . . . are you ready to leave?"

"More than ready. Next stop, the airport?"

"We'll be taking a slight detour."

"Oh? Maybe a little sightseeing? I haven't had a chance to visit Fort Sumter."

"More like Fort Raven. My sister has a journal supposedly written by a shipwreck survivor. I want to see if she still has it. And I want to find out about a certain key."

He hobbled closer to me. "That sounds mysterious and intriguing."

His ultramarine-blue eyes were outlined by black lashes and matching brows, his skin tone now a healthy shade of tan. He reminded me of Matthew McConaughey in *Sahara*—

"Piper?"

"Um . . . yes. Sorry. Woolgathering. There was an article on the internet about a curse—"

"I read it."

"Oh. Well, don't worry, the island isn't cursed, but that legend was, to my knowledge, only ever mentioned in that single book about the area. We're going to swing by Raven's condo and see if she still has it. That reporter had to have had a source." *And if I'm going to see my sister after all these years, Tucker will make good backup.*

Before leaving the room, Tucker moved over to the bedside table, picked up three pebbles, and placed them in his pocket. I wanted to ask what he was doing but didn't want to intrude.

We made it to the car without incident, meaning without notice by the press, and didn't speak for the first few miles. I tried to concentrate on driving, but his presence seemed to fill the confined space and suck up the available air.

The closer I got to Mount Pleasant, the more my mind danced through various scenarios. What would I say to Raven? *Hi. I know we haven't spoken in a long time. Maybe it was my fault—I don't even remember after all this time, but I need to borrow a book. By the way, why did you give me a key ring with a blank key?* Would my sister be happy to see me? Angry? *Would* she even see me? What if Raven slammed the door in my face?

Come to think of it, I hoped I remembered how to get there. Mount Pleasant, located across the Cooper River from Charleston, was one of the fastest-growing cities in South Carolina. New neighborhoods sprang up quickly after Hurricane Hugo in 1989.

Fortunately Raven's condo was in an older neighborhood that had changed little since I'd last visited the area. The town houses were a different color and the landscaping more mature, but nothing else was different. Raven's condo was an end unit, facing away from the other condos. I parked in front.

"Do you want me to come in with you?" Tucker asked.

In a heartbeat. I cleared my throat, ridiculously grateful for his offer. "If you don't mind, that would be wonderful."

Slipping from the car, I grabbed his crutches from the back seat and brought them around to the passenger side. Tucker had already maneuvered from his seat. As he took the crutches from me, his hand grazed mine. A tingling jolt ran up my arm. I snatched my hand away. *Fool. Why am I even thinking like this?*

When he told me about himself, he hadn't mentioned if he was married. He didn't wear a ring, but that didn't mean anything—

"Piper? Hello? You've got a very pensive look on your face. Again." Tucker was smiling at me.

I raced toward the condo before the blush made it to my face. "Just thinking," I said over my shoulder.

I rang the doorbell before I lost my courage. The sound carried faintly through the door. Tucker joined me on the small stoop, and once again I was hyperaware of his presence. I rang the bell again.

"Doesn't look as if she's home." Tucker moved back, then hobbled to the window on the right and peeked inside. "Actually, it doesn't look as if she even lives here. The place is empty."

"You're kidding." I moved to where I could look inside as well. Tucker was correct. The room was bare of furniture. "Oh no."

"How long since you were here?"

"It's been . . . a few years."

"And your sister never mentioned that she moved?"

I looked at my shoe. *Yet another failure on my part.* "It's a long story."

"How badly did you want this journal? Or to see your sister?"

Before I could come up with some lame excuse, a voice came from behind us. "Hello?"

An elderly woman in a leopard-patterned tunic and black leggings, with a bizarre-looking, three-legged dog on a leash, stood in the parking lot behind us. "There's no solicitation here."

Tucker pivoted. "We're not—"

"And you'd better not be one of those door-to-door religious types. So beat it."

My face burned.

"Say, that's a cute dog." Tucker smiled.

"You think so?" The woman reached down and patted the dog's hairless back. The only fur appeared as tufts on its head, tail, and feet. "She's a little odd looking on account of the three legs."

I bit my lip. The three legs were the most normal-looking part of the dog.

The woman straightened. "She's a Chinese Crested. Hypo-allergenic."

"Ah." I couldn't think of anything else to say. Saying some-one's precious dog looked like a refugee from Chernobyl prob-ably wouldn't warm her heart.

Tucker indicated the condo. "We're looking—"

"To buy it? Don't bother." She took a puff on a cigarette I hadn't noticed her holding. "I tried. A bunch of times. I guess they just want the place empty. Pity." She gave Tucker a once-over. "'Course, maybe you might be able to talk them into selling. I could use a good-looking neighbor."

I opened my mouth to answer when Tucker poked me in the back.

"I don't know," he said slowly. "If this place has been empty for so long, maybe there's something wrong with it."

"Nah." Another drag on the cigarette. "Nothing's wrong with it."

"How can you be so sure?" I gave Tucker a sideways glance. I thought I'd delivered that line with conviction. Maybe I was the next Meryl Streep.

She turned and pointed at a solid-looking fence. "See that? Used to be, back when I first moved in, you could drive up to this condo without anyone the wiser. There was a small road there, and a garage where you could park your car out of sight. That's what made it such a catch. Privacy. Then someone had that fence built, the garage torn down, and anyone coming to this place had to come past the other units. A cleaning and maintenance crew comes in once a month."

"So how long have you lived here?" I asked.

"Moved in when it was first built. About eighteen to twenty years ago."

I tried to keep from bouncing with excitement. She'd lived here while Raven did! "Did you know the occupant?"

"Nope." She took a thoughtful drag on her cigarette. "Like I said, private."

"So you didn't see the previous owner?" Tucker asked.

"Maybe once or twice. Years ago. Pretty lady. Saw her husband a few times."

Raven never married . . . at least that I was aware of. She used to have plenty of boyfriends. "I see." How to ask more about this? "Um, when did . . . they move out?" Loosening my clenched fingers, I pasted a hopeful smile on my face. *Please remember something.*

"A long time ago, maybe ten years or more now, a moving van drove up and emptied the place out. While they were busy hauling furniture, I decided to take a look around. I walked in as pretty as you please and wandered through the whole place. No one stopped me. I coulda been a crook or something. The furniture was beautiful, really pricey stuff. Lots of books and knickknacks."

I wanted to ask her the name of the moving company, the husband, anything else she could remember, but considering I was supposed to be interested in buying the unit, that would trigger her alarm. Asking about an old journal would raise the same level of suspicion.

The woman tugged on the dog and pursed her lips. Her gaze went back and forth between Tucker and me, as if regretting saying too much. *Ask about the condo.*

"Thank you so much for the information. The place might be too small, though. We'll keep looking." *Nice, Meryl.* I stepped forward as if to leave.

"It's plenty big." She relaxed. "Two bedrooms on the second floor, one on the third. One of the two bedrooms had been turned into an office. The third bedroom was empty. Not even curtains on the windows."

Tucker nodded. "That does sound big. If I wanted to convince someone to sell, who would I contact?"

"I'd guess the folks who own the whole building."

"And that would be?" I asked.

"Boone Industries."

CHAPTER 10

The older woman didn't move as they made their way back to the car. They drove away in silence. Once more on the road to the airport, Tucker twisted in his seat to see Piper more clearly. The faint flush in her cheeks told him she was aware of his attention. "Did you know your family owned that building?"

"No, but they do own a lot of real estate."

"What about Raven's work? Her job. You could ask there."

"Raven, well, you could say she enjoyed her freedom. Even though she had a degree in business, she didn't hold a job. The family money provided her with enough income, as long as she was reasonable in her spending." She gave him a quick sideways glance.

"Someone in your family should know where your sister moved."

Piper caught her lower lip with her teeth. "Maybe. We, that is, my family, tend to go our own ways. I'm closest to my brother, Tern. I think . . ."

He waited for her to continue.

She gave a tiny shake of her head.

"You think . . . ?"

"Nothing. Never mind."

"What about the family business—maybe you could find out about the condo?"

"I don't know how I'd explain my sudden interest. My mother and brother run the company . . . Well, I should say Tern oversees everything, as Mother appointed him CEO a few years ago."

"Did that make you jealous?"

She glanced at him with a look of genuine surprise. "Not at all. Grandfather started the company, then passed it on to his son, my father, Montgomery. Father died in an accident, so control passed on to *his* son, my brother. I never expected it to come to me."

"You mentioned a stockholders' meeting. You own stock?"

"It's a privately held corporation with Mother, Raven, Tern, Ashlee, and me as shareholders. If anyone passes away, the shares are equally divided among the survivors—except for Ashlee, whose shares don't change." Piper parked in the parking garage across from the airport terminal.

"You mentioned that article. Could someone be trying to cause the company—or the family—problems?"

"Maybe." Piper frowned.

"We could ask the reporter where she got the information," Tucker said.

"That sounds like a plan."

He jumped from the car before she had a chance to ask him to wait and maneuvered his crutches from the back seat.

She pulled out a wide-brimmed hat and put it on. As they moved into the sunshine and crossed the street, the hat allowed a pattern of sun-dots to freckle her face. She looked beautiful.

"How will you recognize Hannah?" he asked once they'd entered the terminal.

Piper scanned the arriving flight information on the screen in front of her. "I'm hoping she'll see me. I said I'd wear this hat. She seemed pretty confident we wouldn't have a problem."

Arriving passengers streamed around them heading to baggage claim. Piper examined the faces of passing women. "This should be her flight . . ."

A striking young woman with long blond hair appeared, staring to her left.

Piper stepped forward and raised her hand.

The woman swung her gaze around, checking the waiting crowd. Massive scar tissue marred the left side of her face. A black eyepatch with a sequin butterfly covered her eye on that side. Her ear was a lump of tissue.

Piper's face drained of color. Tucker fully expected her to turn and bolt.

She raised her hand higher and waved. "Hannah?"

The young woman paused as if waiting for Piper to change her mind.

Piper raced forward and embraced Hannah in a hug. "I am so happy to meet you. Welcome to South Carolina."

He slowly nodded. Piper's complexion was still pale, but she greeted the badly burned woman as if meeting Miss America.

"Anything new on Grandma's whereabouts?" Hannah asked.

"She hasn't shown up." Piper took a deep breath. "But we'll keep on the police." She pulled Hannah out of the main stream of passengers. "How was your flight? Is this your first visit to South Carolina? Do you have luggage?" Piper barely paused for breath. "Are you hungry?"

Hannah opened her eyes wide. "Wow. And I thought you'd be a bit distant. More of, like, a Southern belle. Grandma always said you were, like, proper. That I should be more like you."

"Oh my. Dr. Mueller said that?" Piper ducked her head for a moment. "No one should be like me," she whispered, then straightened. "I *am* being rude. Hannah . . . um, is your last name Mueller?"

"It is now. I took my grandmother's name."

"Hannah, I'd like you to meet my friend Tucker Landry." Piper lightly touched him on the arm. "Tucker, this is Hannah Mueller. Now then, the formalities are over." Piper let go of Tucker's arm. "Luggage?"

Hannah nodded.

He could still feel Piper's hand on his arm. He liked the feeling.

The people by the baggage carousel parted as we approached, glancing at Hannah and just as quickly looking away. Hannah seemed oblivious to their stares. I knew my face would be showing my distress, but I wrapped one arm around the girl's waist. If Hannah could breeze through this crowd with such dignity, so could I.

Once we retrieved Hannah's suitcase, the three of us headed to the car. "I thought you might need to stay at the guesthouse, but the police aren't going to process your grandmother's place, so there's no reason you can't stay there." After placing the suitcase and crutches in the trunk, we got into the car.

"I know she's missing and something bad happened to her." Tears pooled in her unscarred eye.

"Don't worry, Hannah." I turned and gave her an encouraging smile. "I won't let them stop looking."

"Thank you," Hannah said. "You've been awesome."

No one spoke as I maneuvered along the highway heading south. Finally, as the traffic thinned, I spoke. "I have to apologize. I never knew your grandmother had children. I never even thought to ask."

"Grandma just had one daughter, my mother. My parents died in a house fire, which is why I look like this. I ended up living with Grandma."

"How old were you?" Tucker asked.

"Grandma said I was almost five when I came to live with her, which was twelve years ago."

That made her a year younger than my Dove would have been. They might have been friends. *Will I ever get over thinking about what woulda-coulda-shoulda happened if Dove hadn't gone on that boat ride that day? If I hadn't insisted Ashlee take her . . .*

"That must have been a rough time for you," I said.

"Grandma was there all the time, at least at first. She finally sent me to a special boarding school where there were other kids . . . like me. They became like an extended family."

"That explains how Joyce was able to come to the island for the past few years."

She nodded. "She'd leave in the winter when I was in school."

"That must have been hard on you." I watched her expression in the rearview mirror.

She looked out the window and nodded.

Piper took the exit to Marion Inlet, then pulled into a small farmer's market. "Almost there. Just a quick stop."

"Good." Hannah leaned over. "Do I have time to use the restroom?"

Piper parked, then pointed to a row of blue porta potties.

"Mind if I stretch out a bit?" Tucker asked.

"Not at all." Piper brought him his crutches from the trunk. She carried several woven tote bags. They made their way to a double row of white pop-up tents where spicy fragrances wafted through the air. The vendors called out greetings as they passed.

"Afternoon, Miss Piper. I have some spices Mildred might like."

"I've set aside some new baskets for you, Miss Piper."

"Miss Piper! You're looking fine. Check out these new soaps."

"Boiled peanuts, Miss Piper."

Piper would pause at the tent, quickly check out the wares, then make a purchase or move on. Unlike her hesitant approach to life, she knew exactly what she was looking for. He let her move ahead of him, watching her in action.

She passed a few booths without stopping. That's when he noticed it.

Several of the vendors crossed themselves as she passed. One of them made a spitting sound three times.

He was about to catch up with her when a movement caught his attention. A woman with long red hair and pale skin was keeping pace with Piper on the far side of the booths to his left. He crossed toward her through the line of vendors.

Bailey Norton, the reporter from the *Charleston Times*, was snapping photos of Piper with her cell. She spotted him and nonchalantly snapped a few shots in his direction.

"You're following us," he said as soon as he got close enough.

"You're news."

"Where did you get that book?"

"What book?"

Either she was an excellent actress, or she had no idea what he was talking about. "The book about the curse."

"Ah." She raised her eyebrows. "I thought it made a good story."

"Who sent it to you?"

"No one sent it to me, and even if they had, I wouldn't tell you. Would you care to make a statement about the case for the record?" She dropped her cell into her purse and pulled out a small recorder.

"Tucker!" Piper, both tote bags now full, came up beside them. "You!" she said to Bailey.

"How about you, Miss Boone? Care to make a statement for the press?"

Piper spun and practically ran to the car. Tucker attempted to keep up. Hannah was waiting for them.

"Get in." Piper unlocked the car, dropped one of the bags and Tucker's crutches inside the trunk, then jumped in. The minute the doors were closed, she started the engine and spun out of the parking area. "How did she know where to find us?"

"How many ways are there to get to your house?"

"Good point. If she's stalking us, who else is?" Piper shook her head. "I'm sorry. I wanted to say welcome to South Carolina and get some thank-you gifts. Here." She reached into the tote bag and handed Hannah a sweetgrass basket. "The South Carolina craft. The Gullah community, descendants of West African slaves, passed down the tradition of weaving these baskets."

"Thank you, Piper." A smile lit up the undamaged side of Hannah's face.

"For you." She gave Tucker a container of pimento cheese. "Put this on most anything. A local favorite. You'll have a small refrigerator in your room."

"Thank you." He took the container. "If nothing else, I *did* get a chance to ask the reporter about the book. She seemed to know of it, but either didn't know or wouldn't say how she got it."

Piper sighed. "Another dead end." She parked at the end of the road next to a pale-yellow house with a well-trimmed lawn. Beyond it, a dock jutted into the water. "We're here."

I shifted so I could see Tucker and Hannah. "Silva's in charge of our tiny armada and usually pilots the day cruiser, that big one over there." I pointed at the largest vessel. Several smaller boats were also tied up along the dock. A line of boathouses to the right all had rails leading inside from the water.

"Don't you get to the island by bridge?" Tucker cleared his throat. "It doesn't look that far away."

"That's not the island. Let me orient you. We're facing west. The Atlantic Ocean is behind us. What you are calling an island is a wildlife preserve and marsh. Keep going straight ahead and you'll reach the Intracoastal Waterway, which runs from Boston down to Florida, then around to Brownsville, Texas. Over there"—I pointed left—"is Marion Inlet, for which the town is named. We take the inlet to the ocean to get out to the island."

Tucker gasped. His complexion had turned gray. He cleared his throat. "I . . . I guess I didn't realize you had to go by boat . . ."

"But I thought you knew Curlew was an island."

He clutched the door handle. "Like I said, I pictured a bridge . . . or something."

"Our boats are perfectly safe, and Silva is an excellent captain, but if you'd rather stay on the mainland here at the guesthouse . . . ?"

Tucker's gaze was focused on the boats tied up to the dock. "I don't know."

I turned to see Hannah. "How about you? Here or your grandma's place?"

"If you don't mind, I think I'd like to stay here tonight. I don't think I'm ready to face Grandma's place just yet."

"Do you want me to stay with you?"

"Ah, Piper, you're just as nice as Grandma said. I'm fine alone. As long as you have internet."

"Of course. Okay then." I opened the car door. "I'll get Hannah settled while you decide, Tucker. Whatever you are most comfortable with is fine with me." I gave him a reassuring smile, stood, and retrieved Hannah's suitcase from the trunk. Hannah followed me to the split staircase leading to the house.

Hannah paused at the base of the stairs. "Does it matter which side I go up? And, like, why is the house up in the air?"

"The house here and the one on the island are built on pilings in case of flooding, and the split staircase is called petticoat stairs. It's a nod to tradition going back to when women wore hoop skirts. It would be very impolite for a gentleman to follow a lady up the stairs and possibly see her petticoat, so women went up one side and men the other."

"Awesome!"

We kept the key inside one of the rods of the wind chimes by the door. The door opened to a large common area used for both living and dining. The kitchen was on our left and bedrooms on the right. A wide porch overlooked the shoreline ahead of us. The house was aired and had fresh flowers in the vases. A bowl of fruit rested on the counter. A cleaning and maintenance service kept the house ready for guests.

"Awesome possum!" Hannah gave me a lopsided grin.

I set down her suitcase and followed her to the porch.

"I love it here! This is beautiful." As she stared at the water, Hannah's eye welled with tears. "What do you think happened to Grandma?"

"I don't know, sweetheart." The endearment came naturally from my lips. I slipped an arm around her shoulder and gave her a quick hug. "Let's call the police and see if there's anything new." Pulling my cell out of my purse, I looked up the phone number and dialed. After a recording told me I could dial the party's extension at any time, I finally got a human. "I'm calling to see if you have an update on Dr. Joyce Mueller."

"What kind of an update were you looking for?" The woman sounded bored.

"She's missing."

"Did you file a missing-persons report?"

"Yes. Last night. At least I think Mandy filed one."

"What was the name again?"

"Dr. Joyce Mueller. M-u-e-l-l-e-r." I rolled my eyes at Hannah. The clatter of a keyboard carried clearly through the phone.

"Nope. Nothing in the system."

"Excuse me?"

"Look." The woman went from bored to irritated. "You can

file online. W-w-w-dot-Marion-Inlet-police—one word—dot-g-o-v."

"But—"

Click.

"What's wrong?" Hannah asked.

"Um . . . I guess I need to get some more information to the police. Did you find a list of relatives and friends?"

"Yes. I brought her Christmas card list."

"If you don't mind my taking it, I'll . . . update the police on my computer." I moved to the sideboard in the dining room, which held the house phone. "To get in touch with anyone on the island, dial the number on this pad of paper." I pulled open the drawer and pulled out the paper, followed by several menus. "Feel free to order food from these restaurants. They all deliver and know to bill us. The house computer is in that alcove over there. Are you sure you'll be okay here tonight?"

"Yes."

I handed her the key. "Lock up tight. Let me go and see if Tucker wants to stay here as well."

After Piper and Hannah went into the house, Tucker slowly got out of the car and retrieved his crutches from the trunk. The house looked very inviting. He turned toward it, then looked at the waiting boat. *It is time.*

He swung toward the dock. *Think about something else. This is only a dock. Nothing bad happened to you here.*

But something bad *did* happen. Not to him. To Piper.

He stopped. Piper's daughter was abducted from here. He

could see how the crime occurred. A small structure, probably for storing boating equipment, perched at the end of the dock with an inviting gazebo surrounding it. Someone easily could have hidden inside the structure and jumped out when Piper's husband docked.

He moved closer. *That's it.* He needed to not think about his own darkness, his own fears, his own loss. Another step forward. He was an investigator once, before his career ended. Two more steps. He was now at the start of the dock. He slipped his hand into his slacks and felt the pebbles.

The captain of the day cruiser spotted him. "Come on over and get comfortable."

Tucker was far from where *it* happened. This was an inlet, not a river. It smelled of salt and sea creatures, not pine. *Think about Piper's case.* He had offered to help her. "Sure. I'm Tucker, by the way. Tucker Landry."

"I know who you are, Mr. Landry. All over the news. You saved our Piper. Name's Silva."

Keep your eyes on the captain. Move forward. "Call me Tucker. Nice to meet you, Mr. Silva. Or is it Captain Silva?" Almost there.

"Just Silva. Watch your step."

Tucker looked down and froze. Black water, visible between the boards of the dock, lapped less than two feet beneath him.

"I said, are you okay?" Someone gripped his arm.

Tucker jumped. Silva was next to him, holding his arm. The captain's brows were furrowed. "You having trouble with your injury? You're white as a ghost."

"Um . . . yeah. Injury." He concentrated on the colorful pillows decorating the bench seat on the open deck, maneuvering his hurt leg over the boat's side. Silva almost lifted him into the boat. He dropped onto a cushioned seat and swiped the sweat slithering down his cheek.

"Here." Silva shoved a refillable bottle of water into his hand.

Tucker opened it and took a long drink. "Thanks. I guess I'm still a bit shaky." *Concentrate on Piper.* Drawing her daughter. Moving away from That Night. "How long have you worked for the Boone family, Silva?"

"From the beginning, Mr. Landry. From the time Montgomery Boone built the house on the island."

"You must know the family pretty well."

"Well enough."

Tucker took another drink of water. "So. Am I really going to a cursed island?"

Silva's lids dropped over his eyes like shutters. "That's what some say."

CHAPTER 11

Piper appeared, spotted him, and waved. He waved back. She trotted toward them.

Tucker turned back to Silva. "We stopped at a farmer's market just now. Some of the people crossed themselves or spit three times as Piper walked past their booths."

Silva cussed softly under his breath. "Yeah. I saw the article. I'll kill the reporter who wrote about it. Let sleeping dogs lie and all that. Now it's more grief for Piper and the family." He jumped from the boat to the dock.

As soon as she was near, she said, "I take it you've decided to stay on the island after all." She handed her purchases to Silva.

He nodded and tried to stand to help her. Before he could get his crutches placed, she'd lightly jumped on board, barely rocking the boat.

"I'm glad you're coming." She took a seat next to him.

His pulse quickened at her nearness.

Silva untied the boat and turned left. They soon rounded the end of the mainland and headed out to sea.

With one hand, Tucker held the side of the boat in a death

grip. The other clutched the stones in his pocket and squeezed. *Concentrate on something else.* "Kinda windy out here. Did you want to move inside?" He nodded at the cabin.

He felt more than saw a small shiver run through her. "Nope. Too enclosed. I have claustrophobia."

He raised his eyebrows.

She lifted one shoulder. "It started with Dove's passing. My vivid imagination, thinking of the water closing over her head . . ."

Now it was Tucker's turn to shiver. "Yes, I can . . . relate. Well then, since I'm about to meet them, tell me about your family."

She leaned closer to be heard over the boat's engine. "My grandparents William and Lucinda Boone started the family company, which made plumbing supplies." She smiled. "Who would have thought sinks and toilets would be so profitable? Their son, my father, Montgomery, grew the business and branched out into other endeavors." She fluttered her hand in front of her face and drawled, "He married mah mother, the former Car-o-line Beauregard, of the Atlanta Beauregards, a fine ol' Southern family. Grandfather Beauregard died young of a heart attack, leavin' the family, as the sayin' goes, too poor to paint, too proud to whitewash. Grandmother died young too, but my mother married well." Her eyes became unfocused.

He wanted to ask more, but before he could formulate a question, she continued in her usual voice. "There were four of us children. Tern, the only boy, then Sparrow, Raven, then me. As you've read, Sparrow passed in her early twenties."

In the distance, a low mound took shape and grew larger.

"Mother often said Montgomery built the perfect home for the perfect family on the perfect island. But . . ."

"But your daughter died there?"

"Yes. Father died first, then Sparrow." She gave him a quick, humorless smile. "The only other folks are the permanent staff. Silva here." She nodded toward the captain. "Joel, whom you met, and Joel's wife, Mildred. They both live on the island year-round and are like family. I suspect they'd lay down their lives for us."

Tucker felt a pang in his chest. What would it be like to have people care so much? *Change the subject.* The island stretched ahead, with a wooden dock jutting out into the water. The same small structure appeared at the end. Tucker nodded at the building. "What's that?"

"A storage shed. Like on the other dock."

"Is it kept locked?" he asked.

Her gaze sharpened on him. "On the island, no. The one on the mainland is locked with a numeric keypad. And *was* locked the day Dove was kidnapped—if that's why you're asking."

"It is."

"The police said there wasn't any sign of forced entry, that the killer probably hid behind the shed and waited. They said the boat was probably the target—it was brand new—and the killer didn't realize Dove was on board. When he did . . . well, he couldn't leave a witness . . ." She had slumped in her seat.

Silva expertly whipped the boat around until it was again facing out to sea, then maneuvered it to the dock. Before Tucker could move, Silva had secured the boat and jumped back on board to grab Piper's bags. Piper followed him. After handing Piper her things, Silva reached across to help Tucker.

Tucker clenched his jaw and concentrated on the proffered hand. He would not look down at the inky water between boat and dock. Once again Silva yanked him across, bracing him while he adjusted his crutches.

Fortunately Piper didn't see his clumsy movements. She was digging into her bag. "Here, Silva, I brought you some boiled peanuts." She handed him a paper sack. "I got you the Cajun spiced."

"Thank you, Miss Piper. Do you or Mr. Tucker need help getting over to the house?"

"We're fine. We'll take a cart."

As at the mainland house, boathouses were lined up to the right. The shoreline was a combination of pebbles and sand, with a wooden walkway leading to a small, open-sided structure perched above the high-water mark. Three golf carts were parked underneath. The maritime forest provided a lush backdrop and, with the exception of a road, hid any sign of human habitation. A fragrant breeze stirred the foliage, creating a sibilant sigh. Piper stowed her purchases on the back seat of the largest cart, added his crutches, and hopped into the driver's seat. He sat next to her.

The cart quietly purred up the crushed-shell road and meandered through the woods before revealing the house—or rather, the mansion. Like the Boone home on the mainland, this one was raised, but the main entrance was at ground level.

Piper stopped the cart near the front. Just inside the door was a foyer. Raised voices carried faintly from somewhere upstairs. The foyer itself was impressive, open to the sky, with a lush planting of palmettos and ferns in the center, edged with hand-chiseled stone.

"During bad weather, a wall of glass can slide across that opening." Piper pointed to the upper floor overlooking the foyer. "A glass door can seal off the stairs at the top, so you still get the feeling of being outdoors. There's a similar wall in the living room."

"Clever." He moved closer to look at an unusual welded sculpture near the plantings. It was an abstract female figure.

"My father's work." Piper moved next to him. "He was an amateur sculptor. He made a smaller version for the bow of the *Faire Taire.*"

"He was talented." Tucker turned to scan the rest of the entrance. To his left was a small door set deep into the wall. Straight ahead, framed magazine covers and articles about the house and family hung on the cream-colored walls. A hand-carved wooden railing featuring palmettos lined the curving stairs and circled the upper floor.

Piper opened the door, which proved to be a small elevator wallpapered to look like a tiny library. "Ta-da! Useful for groceries, luggage, and an occasional man on crutches."

"I take it your family isn't much for primitive accommodations?" He hobbled inside and hoped she'd join him.

"Nope." She stored her packages next to him. "We have a workout room, study, game room, and media center, which used to be the sewing room. Once you push the up button, watch your hands and feet. The door doesn't open back up if they get in the way."

The voices grew louder and angrier, although he still couldn't make out any words. "Maybe I came at a bad time?"

Piper's face flushed. She gave a slight shrug, then reached inside and pushed the up button. A set of stainless steel doors quietly slid shut, followed by a small whirl and slight jerk telling him he was in motion. He wasn't surprised to see her waiting at the next floor.

The argument was now clear. "So where *do* you suppose that reporter got that information?" a female voice asked.

"Why don't you ask her?" a male voice answered.

"Ask her? I'd like to shoot her!" a second male voice said.

Piper shut the door to the elevator loudly. The voices stopped.

Tucker planted his crutches under his arms with suddenly sweaty palms. He really hadn't thought this through. These people moved in a different stratosphere with power, wealth, family breeding. He was raised by a single mother in a nondescript town and had made a catastrophe of his life. What was he even doing here?

"Come on, Tucker." Piper held out her hand. "They won't bite." Under her breath she muttered, "Much."

A hallway angled to his left, formal dining room on the right, and ahead, the source of the voices, was the living room. He wanted to fall behind her, but she determinedly took his elbow and guided him forward.

He recognized Senator Boone, facing him on the far wall, although the politician was even more imposing in person. Tern, wearing impeccably pressed chinos and a striped shirt, lounged against a six-foot flickering gas fireplace. On his right, a movable glass wall had been folded open to an outdoor deck, which overlooked the sand dunes and ocean. A woman stood in the center of the opening, watching the water. She turned as they entered.

"Tucker, may I introduce my mother, Caroline Boone. Mother, meet Tucker Landry."

Caroline Boone came forward, both hands extended. "Mr. Landry, welcome to Curlew Island. You saved my daughter, which makes you our special guest." Her rich voice held just a slight Southern accent. She had short-cropped white hair perfectly sculpted to her head. Her face was lean and smooth. She wore an off-white, raw silk jacket and slacks with a coffee-colored shell blouse. She reminded him of Glenn Close. "Come, sit down. I'm sure being on your feet must be difficult with those crutches." She led him to the sofa facing the ocean. "I think you'll find our little island very healing. The ocean air, wildlife, sounds of the birds and breezes through the palmettos." She took a deep breath. "Mmm, just smell that air."

Tucker took an obligatory breath. It did smell good.

Before taking a chair, Caroline removed the throw pillow and placed it on the sofa, aligning it perfectly with the armrest.

Piper sat down next to Tucker.

A dark-haired man with intense, deep-set eyes stood near a grand piano. He wore khaki cargo slacks and an open-collared white dress shirt. Without waiting for an introduction, the man stepped forward holding out a hand. "I'm Ashlee Yates."

The ex-husband. "Mr. Yates, nice to meet you." They shook hands.

"Please, call me Ashlee. You have amazing reaction time to have saved Piper like that." He gave Tucker a once-over. "You look like an athlete. What's your sport?"

"Not much right now. I used to compete a bit in the Ironman."

"That explains it!" Ashlee grinned at Tucker, then looked over at Piper. "A 2.4-mile swim, followed by a 112-mile bicycle race, followed by a 26.2-mile marathon. Toughest one-day sport competition in the world. It's on my bucket list." He looked back at Tucker. "Once you've recovered, maybe we could do some jogging. Better yet, have you tried windsurfing?"

Tucker tried not to wince. "I'm currently not much for water sports."

Tern approached him, also with an outstretched hand. "Ah, the hero of the hour, and forever in our gratitude for saving our Piper. Welcome, welcome!" They shook. "What can I bring you? Bourbon? Scotch? We have a wonderful Macallan single malt."

He could feel the rocks in his pocket pressing against his leg. "No, just a glass of water if it's not too much trouble." He adjusted his slacks.

"Ice? Lemon?" Piper asked.

"Sure."

An older, chunky woman wearing a sky-blue housedress and apron appeared, gave Tern a nod, then returned shortly with Tucker's drink.

"Thank you." Piper jumped up and took the glass from the woman. "And, Tucker, this is Mildred. She keeps us all sane and running smoothly. You met her husband, Joel."

"Ma'am." Tucker nodded at the woman.

Mildred gave him a brief smile, then left. Tucker sipped his water and checked out the surroundings. The off-white walls featured original oil paintings of the lowlands. White furniture with matching oyster-colored throw pillows surrounded a hand-knotted area rug. The light-colored wood floor rippled with dappled light, and a slight breeze off the ocean kept the temperature comfortable.

"Have the police—"

"The tropical storm—"

"Go ahead," Ashlee said.

Tern laughed. "I was just noting that the tropical storm's been upgraded to a category two hurricane and named Marco."

"Hurricane!" Tucker glanced outside.

"Don't let Tern alarm you, Mr. Landry." Caroline stood and returned to the open side of the room. She examined a painting, touched the bottom corner to straighten it, then turned and looked at him. "We keep track of such things as a precaution while we're here. I'm sure this hurricane is quite far away, and should anything change, there's a thirty-six-hour advance warning that's issued. We'll have plenty of notice if we are in any danger."

"As long as the hurricane doesn't take an unexpected turn and make a run for us." Tern had moved outside to the edge of the deck to light a pipe. He raised his voice slightly to be heard. "Like Sandy, Katrina, and Florence. A good storm surge would pretty much scour this little island clean."

CHAPTER 12

Mother made sure she had my attention, then shifted her eyes to indicate I was to follow her. As we entered the hall, Mildred was standing in the kitchen doorway. "Miss Caroline, dinner is almost ready."

"I'll just be a moment." Mother took my arm and steered me to the side of the hall overlooking the foyer below. Mildred returned to her dinner preparations. "Piper, I read that awful piece in the paper about the curse. Our family is getting all kinds of attention—the wrong kind. What do you know about it?"

"The reporter who wrote it is stalking us, or at least stalking Tucker and me."

"You know how I hate this kind of thing. Especially now."

I looked away. My brother and mother had worked so hard to craft a wetlands conservation bill that was coming up for a vote. If Tern could garner good press, that would help sway the undecided in the state senate. And he had plans for a higher office. "You'll need to maintain an extremely low profile."

"I understand."

"You need to stay off the press's radar."

"Yes, Mother." What would she say if she knew how much family history I'd shared with Mandy and Tucker? What if they talked to the press?

Mildred leaned around the door and cleared her throat. "Dinner is served."

Returning to the living room, I kept my face down until I figured my color was close to normal. I helped Tucker stand, then followed the family as we passed through the entry to the formal dining room. Mother moved to her usual place at the head of the table, where Tern was holding her chair. She waved her hand for Tucker to sit on her right. I snagged the seat next to Tucker, with Ashlee across from me and Tern opposite Mother. Once Tucker was seated, Mildred took his crutches and leaned them against the wall.

No one spoke as Mildred and BettyJo served the first course and Joel came around the table with a bottle of white wine. Tucker declined. Joel discreetly avoided offering me any. Booze, along with the scars on my wrist, belonged to a past I never wanted to revisit.

Tucker looked down and closed his eyes for a moment while his lips moved.

The man must be religious. The first tiny smudge appeared on his otherwise spotless superhero persona. The rudeness of the thought made my face burn. I bent over the watermelon gazpacho and let my hair curtain my face.

"So, Piper." Ashlee's voice broke into my thoughts. "How did you keep yourself busy today? I mean, outside of throwing cash at a bunch of homeless animals and bailing Tucker here out of the hospital."

"You're not still involved with that dirty animal shelter, are you?" Mother asked. "I do wish you'd find a . . . tidier charity. Like a wildlife refuge."

I clenched my teeth for a moment. I didn't need Ashlee's condescension nor my mother's disdain.

"Many of the animals at the shelter are wild. Does that count?" I smiled, exposing my gritted teeth.

Mother tightened her lips before hiding them behind a delicately dabbed napkin.

Ashlee smirked at me.

Maybe I could shake him up. I picked up my water glass. "I did have an interesting day. Tucker and I went to Mount Pleasant and tried to locate Raven—"

Someone gasped.

I looked up. Everyone was staring at me.

"Why did you want to find our sister?" Tern asked.

"That silly article in the paper." I put down my glass and glanced at Mother. She'd carefully placed her spoon on the table. My heart rate increased. I wished I hadn't said anything. I didn't want, or need, the family to be upset with me.

"Go on," Ashlee said.

"Um, I figured it came from the old journal that Raven had. I wanted to ask her about it. I found out she left her condo a long time ago and—"

"You drove to her condo?" Mother cleared her throat. "Did it occur to you that you could have just asked me? I would have told you she wasn't living there."

"No." My gaze went between Mother and Tern. I dried my sweaty palms on the linen napkin in my lap. I knew what would come next. Mother would glance at Tucker, then Ashlee, then me. It would be her unspoken signal that nothing relating to the family, certainly nothing of an unpleasant nature, was discussed in front of guests. I'd broken our family's unwritten, unspoken code of silence.

"Never mind." Mother smiled slightly at Ashlee as she arranged her wine glass above her knife. "I do hope we'll have a good report from you tomorrow on that market you've been researching."

I balled up my napkin.

Tucker reached over and lightly touched my hand. "'Nobody puts Baby in a corner,'" he whispered.

Warmth radiated up my arm. "*Dirty Dancing*, 1987," I whispered back and took a deep breath. "Tucker and I went to the condo to see Raven and to ask about the journal. An older woman, apparently a longtime neighbor, said Raven moved out around ten years ago. She said she saw Raven's husband—"

Tern leaned forward. "Was she watching the place?"

"No. Just out walking her weird-looking dog. She saw us on the front steps."

"How interesting." Mother looked at Tern. "I have an invitation to speak at the Audubon's Eastern Carolina Center and Sanctuary next month."

Normally I would have slunk down in my seat and concentrated on the soup, but Tucker's light touch still lingered on my hand. *What is so wrong with asking about my sister?* "I was just wondering what you knew about her."

Mother's eyes glinted. "Well—"

"It's okay, Mother." Tern gave me a sympathetic smile. "You've not exactly sought out Raven before now. She stays in touch."

Ashlee started coughing. He covered his mouth and waved at his wineglass. "Wrong pipe," he managed to sputter.

I waited until Ashlee stopped coughing before I asked Tern, "Raven stays in touch with you?"

"And me," Mother said. "She emails me on occasion. And of course she votes on company business by email. Now can we drop the subject?"

Feeling like a chastised five-year-old, I made a point of smoothing out the napkin in my lap. Tern was right. I hadn't even thought about my sister for a long time, certainly not until Mandy had asked me about her. I should have just asked Tern.

"Your daughter Raven sounds like quite a character," Tucker said smoothly. "Maybe even a bit mysterious."

I looked over at my mother. She wouldn't be outwardly impolite and would pass his comments off as Yankee ignorance.

"Yes, bless your heart, you're a peach for asking about her."

Oh boy. "Bless your heart" and calling him a peach in Southern parlance often meant very much the opposite.

"Raven's been . . . finding herself," Tern said. "I believe she's at an ashram in India right now."

"Interesting," Tucker said.

"Thank you for sharing, Tern." Mother's voice oozed syrup.

Mildred placed her hand on my shoulder and squeezed gently as she filled my iced-tea glass. Another subtle reminder to keep the peace. And silent.

I looked around the table at their smooth expressions. Suddenly I felt like a guest surrounded by strangers at a formal dinner party. Maybe it was the annoying pain in my ankle from the shooting. Maybe it was the shock of seeing someone lying dead beside me just yesterday. Maybe it was even the strength of Tucker's presence that made me blurt out, "Tucker has agreed to age-progress Dove's photograph for me."

You could have heard the soft scuffing of the pampas grass outside.

"Piper, I'd like to see you in my room later tonight." Mother turned to Ashlee. "Did you get a chance to read that book I recommended?" She, Ashlee, and Tern spent the remainder of dinner dissecting a recent bestseller.

I wanted to go on and tell them about Hannah and find out if anyone had heard from Joyce, but I knew I'd already committed *the* major faux pas by talking about the family in front of strangers.

Mother finally addressed our guest. "Tucker, won't you join us in the living room for a digestif?"

"Thank you, ma'am, but if you will excuse me, I think I'll lie down and get a few painkillers in me."

Joel quietly moved toward Tucker's crutches.

"Of course. I'll send a few naturopathic pain relievers with Mildred, who will show you to your room. I believe your things are already there."

"I'll do it, Mother." I pushed back my chair. "And if you'll excuse me as well, I'll be going for a walk before going to bed." I stood and moved out of the room with Tucker following.

The dining room opened to both the kitchen and the hall. Tucker looked around, then at me. "Okay, I admit I'm lost."

"Not to worry. You recognize the door over there to the elevator, and the stairs leading to the ground-floor entry."

He nodded.

"So basically the house sprawls out two directions—two wings—from this central living area. Most of the bedrooms are in the north wing"—I pointed left—"along with the gym and media center. The southern wing has my room, the blue room—where you are—the game room, study, and Mother's suite."

"You mentioned a media room that used to be the sewing room. Did someone sew?"

"No." I slowed. "That was originally Sparrow's room. My oldest sister. She sewed a bit and had a machine in her room. When she passed, the sewing stuff stayed for a while, and I guess it was less painful to call it a sewing room than to refer to Sparrow. Later the room was redone into a media center."

"What about your father's sculpture studio? Was that changed into another room as well?"

"No." I stopped. "Funny—not like ha-ha, but strange—but I have to admit I haven't thought about his studio in a long time. Do you have enough energy to see it? It's pretty close."

"I'd like that."

"Take the elevator to the ground floor. I'll meet you there." I took the stairs two at a time and beat him to the foyer. We walked out of the front door and I turned right, passing under the house through an opening in the lattice. It was getting dark, but lights illuminated the walkways. Katydids chattered from the palms, and the ocean crashed and hissed in the distance. The air still carried the warmth from the day. Father's studio was a building originally intended to be a garage in which to store carts and other equipment. Joel and Mildred's apartment was above the garage and accessible by an enclosed walkway leading to the north wing. When the garage was converted to a studio, the garage door had been left in place and proved to be useful when Father needed to move larger pieces. The smaller door had a combination lock on it. "Let's see if I remember the numbers." I tried several sets. No luck. "I tried his wedding anniversary, birthday, and Mother's birthday."

"When did he move to the island?"

"Good suggestion." I bent over the lock. This time it sprang open. The door screeched a protest when I pushed it, and we were greeted with the odors of dust, grease, and stale air. I flipped on the light and the overhead fluorescents flickered on.

Worktables lined the walls, and dusty tools—hammers, calipers, metal rods, gloves, a welding helmet—were scattered across the surface, but the welding equipment had long since been removed. All that remained in the center of the room was a hydraulic table on casters, built by my father to raise and lower sculptures.

Across the open space was an interior door with a window. Yellowed blinds blocked our view of the room beyond. "Father called that his office." A brief memory, my father working over a chunk of metal, flashed across my brain. I was left with a heavy feeling in my stomach and a tightening ache in my throat. I'd been talking about Dove, then Raven and Sparrow. Now I was looking at my father's studio. Both Tucker and Mandy had a way of reaching into memories, challenging me to think about things I'd avoided for years. "We should go back to the house. All the exterior lights will be going off soon."

He followed me out and waited while I closed the studio. "And you turn off the lights because . . . ?"

"They're on timers. We don't want to confuse any hatching sea turtles." We retraced our steps to the main living area, then turned right to go to the south wing. I left him by a table in the hall.

"Wait here." In my bedroom, I opened my purse, found what I was looking for, and walked back to Tucker. I held out a lumpy piece of fabric.

He gingerly took it and examined it. "And this is . . . ?"

"You were asking about different members of the family. This is a pencil holder." I took it from him. "Sparrow made it for me. Of course, it never was able to actually hold any pencils. She accidentally sewed it completely shut."

Tucker was silent.

"Sparrow was twenty-two when she was in the accident. Her room needed to be near the center of the house."

"Why?"

"She had . . . challenges. Seizures. That's what we thought happened in the cart. She wasn't supposed to be driving it." I handed him the photo I'd retrieved at the same time I'd brought out Sparrow's pencil case. "Dove. For age progression. She'd be seventeen now. Almost eighteen."

He didn't speak. Instead his eyes searched my face, then drifted down my proffered arm. He took the photo, placed it on the table, then reached for my hand and lifted it as if to inspect my palm.

My pulse raced. I looked at the floor, not wanting him to see the longing in my face.

He slid my bracelet up, exposing the scars on my wrist.

I snatched my hand away.

"When did you do this?" he asked quietly.

Heat rushed up my neck and I looked away, unable to meet his eyes. "After Dove . . . I couldn't function. Could barely get out of bed. I don't even remember . . . doing it. Ashlee found me at the guesthouse. Unconscious."

He sucked in air as if to comment when BettyJo sauntered up. "Miss Mildred wanted me to be sure you had everything you need. Like towels and stuff."

"Surely you can't be serious?" I asked.

"'I am serious . . . and don't call me Shirley.' *Airplane!*" Tucker grinned.

I had to grin back. "It doesn't count unless you know the year." Tucker had a way of making me feel comfortable, as if pushing back into an easy chair, yet also as if all my senses were in overdrive.

"Huh?" BettyJo stared at me a moment, shrugged, then headed to the blue room. After Tucker picked up the photograph, we silently followed.

Not only had the color and decor changed when Mother converted Dove's bedroom to a guest room, but the layout had changed and a bathroom was added. The only remaining items from my daughter's life—a few books and her favorite stuffed bunny, Piggy—were in a box in my room. Her heirloom christening gown, bonnet, and pacifier were stored in Mother's room.

Joel had placed Tucker's art supplies on the desk by the window. Tucker set the photo of Dove next to a sketchbook. The rest of his things were put away. BettyJo checked the bathroom, turned down the bed, and left.

Tucker looked as if the only thing holding him up was his crutches.

"Will you be okay?" I asked.

"Yes. Thank you."

I left, intending to head for the deck and take a walk along the beach before facing Mother, but I paused at my bedroom door. Today had been a series of firsts. The first time I'd made an effort to see my sister. The first time I'd told anyone about Sparrow. The first time I could talk about Dove without feeling as if a knife were stabbing me. The first time I'd let someone stay in her old room. *I wonder . . .*

Upon entering my bedroom, I strolled to the closet and opened the folding louvre doors. On the floor in the back corner was a sealed box. In my handwriting across the top was a single word. *Dove.*

To reach the box, I'd have to get into the closet. I eyed the narrow space. "It's okay. The doors are open. You have plenty of room. Take a deep breath." Still I couldn't move.

I gauged the distance to the box, got on my hands and knees, then shut my eyes. "Dorothy and the Cowardly Lion," I whispered. "'My goodness, what a fuss you're making!'" Swiftly I crawled forward and snagged the box. "'Well naturally, when you go around picking on things weaker than you are. Why, you're nothing but a great big coward!'" I backed out, dragging the box. "'You're right, I am a coward! I haven't any courage at all. I even scare myself.' *Wizard of Oz*, 1939." I was being ridiculous, but the only thing that helped was focusing on something else, usually movie dialogue.

I sat cross-legged next to the box, stroking the top.

After tearing off the tape with trembling hands, I opened the lid. On the top was Piggy, the stuffed bunny whose ear was still torn.

Picking up the toy, I stood and moved across the room to the small sofa in the corner, where I curled up and cradled the bunny. I closed my eyes. The words to the song I wrote and used to sing to her floated through my mind.

You are my angel, my soul mate, my friend.
I'll be right with you till the end.
And when you fear the stormy gale,
I'll keep you safely on the trail.

Our season together
Will be forever,
My angel.

Squeeeeak. Click.

I jerked upright. I'd fallen asleep. The room was dark. I hated the dark as much as I hated small spaces. Another effect of my imagining Dove's death. Quickly I turned on the light by the sofa.

Had Mother come looking for me when I didn't show up in her room? But hadn't I locked my door? The small floor lamp cast a pale yellow circle around me, leaving the rest of the room in darkness. I shoved upright, and my cuts and bruises added their protest to stiffness from the sofa. I made my way to the door, turning on lights as I moved. My door was unlocked. Opening it to another soft *squeak*, I peered down the silent hall. If someone had checked on me, they were gone now. I closed and locked the door.

The digital alarm by my bed said it was two in the morning. I picked up Piggy from where I'd dropped her, propped the stuffed bunny on my dresser, and crawled into bed, but my thoughts were racing. Why did Joyce call me, then disappear? How did the reporter get a copy of the journal? Why *did* I wait so long to talk to Raven? Could I finally find closure on Dove by age-progressing her image? Why were both Mandy and Tucker able to get me to talk about my family so easily?

After tossing and flipping the pillow for two hours, I gave up on sleep. I showered and dressed, then hobbled through the still rooms to the kitchen, where I made a pot of coffee. While the coffee brewed, I did stretching exercises.

I grabbed a throw blanket from a bench on the deck, wrapped it around me, and sat in a wicker chair to watch the sun rise. As the glow in the east grew brighter, I took a sip of coffee.

"Oomph!"

I turned to see my brother standing in the door, coffee cup in hand but the contents now dripping down the front of his trousers. Ashlee was beside him. "Why don't you watch where you're going?" Tern glared at Ashlee.

"Hey, you're the one who ran into me." Ashlee pivoted and stormed away.

Tern glanced ruefully down at his pants. "Great. Just what I needed."

"I'd be glad to wash your pants for you." I gave him a cheerful smile.

"'S okay." He turned and stalked back into the house, passing Mildred.

The older woman joined me on the deck. "Tern's in a tizzy."

"Ashlee ran into him and made him spill his coffee."

"That would do it." She shook her head. "Both your brother and your mother want everything to be perfect, and my job is to keep it that way, if possible. As your dear mother loves to say—"

"We have the perfect home on the perfect island for the perfect family," I completed for her.

"Right. I'll grab his clothes and get them washed before he can get totally worked up." She started to leave, then turned back. "I almost forgot why I came out here. Lieutenant Gragg called. He has news on the café shooting and will be coming over this morning around ten. He wants the whole family to be here."

My stomach did a little flip-flop. "Sounds significant."

"Mmm." She headed for the kitchen.

I stood. Nana was pacing on the boardwalk leading to the beach. No, he was pacing outside the fence around the empty pool. Did he think there was water in it? Or maybe his water bucket was empty.

As I walked down the steps to the boardwalk, I checked his bucket next to the faucet. Full. Up close, Nana was panting and drooling more than usual. "Come here, Nana. What's the matter, ol' boy? Are you sick?"

The big dog brushed past me and pawed at the pool gate. I spotted something pale yellow fluttering in the deep end.

A crawling feeling wrapped around my neck. "Nana, sit."

The dog complied.

"Stay." I lifted the gate latch and slipped through. My feet weighed a thousand pounds. I didn't want to see what had Nana so upset.

Slowly the pale yellow took shape. My windbreaker. On a body sprawled on the bottom of the pool, long light-brown hair sweeping outward. She looked like me.

CHAPTER 13

I swayed on my feet and backed to the fence. Lifting my arm, I opened and closed my hand. It *looked* real, solid, physical. Could I be dead and not know it?

Would anyone even miss me?

Nana whined and pawed me through the fence. If Nana could see me, I had to be alive.

Slowly I walked to the steps at the shallow end of the pool and descended. *Come on, Piper.* The words Officer Mandy Chou said to me when we were checking out Joyce's home flashed across my mind. *"Ya know, ya pay attention to detail. Ya mentioned the open journal. Tell me what* you *see."* From this angle, I now saw the pants—navy capris.

I didn't own navy capris.

Forcing myself forward, I reached the girl. The brown hair covered her face. With trembling fingers, I brushed the hair away. BettyJo's sightless eyes appeared.

I found myself on my rear, legs splayed in front of me. "No, no, no, no!" I couldn't tear my gaze away from her blank stare.

Placing my hand over my mouth, I stifled the scream that threatened to follow the mindless chant. *Get control. Act, don't react.*

Directly above the body was the chained-off opening where the slide would have been. BettyJo must have thought that was the way to the beach and plunged over the chain. It would have been dark. We kept the lights off outside so as not to confuse the nesting sea turtles.

Better. Pay attention to details.

When I thought my legs would support me, I stood. If she fell in the dark, she would have been here for hours. I approached her again and touched her face. Her skin was cool. I snatched my hand away, turned, and raced for the phone in the kitchen.

The house was oddly silent, as if realizing something terrible had happened. After three tries, I was able to dial.

"Nine-one-one. What is the nature of your emergency?"

"There's been a terrible accident here on Curlew Island. BettyJo . . ." I realized I didn't know her last name. "A woman fell."

"What is the address of the emergency and your callback number?"

I gave her the information.

"Approximately how old is this woman?"

"Early twenties."

"Is she conscious?"

"No. I guess I didn't make this clear. She's dead."

"Are you sure she's not breathing?"

"Um . . . her eyes are open . . . lots of blood . . . her skin is cold . . . she landed on her head in a drained cement pool."

"Okay. Please stay on the line for a moment."

I could hear her speaking in the background, requesting assistance. She soon came back on. "What is your name?"

"Piper Boone."

"Miss Boone, the police have requested you have someone at the dock to meet them and take them to the site. Is that possible?"

"Of course."

"They're on their way."

Mildred was talking to Joel as she entered the kitchen. "BettyJo is late for work. I told that girl—" She froze when she spotted my face. "Oh no."

"BettyJo had an accident."

"Where?"

"The pool."

"How bad?"

"Bad. She's dead."

Mildred reached for the counter. "Did you call—"

"Yes." My brain was fuzzy and I wanted to sit down. "I'm . . . I'm going down to the dock to wait for the police. Could you tell the family?"

"Of course. Should I go . . . cover her?"

Another memory pushed into my mind. Sitting on the ground next to Ami.

"Mr. . . . Lieutenant Gragg, I have to cover her face. It's not right, her just lying there."

"Now, Miss Boone, I know it doesn't seem respectful to your friend, but this is a crime scene and we have to secure and preserve it until the crime-scene folks can process it."

"No. That might compromise the investigation." Why did I say that? BettyJo's fall was just a tragic accident. I bolted from the room before Mildred or Joel could say anything more.

Tern was walking from the north wing looking at his watch. “Can you tell Mildred I won’t be here for breakfast? I’ve got to make a fast trip to the mainland.”

I told him about BettyJo.

His face drained of blood. “Please tell me you’re kidding.”

I didn’t have to answer him. He could see it in my face. “I’m heading to the dock to meet the police and show them where she fell.”

He ran his hand through his hair. “If this gets into the news . . . We need damage control,” he muttered. “Look, Piper, let me handle the police. Hopefully that whole curse thing won’t emerge.”

The phone rang in the kitchen. Both of us turned. Mildred answered, then came to the hall. “Call’s for you, Piper.”

Tern patted me on the shoulder. “Take your call. I’ll take care of everything else.” He trotted off without waiting for my answer.

Mildred had brought me the receiver. “Hello,” I said.

“Hi. It’s Hannah. What’s going on? The police and ambulance and a bunch of other official boats have gone by . . . Oh, wait, that’s the marine patrol boat . . . Um, did they find my grandma?”

I walked into the living room and slumped down on a nearby chair. What kind of a person was I that I forgot about calling poor Hannah? “I’m so sorry, Hannah. No, it’s not Joyce. We had an accident here on the island.”

“Oh no!”

“Tern, my brother, said he’d handle the police. Are you ready to come out to the island?”

“Yes.”

I checked my watch. I didn’t have time to get her and take

her to her grandmother's house before the family met with Lieutenant Gragg about the shooting, never mind the emergency crews arriving to take care of BettyJo. "I'm tied up here for a bit, but I can have Silva pick you up. He works for us."

"You can't come?"

I heard the longing in her voice. "Of course. I'll come as soon as I can. I'll take one of the smaller boats and pick you up. I can take you directly to your grandma's dock."

We disconnected. I trotted out looking for Mildred. I finally found her on the deck staring down at BettyJo's body. Mother was standing next to her, her hands holding the rail with a white-knuckled grip. Both turned as I approached. They had identical looks of dismay on their faces.

"Now, Miss Caroline?" Mildred asked.

"Yes," Mother said.

Mildred nodded, crossed the deck, and descended to the pool level. I moved over to the railing to see what she was doing.

"I just heard." Ashlee raced to the rail next to me and peered over. His Adam's apple bobbed, then he turned and looked at me. "I thought it was you for a moment."

I wasn't losing my mind or feeling paranoid. "Me too."

Mildred entered the pool and walked over to the body.

"Mildred, what are you doing?" I asked.

She didn't answer me. She bent over BettyJo and carefully removed the yellow windbreaker.

"Wait! You can't—"

Mother put a hand on my shoulder. "Piper, stop. We can't have the police making an incorrect assumption—"

"But you're tampering with evidence! A crime scene."

"Evidence? Crime scene? It's an accident, a tragic accident."

Mildred by now had made her way back to the deck, windbreaker in hand. Mother looked at her. "Make that disappear."

Without a word, Mildred left.

Mother glanced back at me. "Because of this unfortunate accident"—she emphasized the word *accident*—"we'll postpone the stockholders' meeting for a day or two."

"That's a good idea. I was going—"

"Now I do feel a headache coming on." She walked into the house without a backward glance. Ashlee and I were left alone.

Ashlee was handsome in his late twenties when we first married, and the passing years had treated him well. He was lean and fit from daily workouts, and his deep, sepia-brown hair had silver-white streaks, contrasting with his tanned face. A few lines furrowed his forehead and around his hazel eyes. He'd been considered the catch of the season, and I was stunned when he asked me to marry him. My family approved, and our wedding had been *the* event of the year.

"Good. I have a chance to talk to you while we're alone." He looked me over as if he were judging a hog at the county fair.

"You're looking good, Piper. Put on a few pounds." He smiled, exposing his perfect teeth.

He was too near, crowding my personal space. I stepped away and folded my arms. We may have been married at one time, but his nearness now gave me the chills.

He closed the space between us, still smiling. "Watch it that you don't put on too much weight. You wouldn't want to become fat."

I really hoped I'd see a hunk of spinach caught between his two front incisors. I stared at his teeth as if willing a green spot to appear.

He glanced away and did a quick dental check with a finger.

Gotcha.

"I think she looks spectacular." Tucker hobbled across the deck.

Okay, Tucker was now officially the greatest human on the planet. I made a point of looking for Nana so my face wouldn't radiate hero worship.

Ashlee left, leaving behind a cloud of Clive Christian aftershave.

Tucker maneuvered over to me and leaned against the rail. He jerked upright. "Oh my sweet Lord!" he whispered. "That looks a little like you."

"Before Mildred removed my yellow windbreaker, she looked a lot like me."

"Huh? What happened?"

"It's BettyJo. She fell. Police are on their way."

Tucker closed his eyes and bowed his head. *Lord, give BettyJo's family peace in this very trying time. And, Lord, let me be salt and light to the Boone family. In Jesus' name I pray, amen.* He glanced at Piper. She was staring at him.

"Did you pray just now?" she asked.

"Yes."

"What for? Do you really believe in God?"

"I do. He carried me through some tough times—"

"What do you know about tough times? Death?" Red blotches appeared on her cheeks. "Losing everything? Your God abandoned me long ago." She turned to leave.

"My wife and unborn son died in a car accident."

Piper froze.

"I know what it's like to have my world destroyed." He dried his damp palm on the side of his slacks. Brushing against the lumps in his pocket reminded him of the stones he'd placed there.

She turned and stared at him, her eyes huge. He couldn't meet her gaze. *I didn't need to tell her that. Not now.*

Before she could answer, Tern arrived leading several men and women wearing coveralls and carrying bags and cases. "She's down there." He pointed. "You can reach the pool from those stairs."

Lieutenant Gragg followed the group of first responders. "Hello, Piper, Tucker. If you two and Senator Tern would show me to someplace quiet, I can share some information with your family. We need to leave these people so they can do their job."

A woman's voice came from the steps. "I think we have a problem here. There's a grizzly bear or something . . ."

"Oh." Piper leaned over the railing. "It's a Newfoundland. A dog. He's very gentle." She clapped her hands. "Nana, come! Come on, boy."

The giant dog trotted up the steps, crossed over to her, and sat. "Go see if Mildred has a cookie—" Nana charged off into the house.

Tern escorted Lieutenant Gragg toward the living room. Tucker hesitated. "Please join us," Piper whispered. "And I'm so sorry about your family. I didn't know. I apologize for my outburst."

He wanted to take her in his arms and make things right again in her life. *Who am I kidding?* He'd barely gotten his own life back on track.

Tern and Ashlee were both already seated in the living room.

Mildred was serving coffee from a side table. Lieutenant Gragg grabbed a steaming mug and moved to a chair. Tucker and Piper sat on the sofa.

"Is Mrs. Boone joining us?" Gragg asked.

"Miss Caroline is lying down. She isn't feeling well." Mildred handed Piper a cup, then raised her eyebrows at Tucker. He nodded. After serving him, she moved toward the door.

"Mildred," Gragg said. "I'd like for you to hear this."

She gave a small nod and took a seat near the wall.

"I wanted to be the one to tell you rather than you hearing it from the press," Gragg began. "We found the man who opened fire at the café."

"I hope you're going to throw the book at him," Tern said. "Toss him in prison and make sure he never sees freedom again."

Gragg placed his mug on the coffee table. "I should have phrased that differently. We found the body of the man responsible for the shooting. He committed suicide. Poison."

"Are you sure it's the shooter?" Ashlee asked.

"We're doing ballistics on the rifle we found with him." Gragg glanced at Tucker. "He looks like the composite you two did, and he was wearing the same type of clothing you described."

"Who was he?" Piper asked.

Gragg took out a small notebook. "His name was James Vincent Cave. Up until two years ago he was an accountant. He was fired, couldn't find another job, his home was repossessed, wife and family left him. He was living on the street and in a homeless shelter when they could find space for him."

"If I could ask a question here?" Tucker leaned forward. "If he was destitute like you say, how did he come by the rifle and ammunition? Both take money."

"Well, that's one of the things that makes this all very interesting. The rifle was a ghost gun."

"Ghost gun?" Piper asked.

"A rifle made with an unfinished receiver that holds the firing mechanism," Gragg said. "Anyone can buy parts to finish the rifle and they're not illegal to own, only to sell, and they're untraceable. He had an AR-15. A so-called assault rifle."

"Why do I get the feeling there's more to this story?" Piper said.

"Yes, there is." Gragg looked at Tern. "Cave was fired from Boone Industries. It appears your family, or at least Piper here, was the target."

CHAPTER 14

I stared at Lieutenant Gragg, my mind blank. Then everyone spoke at once.

"Are you saying—"

"Impossible. Who would want—"

"Maybe it was a coincidence—"

"Please, please." Gragg raised his hands to stem the flow of outrage. "We are investigating every possibility, but we'd been suspicious from the beginning. All of the injured and dead were young women around Piper's age."

"Well then." Tern cleared his throat and moved to the center of the room. "I might have something to add. The other night someone tried to run me off the road. I thought it was a case of drunk driving, or even road rage, although I did nothing to cause it. Now I'm not so sure."

"Did you report it?" Lieutenant Gragg asked.

"No. I thought about it, but so much else is going on and I wasn't hurt. My car didn't receive any damages."

"Driver? Type of vehicle?" Gragg asked.

"Like I said, it was night. Just headlights."

"Was this before the shooting?" Gragg asked.

"I think so."

"I think you need to report it anyway," Gragg said. "We need to stay on top of this."

"You still didn't answer the question I asked," Tucker said. "If the shooter was so poor, how did he come by the rifle and ammunition?"

Gragg stood. "We have to hold some information back for investigative purposes."

"Is there a chance that Cave wasn't working alone?" Tucker nodded toward Tern. "Perhaps other members of the family are at risk?"

"Like I said, we're investigating." Gragg looked at Tern. "I'd like to interview or reinterview all of you in light of our new information. You could come down to the station, or I could do it here if you have a quiet location."

"That would obviously be preferable, Lieutenant Gragg." Tern moved toward the door. "Take a look at the study and see if that . . ." His voice faded as he accompanied Gragg out of the room.

I turned to Tucker and whispered, "I have to get Hannah and take her to her grandmother's house. I'm going to duck out and catch up with the lieutenant later—"

"Piper, didn't you hear what he said? That fellow they just found was trying to kill you—"

"And he's dead."

"What about the attempt on your brother?"

"He didn't think it important enough to report. It was probably nothing." A tiny shiver went up my spine. I ignored it. "I have to go. You could come with me."

His eyes opened wider and a sheen of sweat broke out on his forehead. "I . . . I could if you needed me to."

I'm trying very hard not to need you. "I have a better idea. Could you work on Dove's age progression? After I take care of Hannah, I'll need to know what to ask Lieutenant Gragg about the investigation into Joyce. You said you'd help me."

"I will. I'll come up with a list of questions and start on the art, but you have to promise me something."

"Okay."

"Promise me you won't do anything rash."

"Of course." I stood to leave.

"Piper, Lieutenant Gragg would like to speak to you first." Tern waved me toward the door.

Rats. So much for a fast escape. "Coming."

The lieutenant stood as I entered the study, located in the same wing as my bedroom. "I don't know what more I can tell you—"

"Have a seat, Miss Boone." He indicated the caramel-colored leather chair facing him. After I sat, he asked, "What brought you to the café the other day?"

"I often eat there, so I suggested it when Ami wanted to get together."

"She wanted to ask you for money."

"She . . . I beg your pardon? No. We were high school classmates. She said she'd been thinking about me and suggested a meal. Why do you think it was about money?"

"Your brother told me. He said Ami called him and asked if your family would donate to the Women's March. He turned her down. I guess she then tried you. You have a bit of a reputation for generosity."

I blinked, trying to think of something to say. "Um . . . what were the women marching for?"

"I have no idea. You mentioned you often ate at the café. How often?"

"Maybe once or twice a week."

"You meet your friends there?"

Friends? "No. I dine alone." I sounded lonely. "I enjoy my times alone." From lonely to pathetic. "Um, how hard would it be for me to see police reports?"

Now it was Lieutenant Gragg's turn to blink at the change of subject. "Depends. Shall we get back to my questions?"

"I'm sorry. I thought we were done."

"Almost. Did you know James Vincent Cave?"

"The shooter? No."

"Have you ever heard the name before?"

"No."

"Do you have any enemies?"

"No." *Nor apparently any friends.*

"Have you noticed anyone hanging around or any unusual activity? Anyone paying you more attention than usual?"

"Before the shooting, no. Now, of course, there are the reporters. I'm sorry I can't be of more help."

The lieutenant nodded and stood. "Thank you, Miss Boone. If you think of anything, give me a call." He handed me a business card.

"I have quite a collection of these."

He handed me two more and grinned. "And I want to order new cards."

I took the cards and stuffed them into my slacks, then left, heading for the back door. Ashlee cornered me before I could reach it.

"Piper. Wait. I need to talk to you."

"I'm in a hurry, Ashlee. Can't this wait?"

He planted himself in front of the door, effectively cutting off my escape. "No, it can't."

"Are you concerned about my weight? I promise not to get fat today." I folded my arms.

"Earlier there wasn't time. I need to tell you something and I wanted you to hear it from me. I'm engaged. Getting married at Christmas."

"Why?" The word slipped out before I could catch it.

His brows drew together. "What do you mean? Why not? I'm not content to sit around and grow old. I'm not living in the past."

"Neither am I."

His eyes narrowed. "Then you're more delusional than I thought. After our daughter died, you built a wall around you that no one could breach. I tried. Every time I'd reach for you or touch you, you'd cringe. You clutched that wall around you and ran from anyone or anything that would dare break through. When Dove died, you died."

"Don't you dare say her name!"

"Why not? Do you think you were the only one who lost a child that day?"

"That's the point," I practically spat. "*I* didn't lose her. *You* did. You let someone take her—"

"You know that's not how it happened. I told you she'd fallen asleep in the forward cabin. I didn't want to wake her until I'd tied up. No one *took* her. No one knew she was on board—"

"*You* should have died trying to save her!" I pushed past him, but he caught my arms and pulled me close.

"So you finally said it! The thought that has gnawed at your soul all these years."

"You're wrong—"

"Listen carefully, princess," he whispered in my ear. "Everyone's been tiptoeing around you for the past fifteen years. I'm done with that. When are you going to get over it?"

"Losing a child isn't like getting the flu! I'll never 'get over it.' The best I can do is get up every morning—"

"See? 'Poor Piper, she's gone through so much.' You're the perpetual victim. The enduring martyr. But you're nothing more than a bitter, angry woman running away from life, and I'm glad I've finally found happiness without you."

I jerked my arms away and ran to my room. I would not give him the pleasure of seeing how his words had stabbed me with the precision of an ice pick.

CHAPTER 15

After Piper left the living room, Mildred stood and started collecting coffee cups. Ashlee checked his watch, then hurriedly left.

Tucker waited to stand until Mildred finished. The only sounds now were the distant voices of the team working to recover BettyJo's body. The voices grew, then faded as they transported her body around the house and toward the dock. *Poor girl.* He prayed for her family again.

He felt too restless to draw, but he needed to keep busy. He grabbed his crutches and hobbled to his room.

He'd done age progressions after training with the National Center for Missing and Exploited Children. Their work was all done on computer using Photoshop and special programs. He'd left his computer with that program at home; however, the method was similar with hand-drawn art. He pulled out a light box and plugged it in, then lifted the photograph of Dove and taped it to the glass. Carefully he traced the upper half of her face onto a piece of bristol paper. Sliding the paper down, he then traced the lower half, lengthening her face. In young children, the upper part of the head is larger than the lower half. As children age, the proportions end up evenly divided between the upper and lower face. The nose grows forward and downward, lips stretch over adult teeth, the jaw lengthens and widens, and eyes grow larger. Normally, in addition to the photograph of the child, he'd study and utilize the images of the parents—both as children themselves and their adult features. He incorporated Piper's and Ashlee's features into the drawing.

I stood in my bedroom, breathing deeply after my encounter with Ashlee. I wasn't a bitter, angry woman. I wasn't sitting around growing old. I wasn't a perpetual victim or an enduring martyr.

I was . . . I would be on a mission.

I'd find out what happened to Joyce.

Right.

People didn't need to tiptoe around me. I was fine.

I found myself staring at my half-packed suitcase. Was *that* fine?

Stop it. I didn't need to psychoanalyze myself. And how dare Ashlee talk to me like that! After this he could just stay on the mainland and come over for the meeting. Better yet, I'd buy out his shares. Or get Tern to fire him.

You don't have the money, or the power, to do anything to Ashlee. You're pathetic.

I picked up a pillow from my bed and hurled it across the room. It hit the wall and bounced onto the floor. I gave it my best soccer-ball kick. The pillow flew up and landed on my purse.

My oversized, overpriced Coach purse. A gift from Ashlee that I'd been too cheap to toss. I'd forgotten that. My vision narrowed, and the room receded. With a guttural roar, I kicked the purse as hard as I could. It flew up and smashed into a *Signs* movie poster. The poster canted sideways, crashing into the framed article about my father. Both pieces dropped straight down to the overloaded shelf below, shooting books, sweetgrass baskets, a line of candles, and glass into my open suitcase and onto the floor beyond.

The sound of shattering glass and crashing objects seemed to go on forever. My mouth dried. I stood rooted to the spot, breathing heavily, my hands opening and closing convulsively. Somewhere outside, Nana barked. The rancid odor of my own sweat burned my nose.

I struggled to remain standing on wobbly legs.

Under glittering shards of glass, a pair of jeans next to a couple of T-shirts peeked out from the suitcase.

The purse had upended, then landed on its side, spewing the contents.

I stumbled backward to a chair and sat. I was empty, hollow, unable to formulate thoughts or words.

Someone knocked on my door. Then knocked again. "Piper?" Mildred called. "I heard a crash. Are you okay?"

No. I'm not okay. "It's nothing, Mildred," I managed through numb lips. "I just dropped something."

After a few moments, I heard the tapping of her shoes as she walked away.

As soon as my legs felt like they could support my weight, I stood, stomped across the room, and closed the suitcase, glass and all. I picked it up and dumped it into my closet. Returning to the corner, I picked up the larger pieces of glass and placed them into the trash basket.

I didn't want to even touch the purse. Finding an empty plastic shoe box, I placed my wallet, keys, a container of mints, compact, comb, and Sparrow's sad pencil case inside. My journal went to the bedside table. The final item was a small bound notebook. The book I was going to write. I knew what was inside. A few notes and the pink slip from my publishing employer. *Due to financial difficulties, we will no longer be in need of your services. Please pick up your final check from bookkeeping.* The reason for my return to the island. I couldn't afford to live on my dividends and support all my causes. Four Paws Rescue and injured goose: 1. Independent lifestyle: 0.

I shoved the notebook into a drawer. The purse followed the glass shards into the trash. Ashlee's voice pounded into my brain. *"You're nothing more than a bitter, angry woman, running away from life."*

Not true.

The hall outside my room had a cleaning closet with a vacuum cleaner. I grabbed the vacuum and vigorously cleaned the floor. I returned the vacuum cleaner and pulled out a duster. Attacking the shelves, I jabbed at the surfaces, replacing the baskets and candles. The leather band around my wrist that covered my scars came into focus. *Running away from life . . .*

The romance books and sappy movies surrounding me were evidence of my attempts to escape. I'd slapped on a hundred-pound backpack to climb a steep hill with no summit in sight.

How could I *not* be the very thing Ashlee said I was?

In the bathroom, I stared at my reflection. Was that what everyone saw when they looked at me?

Tucker didn't.

"Maybe that's because Tucker doesn't know me."

Returning to my room, I strolled over to where Piggy stared at me through button eyes. "I know. You don't have to remind me that I just had a temper tantrum worthy of Dove. And now I'm talking to a stuffed rabbit."

The walls seemed to move inward, and the air became thicker. I grabbed a jacket and rushed from my room, almost colliding with Mother. "Oops. Excuse me."

"What's the matter, Piper?" Mother brushed my hair away from my face. "Mildred told me she heard noises coming from your room. I was just coming to check on you."

I moved out of her reach. "Why would you need to check on me?"

"We're concerned." Tern came up behind me. "You were almost killed, then finding BettyJo's body . . . Well, that's a lot of shock." He put his arm around me and gave me a hug.

I untangled Tern's confining arm from my shoulder. "Thank you, Tern, Mother. I'm fine. Maybe . . . more than fine." Turning away, I could feel their eyes on me as I walked to Tucker's room and tapped on the door.

Tucker answered, his gaze going from my face to my family. Without saying a word, he stepped back, allowing me to enter, then firmly shut the door behind me. "What's going on? Your brother and mother just gave me the strangest looks. Are you okay?"

"Yes. I mean, no. I mean, it's time."

"Time for what?"

To grow up? Stop running? "Would you help me find out what happened to my daughter?"

"Don't you pretty much know all the details?"

"I know she drowned, that her body washed up on Curlew.

But what happened before that? What if someone . . . did something to her before throwing her into the ocean? And who did it? Why?"

He studied my face intently. "Do you really want to know all that?"

I closed my eyes. "Yes. I have to. I need to. And I have to make her killer pay for what he did."

"Revenge is a caustic companion."

"Then call it justice."

He stared at me for a long moment. "I hope I can eventually call it forgiveness and redemption. Yes. Of course I'll help as much as I can."

I kissed him on the cheek.

He leaned against a chair, wrapped his arms around me, and kissed me on the lips.

I was afraid my suddenly wet-noodle legs would give way. The world took a step backward, leaving me in the center of an electrical storm.

When he let go, I almost did fall. We stared at each other for an awkward moment.

"I . . . The time . . . I promised I'd pick up Hannah. She's probably standing on the dock right now." I turned and fled.

I didn't stop running until I arrived at the dock. BettyJo's body must have been transported to the mainland already, as only one official boat was tied up, presumably Lieutenant Gragg's.

I opened the door to the boathouse, took out a key to one of the smaller vessels, climbed aboard, and headed for the mainland.

The fresh air cooled my hot face, and the sea was relatively calm. I concentrated on driving the boat, but my thoughts kept bouncing around in my brain. He kissed me. And I liked it. But was I simply reacting to Ashlee's engagement announcement, or did I really feel something for Tucker?

Tucker watched Piper race across the foyer and out of sight, mentally kicking himself for his rash kiss. What made him do that? He'd vowed during The Darkness following his wife's death that he'd never seek another woman. That was his personal penance for losing her and their baby.

Piper had only come to his room to ask for help. He'd probably just made it too awkward for the two of them to work together. *Stupid, stupid, stupid.*

He returned to his desk and sat. The three stones in his pocket jabbed him. He pulled them out and lined them up on top of his desk. At this point, the best he could do was finish the drawing.

Two hours later he laid down his pencil. A very pretty young version of Piper smiled out at him. She looked so familiar.

He placed a hand over the left side of her face. Now Hannah stared back.

Hannah was waiting on the dock and raced toward me as soon as I'd tied up. I had to admit she made me smile. She had a way of lifting my spirits.

"I didn't know what to think!" Hannah said. "I was afraid they'd found Grandma, then afraid they hadn't found her. I didn't want to be alone."

"You're not alone. I'm here." I liked the way that sounded. "I didn't think to check for food at Joyce's place. Maybe we should visit a grocery store first."

"Absolutely."

Watching out for lurking reporters, I drove to the nearest Publix market. As we stepped from the car, a little boy walking by with his mother pointed at Hannah's face and burst into tears.

Hannah glanced at me, gave a slight shrug, wiggled her fingers at the boy, and moved toward the store entrance.

I slowly followed. Who should be uplifting whom?

Tucker leaned back in his chair, staring at the drawing. Obviously meeting Hannah had played into his sketch, adding a resemblance he hadn't intended. He reached for his computer and booted it up. The internet connection needed a password.

Standing, he grabbed his crutches and made his way to the kitchen to find Mildred. He found Tern instead. "Sorry to bother you, but I'd like to get on the internet and need the password."

"Boone, capital *B*. Not very creative, but it's not as if we have a lot of people wanting to use it." Tern checked his watch, then glanced toward the kitchen.

Tucker took the hint and started to hobble away.

The phone rang.

Tucker moved around the corner and out of sight, then paused to listen. He was probably being rude, but he was curious.

"Yes, this is me. What do you have for me? Really?" Tern was silent for a few minutes. "I agree. I have another name I want you to look into—a BettyJo Wilson. Right. No, look into the family. Hopefully she'll not have any. It's important that we keep this out of the news. Have you found out anything about that reporter, Bailey Norton? Okay, then get on it as soon as you can. Right. Get back to me as soon as you have something."

Swiftly Tucker moved toward his room, not pausing until he'd closed the door. He guessed politicians wouldn't want news of a dead woman found at their home splashed all over the media, even if it was an accident. More fodder for the island-curse legend.

His computer was still on. He logged on to the internet to learn what he could about Dove. A quick search didn't add any more to what Piper had already told him. If he were still in law enforcement, he'd have had access to more detailed information than what the police would share with a civilian. His former colleagues wouldn't help him. They'd made it clear he was on the wrong side of the thin blue line.

He could resurrect his college hacking skills. He'd have all the reports, bank records, travel information, even the link analysis charts from the initial investigation.

But accessing those would mean he'd be breaking the rules of Clan Firinn, which had literally saved his life. He said a quick prayer, then returned to his computer screen.

Television shows and movies often showed detectives, agents, or other officers discussing an investigation while gathered around complex wall displays. Glossy photos of the crime scene, victims, and suspects would remind the viewers of the characters. In reality, detectives usually worked multiple cases at the same time, and wall space for such lovely charts was limited. But Tucker had a link analysis program that would allow him to create a virtual wall, albeit without the yarn, Post-it notes, maps, and photographs.

The police assumed the theft of the boat was the motive behind the attack on Ashlee. He would interview Silva to find out more. He started a file on the boat in his link analysis program. The value of Dove as a ransom victim was another avenue he could explore; however, there was no ransom note. Maybe someone had killed Dove before the note could be sent. The criminal element was at best unreliable. Under the heading of Suspects, he wrote *unknown/stranger, family, staff, neighbor, business associate, friend*. That narrowed the suspect pool to everyone.

We returned to the dock with Hannah's groceries and loaded the cruiser. Hannah had been silent since the incident at the store. I didn't know what to say to her. I settled on a bland, "Have you been out on the ocean before?"

"No, although Wisconsin does border both Lake Michigan and Lake Superior, both pretty big." We pushed off the dock, aimed for the inlet, then turned east toward the island. She sat beside me and raised her voice over the engine. "That bothered you, didn't it?"

"What?"

"The little boy's reaction at the store. I could see it in your face."

"Yes. Very much. You . . . you were so gracious. Didn't it bother you?"

She turned so I could see both sides of her face—her peaches-and-cream skin paired with the brown, deeply scarred side. "I've learned to run with endurance the race set before me."

"That sounds like a quote." The island was growing larger in front of us. I turned north.

"It is. From the Bible. Hebrews 12:1. That's what gives me strength. And hope."

Something twisted inside me. "You are a most remarkable young woman."

She gave me a lopsided grin. "And you are everything Grandma said you'd be. Do you really have an entire rescue place for animals? I'd love to go there."

"Well, technically I just support some of the animals. Make that a lot of the animals. You could say I'm a critter patron."

"Could we go visit?"

"Sure. There's a goose that's honking to meet you." I nodded ahead. "We're almost there."

She shaded her eye to see the island better. "It's beautiful."

Joyce's dock appeared and I slowed the boat to just above idle, stood, and chucked the fenders over the side. I stopped the engine and let the boat drift close. Before I could say anything, Hannah had grabbed the line in the bow and jumped onto the dock. I did the same in the stern. A moment later we were tied up. Hannah picked up her suitcase, and I grabbed the groceries.

A path led upward to the small bluff Joyce's house was built on. To my right was the spit of rock and sand with Dove's rock cairn at the natural seawall. I still needed to replace the fallen stones.

"Piper?"

I realized I'd stopped to stare at the cairn.

"Is that where they found your daughter?" Hannah indicated the small monument.

"Yes."

"Grandma told me a bit about it. Did you want to go over and put the rocks back?"

I shook my head. "We need to get your groceries into the refrigerator. I'll see to it after that."

Joyce's house looked the same, but some of the pages of the open birding journal were starting to curl in the slight humidity. I closed it as I passed, then showed Hannah into the kitchen.

A loud panting came from the other door into the house. Nana, with uncanny insight, waited outside the screen for a cookie.

"Nana!" Hannah opened the door for him. Nana paused long enough to acknowledge the greeting, then charged toward the closet with the cookies.

"You know his name!"

"Sure. Grandma talked about her." Hannah furrowed her brow. "Shouldn't Nana be black?"

"This Nana is a male, and yes, most Newfoundlands are black, but they also come in brown and gray. And some are even black and white, which are called Landseers."

"But I thought Nana was black and a girl dog."

A slight chill went through me. The last black female Newfie we had was before Dove had passed. That Nana died two years later, replaced by a Landseer, then the brown version we had now. "Joyce must have talked about an earlier dog."

"I guess."

Nana had planted himself in front of the hidden closet and was staring at it intently, as if he could will the cookie from the box and into his mouth. A long, ropy strand of drool extended from his jowl to the center of his chest. I snatched a paper towel and captured the slobber before it hit the floor.

"That is so gross." Hannah moved backward.

"Well, it's much grosser if Nana shakes his head and launches the drool in all directions." I opened the closet, pulled out a dog biscuit, and handed it to the canine. "Then again, you haven't lived until you've been hit with a Newfie spit bomb." He politely took the biscuit and trotted outside.

"You love that dog though, don't you?"

"I do, but how did you know?"

"Your face. When you see something you like, your eyes grow wider, your mouth opens slightly, and then the corners of your lips tighten into a tiny smile."

"You are unusually observant." I looked around the room. "Are you sure you're going to be comfortable here?"

"Yes. I'm near my grandmother here."

"Do me a favor? If you think of anything, or even if you get lonely, call me." I wrote my cell and house numbers on a pad of paper next to the phone.

"Will do."

I gave her a hug, surprising both of us, then trotted from the house. I couldn't get Hannah's comment out of my mind. *"But I thought Nana was black and a girl dog."*

CHAPTER 16

Tucker popped a couple of painkillers, grabbed his crutches, then moved outside, not encountering anyone on his journey. He needed more information about Dove's disappearance, and a logical starting point would be Silva, the captain of the stolen vessel. Hopefully Silva would be on the island, not the mainland.

He also needed to get that kiss with Piper out of his mind.

Not sure of the protocol on using the family's carts, he opted to walk down to the beach. Gray clouds had moved in, casting the surroundings in dusty shadows. The briny air smelled of rain while seagulls emphatically cawed overhead. He could easily get used to living here—if only he didn't have to get here by boat.

He breathed a sigh of relief when he spotted the day cruiser tied up. Silva himself was busy wiping down a spotless bench seat.

Tucker kept his eyes on the man as he negotiated the dock. The slapping of the water under his feet was enough to increase his heart rate.

Silva paused when he spotted Tucker. "Need a lift?"

"Nah. Just out for a walk. I'm curious. Do the family members call you when they need a ride?"

Silva leaned against the seat. "Call or leave me a note. I practically live on this boat, so I'm easy to find."

Tucker raised his eyebrows. "You live here? How big is this thing?"

"This sweet baby, *Taire*, is a fifty-four-foot Cantius Cruiser. Three cabins, two heads." He noted Tucker's expression. "Two bathrooms. I keep her in running condition, and when the family's not wanting to go to the island, I go fishing. Just me and the ocean. The way I figure, this is pretty much paradise and I have the perfect job. When the time comes to retire, I plan on getting a boat like this and fishing full-time." He relaxed and studied the sky. "Storm's coming."

"So I see. What about the boat that was stolen? Was it like this one?"

Silva caressed the railing with the cleaning cloth. "The *Faire Taire*. An eighty-two-foot Hatteras High Spirits."

"What does the name *Faire Taire* mean?"

"I was told it meant something like 'be silent' or 'hush.' I figure it must refer to the engine. She was a beauty. Not so much cruiser as yacht. Had five staterooms. Mr. Boone—Montgomery, Piper's father—used it to entertain clients. Even had his sculpture on the bow."

"And you would pilot it?"

"Sometimes. I suppose technically no one needed to pilot any of the Boone boats. They all have some form of autopilot. Sometimes Mr. Boone took it out. Sorta gave me a break." Silva looked away and pulled on his ear, then cleared his throat.

Interesting reaction. "Mr. Boone took it out when he had certain clients he wanted to entertain?"

"I didn't say that." Silva's jaw clenched.

Change the subject. "If I could ask, what's a boat like the *Faire Taire* sell for?"

"Double this one. Somewhere between four to five million new."

Tucker gave a soft whistle. A yacht worth that amount would certainly be a target for theft. And a family rich enough for a full-time captain to pilot the multimillion-dollar boat would make a good target for kidnapping. What ransom would that little girl have been worth? "A boat, make that yacht, must be difficult to maneuver. Was it usual for Piper's husband, Ashlee, to take it out without you piloting it? Especially since it was, after all, your home."

"Police asked me the same thing. I said it was *practically* my home. I have a small place on the mainland. Yeah, Ashlee wasn't much for boating. Oh, he could steer and dock it if he had to—just needed to be careful. Anyway, the only boat at the island that day was the Hatteras." His voice drifted off as he made a fuss about loading tobacco into a pipe he'd pulled from an inside pocket.

"Piper said everyone was on the island that day for the annual meeting."

"'S 'at how she remembers it?" Silva didn't look up. "Not surprising. The whole thing nearly killed her." He lit the pipe and puffed a few times. "That's why there weren't any other boats besides the yacht. Almost everyone in the family had arrived for the meeting but were doing errands on the mainland. As far as I know, only Piper, Joyce—the neighbor lady who lives at the other end of the island—and I were on the island when the *Faire Taire* was stolen."

Tucker shifted his weight. "So technically, almost no one had an alibi for when Dove was kidnapped and killed?"

Silva stared at him for a moment. "You sound like a cop."

"No." Tucker tried to give him a reassuring smile. "I'm just an artist. Piper told me a bit about what happened to her daughter."

"That's the problem, of course. No one really knows exactly what happened that day."

"Where were you when Ashlee took the boat? And wasn't taking off with the *Faire Taire* . . . well, stealing?"

Silva carefully emptied his pipe into a nearby container, then looked Tucker over from head to toe. "You're asking a lot of questions for just being an artist."

"Piper asked me to look into her daughter's disappearance, that's all."

"Did she now? Well then, 'bout time."

What does that mean? He held his tongue, hoping Silva would elaborate. The captain reloaded his pipe, tamped down the tobacco, then lit it. After a few puffs, he said, "Ashlee was a family member—at least he was then—so it wasn't stealing. As for what I was doing, not that it's any of your business, but if Piper asked for your help . . . Well, I was visiting Joyce Mueller. She was a friend of mine."

"Was?"

"After Dove's disappearance, Joyce stopped coming to the island. At least for a few years. She made no effort to contact me, so I figured she'd just . . . moved on. Got me a lady friend now, so I guess I moved on as well."

"When exactly *did* Joyce leave the island? Was it sudden?"

"Nah. She'd been planning on heading back to Wisconsin for

a couple days. That's where she was from, you know. All packed up. I think she was selling her practice or her house or something. Papers to sign, all that."

"So nothing unusual that day? No reason . . . ?"

"I suspect if I hadn't stopped by, she would have been gone sooner."

"Joyce is missing. Where do you think she's gone to now?"

"Like I said, we've moved on. She always did whatever she pleased. Not to be rude, Mr. Tucker, but I have things on the boat to attend to, so if you'll excuse me." He didn't wait for an answer but ambled into the boat.

Tucker turned and hobbled back to the house. So the only three on the island the day Dove died were Piper, Joyce, and Silva. Joyce was Silva's alibi. And Joyce was missing.

I stood in front of the rock cairn running Dove's amber teething necklace between my fingers. No one would let me see what was left of my daughter after they found her. She was initially identified by the necklace. I'd opted to have Dove cremated and placed aboveground in a cremains niche wall. I wanted to be sure no water would seep into her coffin. I had flowers delivered there once a week. Daisies. Her favorite.

It didn't take long to clean up the driftwood debris and restore the stones.

The breeze picked up and the waves grew a bit higher. I headed for the boat before it started to rain and the water got too rough. Fortunately the waves were not as bad on the leeward side of the island, and I made it to our dock in good time.

The *Taire* was moored but Silva was out of sight. Lieutenant Gragg's official boat was still tied up. Apparently interviews were still going on. I returned the boat keys to the storage shed and trotted up to the house.

Mildred clattered around in the kitchen, pausing long enough to wave to me.

"Gragg still interviewing people?" I asked.

"I think he's about done. He's been invited to lunch if you need to talk to him."

"Thanks. Do you need help?"

"Joel's here. And more help is coming later today."

I aimed for my room. I needed to see what Tucker had come up with for a drawing, but I knew I'd turn some shade of unpleasant orangey red. "Stop it, you fool!" I whispered. "What are you? Twelve? It was just a kiss. You know your face gives away your every thought. You must have given him a look that you wanted to be kissed."

So how to keep that look off my face? Assuming I didn't want to be kissed again.

Tucker left his door open a crack to listen for Piper's return. He owed her an apology. She could ask him to leave, and that would be the end of all this, but at least he could give her all he'd uncovered. In the meantime, he'd added Silva's information to his link analysis program. He also added a list of questions that the new information had raised. He really needed to see what the police had uncovered in the initial investigation and look for undeveloped leads or evidence.

The ocean breeze had freshened, increasing the scent of rain. He checked the windows, started to close them, then left the one next to the desk open. The gray day matched his mood, and the wind added to his restlessness. His work with Clan Firinn kept him busy and gave structure to his life. His faith gave him meaning. Piper had brought him a challenge.

Someone tapped on his door. He opened it. "'Hello, gorgeous.'"

"*Funny Girl*, 1968." Piper grinned and entered. "'Snap out of it!'"

"*Moonstruck*, 1985?"

"1987."

He let out a deep breath. She didn't appear to be angry with him. "Look, I'm sorry—"

"For what? Kissing me?"

"No. I wanted to kiss you. I'm sorry if that bothered you or made you uncomfortable."

Her face flushed slightly. "Can we just move slowly?"

"Yes." He sucked in a deep breath and made an effort to control his erratic breathing. Reaching into his pocket, he squeezed one of the stones.

"Then for now, just forget about it. Did you get a chance to work on the age-progression drawing?"

He nodded to his left.

She advanced to the desk, her steps getting slower as she drew closer. Finally she stopped and gasped.

Parents, when presented with the age-progressed drawing of a child who'd passed, usually broke down with sobs dredged from the innermost corner of their soul.

Piper spun, her face white. "Dove! Hannah is Dove! She isn't dead! She lived—somehow she lived!" She snatched up the drawing, then charged for the door.

Tucker caught her arm. "Wait, Piper—"

"You can see it, can't you?" She shoved the sketch at his face. "Your age-progressed drawing of Dove is the spitting image of Hannah."

"It does look like her." He eased the hand holding the drawing away. "I suspect I had a bit of mental contamination from seeing Hannah's face and unconsciously merged her image into the drawing. Forensic artists try to be aware of that possibility, but it happens."

"No! It's her! What about the dog?" She shook off his restraining arm. "What about Nana?"

"What?"

Piper's face was white and she was huffing as if she'd just run a marathon. "Hannah identified Nana as a black female Newfie, just like the dog we had when Dove was a little girl. How could Hannah possibly know that?"

"Joyce could have told her."

"But I *feel* something for Hannah. I feel close to her. I've never felt like that . . . since . . ."

"I like Hannah as well, but think about it, Piper. A second three-year-old girl drowns at exactly the same time as Dove, washes ashore *here*, and no one ever reports a second girl as missing or lost?"

"But—"

"And this second girl just *happens* to be wearing the same necklace?"

She grabbed the necklace and held on. "But—"

"What about her age? Hannah is a year younger than Dove would have been."

Piper shook her head. "A mistake . . ."

"I'd bet they ran DNA on the body."

She became very still.

"Did they gather DNA from you for comparison?"

Slowly she nodded. "The police came and asked for something from her, like her toothbrush or hairbrush. They took the hairbrush."

"And?"

"A match," she whispered.

Abruptly the heavens opened in a torrent of rain, splashing against the open window.

He moved to the window and slid it shut. When he turned to look at Piper, she was staring at the drawing. "I don't know how, I don't care why, but I know, absolutely in my heart, that Hannah is Dove." She started for the door.

"Wait. Where are you going?"

Piper paused, one hand on the door. "To see her, to tell Hannah who she really is."

"Think about that, Piper. If what you believe is true, Hannah has lived a lie her whole life. The person she loves the most in this world is Joyce, and you'd be saying Joyce wasn't her grandmother. In fact, Joyce has deceived her. She'll be confused and scared, and she'll hate you for it."

She let go of the knob. "Not if I explain it right."

"There's no way to explain it that won't seem like fiction. And you need to consider one very important factor."

"What's that?"

"*If*, and that's a very important if, somehow, some way, Hannah is your daughter"—he moved closer—"then someone, or a group of someones, has gone to a great deal of trouble to hide that fact. And they've done an excellent job of it for fifteen years. I suspect whoever is involved will go to great lengths to keep it a secret."

"What should I do?" He expected to see her eyes glittering with tears, but she was flinty-eyed, her jaw set in determination.

The rain tapped against the glass and wind tossed the palmetto fronds.

He knew he couldn't talk Piper out of her conviction that Hannah was Dove, but maybe he could direct her toward logical, rational reasoning. And caution. "You don't want to put Hannah in danger, or yourself. How many people know she's here?"

"As far as I know, just you, me, and Officer Chou."

"Who's Officer Chou?"

"Mandy Chou, marine patrol. She was looking into Joyce's disappearance."

"Let's keep it between just us."

Piper moved away from the door. A blast of wind sent rain against the window, rapping the glass with a persistent drumming. "Joyce called me a couple of days ago. Mildred said Joyce sounded scared. Maybe Joyce wanted to talk to me about Hannah. Maybe that's what happened to her." Her eyes opened wider. "Oh my gosh! I took Hannah to Joyce's house. That's where Joyce disappeared. I've put Hannah in danger!" She turned toward the door.

"Wait. If only the three of us know she's even here, she should be fine for now. No one is going to go anywhere in this storm. But I agree we need to move Hannah someplace safe, at least until we can find out more information."

Piper nodded.

"Lieutenant Gragg is still here. He would have computer access to the original report. Shall we go find him?" He didn't wait for her response but headed out the door and toward the study.

Gragg was standing over the desk tapping papers into order. He looked up as they entered. "Tucker, Miss Piper, how can I help you? Did either of you two remember something?"

"No," Piper said. "I'm here about the police report. About Dove. Could I see it?"

Gragg sat. "I'd need access to a computer—"

"Behind you." Piper opened a door in the pale aqua–stained cabinet and pulled out an iMac. In a moment she'd logged on, then stepped away to give Gragg access.

Gragg rolled his chair over, typed for a few moments, then stood and moved away. "Here's the narrative."

Piper sat. Only the tapping rain broke the silence. Finally she looked at him. "You were the first officer on the scene. You were involved from the first day."

"I was on patrol and answered the 911 call."

Piper rose. "Tucker?"

He took her place and rapidly scanned the report. "The call came from a passing boater?"

"Yes." Gragg took one of the leather chairs. "They saw someone lying next to the boathouse on Marion Inlet and called it in. You couldn't see Mr. Yates from the land side."

"Did you eventually learn what knocked him out?" Piper asked.

"An oar with blood on it was recovered. He was dragged behind the shed and tied up with duct tape, so they came prepared. They put duct tape across his mouth as well."

"They? Did you think more than one person was involved?" Tucker asked.

"That's a possibility. This was a daring theft, and someone had to be ready to conceal the boat until changes could be made to alter its appearance. Organized boat theft rings will target a specific boat, but they usually like to work at night. We also couldn't rule out a crime of opportunity. Silva's a big, powerful man who lived on the boat and was known to be armed. But the boat was docked by Ashlee, so if someone was watching for a chance, well . . ." He shrugged. "No other signs of foul play. We searched for over a week, sent out BOLOs—be on the lookout—all up and down the Eastern Seaboard, but the boat simply vanished. The only thing we recovered was, as you know, your daughter's body and maybe the dinghy."

"*Maybe* the dinghy?" Piper asked.

"We couldn't get a positive identification. The dinghy on the *Faire Taire* was an inflatable type, as was the one we found. The recovered dinghy had the air out of it and had washed up a couple of days after the boat went missing."

"The DNA report?" Piper asked. "Could there have been a mistake?"

Lieutenant Gragg indicated the computer. "Give me a moment and I can look it up."

Tucker relinquished his chair and Gragg sat. While he typed on the keyboard, he said, "I remember someone bringing a hairbrush . . . Here it is." He leaned backward so they could see the screen.

A hairbrush with a green animal adorning its handle rested in a clear plastic evidence bag. Next to it was the chain-of-custody form.

"What's that?" She pointed to the form.

"From the time the evidence is collected by police, everyone who touches, analyzes, or controls that piece of evidence has to sign for it. That way there's never any doubt that the same piece of evidence collected is the one analyzed and, if it ends up in court, is the one presented. Do you recognize the brush?"

"Her sea turtle brush." Piper straightened.

"You recognize it?" Gragg asked.

"Yes. I had it made for her. She loved sea turtles. It was one-of-a-kind." She glanced at Tucker. He expected to see a look of resignation, but her eyes had the same glint of determination.

"Do you have a list of who you interviewed and the time line for everybody?" Tucker asked.

Gragg raised one eyebrow. "Sounds like you suspect someone in the family was involved."

"Perhaps someone near the family. It just seems strange that the one time Ashlee pilots the boat by himself to the mainland, someone just happens to be waiting for him. That's all." Tucker leaned back in the chair. "I'd also be curious if you found anyone with motive, someone needing money, for example."

Gragg chewed his lip for a moment. "It's been fifteen years . . ."

Tucker took a deep breath. "Let me guess. You discovered no one had an alibi, and everyone had a motive."

CHAPTER 17

I was lucky to be sitting. Gragg didn't deny Tucker's statement.

"What do you mean, no one had an alibi and everyone had a motive?" I asked.

Gragg leaned over the computer and turned it off. "I've said enough, really. Rest assured that our cold-case officer is working on it. I've already given you what you wanted to see, which was the initial police reports."

I gripped the chair. "But—"

"I need to get back to the mainland. You have my number should you think of anything else to add on the café shooter, James Vincent Cave." He started to leave but paused. "I won't be staying for lunch. If I don't see him first, please thank Tern for the offer." He left.

A gust of wind sent a flurry of rain against the window.

"What now?" I asked.

"Now it's time to do some digging. I'll start here on this computer. You mentioned you have a media room."

I blinked. "Ah, yes, but—"

"But what does that have to do with anything?" He smiled at

me and I took a quick breath. "Is it just for television and movies, or do you have family videos?"

"There are older family videos."

"Perfect. I need you to go through them and watch for anything . . . out of the ordinary."

"Like what?"

"I don't know. There may be nothing."

I stood. "Do you honestly believe a member of my family did this?"

"I don't know that either, but we have to start somewhere."

Leaving the study, I passed the game room. Joel lay under the air hockey table, tool kit open on the floor beside him as he repaired something. Tern and Mother were in the living room deep in conversation. I overheard, "My campaign manager called a bit ago."

"Oh," Mother said. "And?"

"He confirmed that the café shooting boosted my approval with the sympathy vote."

"I told you it would. Now, back to the wetlands proposal. If we amend it to read 'not to exceed' and add the words 'fiscal year' . . ."

Sympathy vote? I thought about interrupting and reminding them it was a mass murder. Of course, they'd just look at me with their usual bland expressions. The media room was next to the kitchen. Mildred was stirring something on the stove. "Where's Ashlee?" I asked.

"Did you want to see him or avoid him?"

"Avoid."

"He should be working out in the gym."

The gym was across the hall from the media room. Hopefully the door would be shut. "Thanks."

The door was open, but Ashlee seemed intent on watching himself lift free weights, and I was able to slip into the media room and lock the door without notice. Two rows of black leather sofas with built-in drink holders rose in tiers in front of a big television screen. Behind one wall was a library of home movies, most of which had been converted to DVDs. The bulk of the DVDs were arranged by date and had been recorded prior to Father's passing, but I found one dated the July after his accident. That was the year I married Ashlee, the year I became pregnant with Dove.

I put it in the player. A football game between Carolina and Clemson came on. *Rats.* Someone had taped over the original video. I hit fast-forward. More game. I was about to shut it off when a brief scene appeared at the end. I stopped the DVD and backed up.

I recognized the beach in front of the house. Raven and I were playing in the surf with Nana the black Newfie. I wore a black one-piece suit. My baby bump wasn't evident, but I was spending most of my days being sick. I must have caught a break this day.

Raven wore a blue bikini that showed off her perfect figure. The camera stayed glued on my sister. I'd forgotten how breathtaking she was. Her long, thick hair had a red tint to it and swirled around her face. She laughed with abandon when Nana shook water all over both of us.

Raven found a shell, held it up, then made it disappear. Her famous sleight-of-hand trick.

A lump formed in my throat. I'd forgotten her laugh, her infectious sense of humor. Why *had* we not seen each other or spoken in so long? I'd get her email address and reach out. I could almost hear Mandy drawl, "'Bout time."

We both waved at the camera and the edge of a hand waved back. One last closeup of Raven's face and the DVD ended.

I found a few more family movies, but they all seemed so far in the past that I couldn't see how they would be useful. Until I found the DVD of Sparrow.

Tucker stood and returned to his room, where he picked up the three stones and looked at them. He was most decidedly at another fork in the road. He had the ability to get Piper the answers she thought she wanted, but was that the best path? What could that cost him?

It would give Piper a second chance. What if she could have her daughter again?

What would he give to have another chance with his family? To bring back his wife and baby? His career? All that he'd lived for and then thrown away? To make That Night go away?

He kept the rocks in his hand as he returned to the office. What did Scott mean when he said, *"When the time comes, you'll know what they are and what to do with them"*? Were they a magical talisman, some kind of rock dice that would show him how many moves he had? Did they change color with his mood, or should he paint on them? As far as he could tell, all they seemed to do was weigh down his pants on that side.

He dropped them into his pocket.

Piper hadn't returned by the time he'd found his way to the office. He eased into the computer chair and stared at the blank screen. Scott had left the door open to reach out when he needed support.

Tucker turned on the computer and began typing an email.

Hey, Scott, You asked me to keep in touch. Without going into details, I need some advice.

He hit Send before he could change his mind.

The answer came almost immediately.

Tucker—glad you reached out. Do you still have the rocks?

Tucker smiled grimly.

Yes. Am I to consult them? Get stoned? Become a little boulder?

He hit Send.

Good to see your humor, or should I say sarcasm, is intact. What's the problem?

Tucker rubbed his mouth.

What if I could help someone like you helped me, believe in someone who has lost hope, encourage someone even if it costs me?

He read that over, then deleted it.

I'm just not sure what to do about—

He hit Send before he finished the sentence.

Scott answered.

In the words of Corrie Ten Boom, "Never be afraid to trust an unknown future to a known God."

Tucker leaned back, then folded his hands.

Yes.

This time the shot on the video was of the front of the house on the island. Tern, looking impossibly young, stepped outside. He was dressed in tan slacks and a blue button-down Oxford shirt, and he carried a small suitcase.

"Wave at the camera, Tern." Mother's voice was loud. Obviously she was the cameraman.

Tern waved self-consciously. Behind him, also holding luggage, came me, then Raven, and finally Sparrow. I must have been around sixteen or seventeen at the time.

"Raven, do a trick for us," Sparrow pleaded.

Raven grinned. "Later. I'm driving." Tern, Raven, and I raced for a cart. Tern got there first. "*I'm* driving." He stowed his suitcase in the back and started to slide into the seat.

"No, you're not." Raven dropped her bag, grabbed him around the waist, and pulled him away.

While the two were laughing and struggling, I jumped into the driver's seat. "It's my turn."

Sparrow stayed by the door and watched.

Raven released Tern, jogged over to Sparrow, and playfully tugged her toward the cart. "Come on, Sparrow. You can sit in the front this time."

Sparrow jerked her hand away. "No!" I leaned forward and froze the action. Sparrow's eyes were wide open, her complexion white, her mouth twisted in fear.

How did a woman who was terrified of riding in a cart end up dying while driving one? Now that I thought of it, Sparrow had never wanted to be the driver.

I turned off the TV. After collecting the two DVDs, I crept past the gym. I didn't need to be careful, it turned out. Ashlee must have finished his workout. Tern and Mother were also gone from the living room, although Joel was still tinkering with the air hockey table in the game room.

I opened the door to the study and held up the recordings. "I'm not sure what I was looking for, but I did find something interesting."

"So did I," Tucker said. "You might want to sit down."

I didn't like the sound of that. I sat.

"Before I start, what did you find?" He took the chair opposite me.

"This one"—I placed the first DVD on the coffee table between us—"is mostly a football game, but at the end are some good shots of Raven. It's probably one of the last times she was here on Curlew, at least that I know of. And this one"—I set the second DVD on top of the first—"is downright creepy. It has the four of us kids getting ready to take a short trip. At least based on the size of our suitcases."

"That would put the timing . . . ?"

"Possibly the year Sparrow died. The weird part is that Raven tried to pull Sparrow into one of the carts, but Sparrow was afraid of the carts." I let the significance of that fact sink in.

He frowned. "But you said she died while driving a cart."

"Right. Or so we were told."

"Can you show me?"

I opened the cabinet below the small flat-screen television, grabbed the remote, turned on the player and television, then loaded the DVD. The entire scene lasted less than two minutes. I played it through once, backed up, and the second time froze the screen on Sparrow's expression.

"I see what you mean." Tucker leaned back in his chair and rubbed his chin. "Maybe, maybe," he whispered.

"What?"

His gaze sharpened on me. "I'm trying to put this new information into what I discovered."

I returned the Sparrow DVD to its case, then loaded the second DVD into the player. "Did you want to see this one?"

"Not just yet. Before I tell you what I found, I have to ask—are you sure you want the truth, no matter how painful?"

I sucked in a quick breath. "Yes."

"Okay then. I should first tell you that in college, in addition to art, I had certain . . . skills. Computer skills. Hacking skills."

I jumped up and began pacing. The rain outside usually made this room seem cozy, but today the patter on the window sounded like drumming fingers. "Go ahead."

"Okay, so I want you to look at this." He stood and moved to the computer. A few clicks on the keyboard and a line chart appeared. "This is the Boone Industries profit and loss statement for the past twenty years."

I stopped and stared at him. "You hacked into the Boone Industries accounts?"

"I told you I was going to look into what happened, but in this case, I didn't have to hack. This computer was dedicated to Boone Industries and is unprotected here."

"Probably because it is Mother and Tern's computer."

"I always start with money. The company posted losses for

two different periods." He pointed to where the line shot downward. "The first starts here in 1997, when your father purchased the *Faire Taire*, and continues until 2001, then it dips into the red again in 2005."

"There are always ups and downs, and twice we came out of it."

"Your father died in 2001—"

"My father?"

"Let me finish. When I interviewed Silva, he mentioned that the *Faire Taire* was used by your father to entertain clients."

"Yes, that's true."

"In the four years after the purchase of that boat, the upkeep, combined with building this house on the island, put Boone Industries into a cash-flow crisis."

I slowly sank down on my chair. "I'm not sure I want to hear this."

"I think you should. In 2001, your father's death, or should I say your father's life insurance, carried by the company, bailed out Boone Industries. The second time, the insurance on the yacht brought in a much-needed boost, which it needed to cover payroll for expansion and new hires."

"That can't be true. My family owns the house and boats—"

"No. The corporation does."

I started to shake. "Are you trying to say that to save the company, someone in my family stole the yacht and my father committed suicide—"

"Your father may very well have been murdered."

The door to the study flew open and hit the wall, revealing my furious brother, nostrils flaring, teeth bared. "How dare you!"

CHAPTER 18

I leaped to my feet. "Tern! This is important—"

"This is how you repay our hospitality?" Tern stomped into the room and jabbed a finger at Tucker. "Hacking into our company's computer?"

"Wait, Tern." I grabbed his arm. "I told him to—"

"To what? Make up lies? Our father died in an accident. It was the most common accident among welders. We brought in experts."

Tucker was standing by now. "I'm sorry—"

"Get out!"

"But—"

"Get out of this house!" Tern's voice shook.

"Let me explain—"

"I don't want to hear it."

My heart pounded like a drum in my ears. I leaped between them. "Listen to him, Tern."

Tern spun on me. "No, you listen to me, Piper. I looked into your so-called hero, Tucker Landry. Or should I call him Tucker Canmore?"

"What?"

"He works for a company called Clan Firinn."

"He told me that."

"What he probably left out is that Clan Firinn is a halfway house for washed-up, discredited law-enforcement and forensic experts. They've destroyed their lives, devastated their families, and shattered their careers. Clan Firinn picks up the pieces, dries them out or gets them off drugs, changes their identity, and puts them back to work." He glared at Tucker. "You probably got religion while you were there, right?"

Tucker didn't answer. He was staring at me.

"I'm sure he not only didn't tell you about his work but left out the best part." Tern's voice dropped to almost a normal volume.

I didn't want to hear. I tried to get around Tern, but he wouldn't let me pass. "Did he tell you he was a drunk?" Tern smiled unpleasantly. "That while soused he drove off the road and into a river, killing his pregnant wife? That he went to prison for it?"

I flinched and looked at Tucker.

Tucker took a half step backward, placed a splayed hand on his chest, and looked down. His shoulders hunched as he hobbled from the room.

I started to follow him.

"Where do you think you're going, Piper?"

I practically spat at him, "It's none of your business!"

"Anything to do with this family is my business. Mildred's about to serve lunch, so I suggest you forget about Tucker and join Mother in the dining room."

My mouth dropped open and I gawked at him. "Are you *serious*?"

"Do you want to know just how serious I am? If you do even *one* thing to contact Tucker, I'll have him arrested."

"You wouldn't dare—"

"Wouldn't I? I'll also call Clan Firinn and let them know what he did. He'll be dropped from the program so fast he'll never recover. I'd bet he'd be back on the booze before you could say Jack Daniels. Is that what you want, Piper?"

I put my hands up as if to ward off his words.

"Be reasonable and rational. Go wash your face and go to lunch. Forget about Tucker and anything he told you."

After stumbling from the study, I somehow found myself in my room. Tucker had lied to me about his past . . . No, he hadn't lied. He told me about his wife. He just left out his part of it. And who he really was.

I walked to the bathroom, turned on the cold water, and splashed my face. The mirror showed a pinched face with flushed cheeks. "I should move on, do as Tern said, forget about Tucker. That's what the reasonable and rational Piper would do."

But I wasn't reasonable and rational at the moment. Someone had tried to gun me down. Tucker uncovered evidence that my father may have been murdered. The video I found indicated Sparrow's death might have been more than an accident. My daughter had somehow survived and another child had died.

All I had to do was prove it was all true.

Tucker wanted to vomit. Closing his eyes, he dry-scrubbed his face. He'd blown this big-time. Why hadn't he told Piper everything? Better to hear his story from him, along with how he'd changed his life, rather than the way she'd found out. She'd believe he'd lied to her and betrayed her trust. She'd never speak to him again.

I don't deserve Piper anyway. Better it ended now.

He made his way to his room. Asking Joel, or anyone else, to help him with his suitcase would open him to questions he didn't want to answer. He'd leave most of his clothes and art supplies here for now and send for them later. Placing his laptop into a messenger bag, he added a change of clothing, toiletries, and pain pills. After pulling on his rain jacket, he started for the door. He stopped, returned to the desk, took out a page from his sketchbook, and wrote, *I'm sorry. Forgive me.* Underneath he wrote his cell number.

He hobbled to the nearest exit and out into the rain.

Even with the jacket, Tucker was soaked by the time he arrived at the dock. A light was on inside the boat, and he focused on the illumination to take his mind off the dock and water below.

Silva must have heard his movements over the splashing rain. He appeared just inside the open galley/saloon. "Bad time to go for a walk."

"Would it be possible to go to the mainland?"

"I suppose. Is anyone else going over?"

"Not that I know of."

"Do you know how long you'll be?"

"I . . . I'm not coming back."

Silva pulled on his ear for a moment. "That so? Well, well, well. Let me help you on board."

Once again Silva approached, grabbed Tucker's arm, and

drew him swiftly on board. Tucker trailed the captain into the saloon. On the left, a single plate with the remains of a sandwich rested on the otherwise immaculate counter of a small galley kitchen. Silva slid the plate into the sink as he passed. "Would you like some water, or a drink, or . . . ?"

"I'm fine." Tucker sat on the light-gray sofa.

Silva grabbed a yellow slicker, ducked outside to untie the boat, then returned and powered up the engine. The wind and rain made for a bumpy ride, and Tucker kept a tight grip on the edge of the sofa. He couldn't leave Piper alone to combat whoever was trying to kill her and destroy her family. He'd need to stay close, but how to do that when they were on an island—and he was terrified to cross any body of water?

Closing his eyes, he prayed. *Dear Lord, guide me, direct me, show me what I should do. I'm lost. Amen.*

He kept his eyes shut, listening for an answer. The words nudged into his mind. *Piper is the one who's lost. You must finish what you started.*

"I don't know if that's You speaking or not, Lord," Tucker whispered. "So if I am to finish, to help Piper, show me a way."

Before I headed for the dining room, I returned to the study. Both of the DVD cases were missing. Tern must have taken them. I opened the player and breathed a sigh of relief. The one with the game on it was still loaded. Tern must have checked, then concluded it was just a football game. I removed the DVD, shot back to my room, then looked for a place to hide it. I didn't know if that brief video of Raven and me on the beach at the end of the football tape was important, but at this point anything could be significant.

The *Signs* movie poster gave me an idea. I selected that movie's case, removed the DVD and placed the Raven DVD in the case, then replaced the movie DVD on top of it. Not perfect, but I had thousands of movies and it would take more than a few minutes to go through all of them.

I headed to the dining room. Mother was seated at the head of the table, her expression pressed into frozen neutrality. Tern, opposite of Mother, was just about to sit down. He paused, waiting for me. Across the table from him was Ashlee. I could see from their faces that they'd all heard about Tucker.

"Piper, you remind me of the old saying about not having enough sense to get out of the rain." Ashlee took a sip of wine. "Your face is wet."

"At least my nose wouldn't be up so high as to drown."

Mildred entered with a soup tureen. "Turnip greens soup and a chopped quinoa salad with cranberries." She ladled out the soup. I had no appetite. Using my fork, I rearranged the food on my plate. I had to move Hannah out of danger, get off the island, and find Tucker before he left town—and I had to do it without Tern knowing. Without anyone knowing.

"I understand the hurricane is moving up the coastline." Mother spoke to Tern. "They're keeping an eye on it. I'm not worried, but the rain could affect the turnout at some of your speaking events."

The phone rang. "Boone residence." Mildred's voice carried clearly from the kitchen. "She isn't available at the moment. May I take a message?"

No one spoke.

"I see. Hold on, please." Mildred entered the dining room, her lips pinched and brows drawn. "Miss Piper, a woman is on the phone. She won't tell me who it is, but she says it's important that she speak to you."

Mother hated anyone taking a phone call during a meal.

I stood and moved toward the kitchen. "Thank you, Mildred."

"Piper!" Mother's voice was slightly higher than usual.

"If you'll please excuse me." Entering the kitchen, I picked up the receiver. "Hello, this is Piper."

"Hey, Piper, it's me, Mandy Chou. I hadn't heard from ya and wondered if ya found the journal?"

"No." I peered around the corner. Mildred was approaching. "Sure, I'd love to see you for coffee this afternoon."

"Are you okay, Piper?"

"Fine, but I will take you up on your offer to pick me up in your boat."

"So, ya can't talk openly. Gotcha. The weather is supposed to clear up around three this afternoon. Will that work?"

"Three o'clock it is. Maybe we can take in a movie."

"I'm off work and will come in my own boat. Give me a hint, though. Did y'all find some buried treasure, or a shipwreck, or graves, or something?"

"I agree. I'm also in the mood for a good murder mystery."

Tucker made a point to move away from the docked *Taire*, knowing Silva would be watching his every move and would undoubtedly report back to Tern. He had no idea where he'd go. After passing the family home, he knew he was out of sight.

The house gave him an idea. The information about his past as well as the work of Clan Firinn wasn't public knowledge. That meant that Tern had a lot of power to dig up hard-to-find information about people. Should Tucker remain in the area by staying in a hotel or bed-and-breakfast or renting an apartment, Tern could find him quite easily.

He *could* hide in plain sight. He'd heard a slight tinkle of wind chimes when Piper had taken Hannah to the house. Keeping the house between himself and the landing, he walked up the front steps, then inspected each rod of the chimes, making sure they didn't clank against each other. The key was in the third rod he checked.

He unlocked the door and entered the house. Now to find someplace in the house where he could operate yet stay off the radar.

I didn't return to the dining room but made my way through the kitchen to the foyer, then to the south wing. As expected, Tern followed me. "You remember what I told you," Tern said.

"Don't worry, brother." I kept walking, keeping my face turned so he couldn't read my expression. "Tucker betrayed me. He didn't tell me his past, not all of it, and I'm sure he was here to cause trouble." I delivered that with my best Meryl Streep performance. I wasn't sure he bought it, but soon his footsteps moved away.

I had an hour and a half to kill before Mandy showed up. If I took Piggy over to Joyce's house and showed Hannah and she identified it, that would prove that Hannah was Dove.

Unless Joyce had told her about the toy. Hannah recognizing Piggy would be like her knowing the right dog—intriguing, but hardly proof of anything.

Don't forget, Hannah said she'd never seen the ocean. "She blotted that out. She was just a tiny child."

What excuse could I give for taking my purse and the toy to Joyce's house? *Oh yeah, I just suddenly developed an interest in walking in the rain. You're wondering about the stuffed rabbit under my arm? I wanted company.*

I couldn't even call over there, not with Mildred in the kitchen by the phone all the time. I had no doubt Mildred would help me no matter what I did, but she was also fiercely loyal to my mother. Should Mother ask, Mildred would tell her the truth.

I could organize my thoughts and run them past Mandy. She was in law enforcement, just like Tucker used to be. Until I could talk to him safely, maybe Mandy could advise me. By now I'd reached the game room. Snatching up a pen and small pad of paper used to record game scores, I thought of where I could work.

My room was too obvious, and I didn't want to run into any member of my family. *Nana's realm?* I crept toward the breakfast nook. With window seats on three sides and a small table in the middle, it used to be a favorite spot for morning coffee. Then the current Nana had claimed the area under the table as his cave on hot, humid days. The smell of wet dog, the possibility of drool-draped clothing, and the occasional special treasure he'd retrieved from the ocean and snuck into the house ensured Nana had exclusive use of the area.

Nana was obviously outside enjoying the rain, though a chewed piece of driftwood marked his spot. I crawled into the window seat that was hidden from any casual passerby.

What had Tucker said to Lieutenant Gragg? *"Everyone had a motive. No one had an alibi."* What kind of secrets had my family kept from me? Beneath the bland conversations and polite smiles, what did they know or do?

Did Ashlee know his assailant? Did he really have an alibi because he was the victim? Or did he plan his own attack to make himself look innocent? Was he delivering the boat and taking a cut? Was Dove collateral damage?

If that was the case, I'd assured my daughter's fate by putting her in his arms that day and insisting he take her.

No. I wasn't going to take on that burden. I wrote down Ashlee's name.

Motive? There was no doubt that Ashlee liked the good things of life. And those good things cost money.

But Ashlee wasn't around when Sparrow died, nor when Father did.

Their deaths could be unrelated. Or maybe, inspired by the infusion of money after Father's accident, Ashlee decided to use insurance money from the boat theft to prop up the company. He owned shares and would certainly profit by doing so. He had extremely expensive taste.

But why wouldn't he tell his accomplice that Dove was on the boat? Why would he later hide the survival of our daughter from me? I placed a series of question marks after Ashlee's name.

Tern. I wrote his name next. *Alibi?* He was on the mainland when the boat was stolen and Dove taken. I hadn't asked what he was doing that day. What about motive? Did he need more money to campaign for office? He was big and strong enough to cold-cock Ashlee and drag him out of sight. Dove would recognize her uncle Tern.

That didn't make sense. Tern could have borrowed money if he needed it.

But he was around for Father's and Sparrow's deaths. And the attempt on my life. And on his. So he said. What if he was just making that up?

He received a lot of attention in the press whenever something happened to his family. Tern loved attention and power—which could translate into motive. But would he kill for that power?

Mother was next. *Alibi?* I didn't have a clue. I'd never asked about her either. Was I going to believe my mother murdered her only grandchild to get the insurance money on the boat? But Mother had never made a fuss that Raven didn't come around anymore, and she hadn't seemed to mourn Sparrow's death. Maybe she was incapable of feeling anything for others. Except for Tern.

I jabbed the paper with my pencil. My brain just wasn't wired to look for the whys or whos of a case. Could I believe Mildred and Joel were capable of this? Mildred was shopping that day. I saw the receipt, and the police would have checked her alibi. What motive could they have? Money? They lived simply, and they'd loved Dove. Neither would have profited from anyone's death.

But if Mother was involved up to her teeth, maybe she could get Mildred or Joel to do her bidding. Mother's world had to be perfect, and Sparrow was far from perfect.

Silva? As far as I knew, he was content with his life. What would he gain? But like Mildred and Joel, he was loyal. Just how loyal was the question.

Raven?

My hand hovered over the notepad. Where exactly *was* Raven? Tern said she was at an ashram in India, but I'd never known Raven to have a religious bone in her body. Of course, that woman at the condo also said she was married. Maybe Tucker could draw the husband and I could figure out who he was. I'd certainly be talking to Raven's neighbor again.

A lot can change in a person in fifteen-plus years.

Raven wasn't expected to attend the meeting the year Dove supposedly died, and Mildred hadn't prepared her room for her. In fact, she'd missed the shareholders' meeting for several years. Mother and Tern said they'd stayed in touch, but you could email from anywhere. How was she paying for her travels? Her motive could certainly be money.

Of course, the most obvious motive for anyone in the family to become homicidal would be the shares in Boone Industries. Mother was the last in her family. Father had been an only child. The last survivor of the family would own it all.

Tucker was right. No one had an alibi, and everyone had a motive. Money. Checking my watch, I found I had just enough time to grab a raincoat and purse and meet Mandy on the dock. She pulled up in an older blue-and-white Bayliner and I jumped in.

"Is there a chance that someone was watchin' ya?" She sped up, heading for the mainland. "I thought I saw someone up in the bushes."

"A really good chance. Do me a favor. I need to get to Joyce Mueller's place without anyone knowing about it."

She altered her course. "I'll aim for the harbor. That will put me out of sight of anyone spying on ya. Then I'll double around to the north. But only on one condition."

"What's that?"

"Ya fill me in on all this cloak-and-dagger stuff."

"I will. But first I need to get my daughter and this time make sure she's safe."

CHAPTER 19

Starting in the kitchen, Tucker explored each room. He knew Hannah had spent the night here, but it appeared as if the cleaning staff had already done their job. Did they come daily, weekly, when someone spent the night? Did they report to the family when someone was present? Piper said she'd only told Chou and himself of Hannah's arrival, but eventually someone else would know. He'd need to stay vigilant and work fast.

The main floor yielded no solutions for a concealed stay, but did give him the meal information, the house internet password, Boone12345, and the code to the lock on the boathouse. He moved upstairs. At the top of the stairs he spotted a hatch in the ceiling with a small rope dangling. He pulled on the rope and drop-down stairs appeared.

He left his crutches on the floor and clumped up the steep stairs. The attic itself was dusty and stretched the length of the house, with a window at either end, allowing views of both the street and the dock. He could stand up in the middle of the room. Stacked under the eaves were outdated Christmas decorations, plastic tubs of clothing, and white corrugated boxes.

In the corner he found camping gear, including an inflatable air mattress and a sleeping bag. Perfect.

The sound of a boat engine brought him to the window overlooking the water. Silva pulled up, docked, then began moving boxes and luggage onto the dock. A woman driving a small U-Haul truck parked next to the dock, and the two of them loaded up. The U-Haul left and Silva returned to the boat. He went into the cabin.

Tucker moved down to the living room to work, leaving the drop-down stairs extended in case he had to hide quickly. All of the windows had either closed blinds or sheer panels with drapes on them. The sheers allowed him to look outside without being seen during daylight hours. He booted up his laptop, but the sound of an approaching car engine made him pause. Carefully, so he wasn't backlit, he moved to the window overlooking the road. A paneled van parked across the street and the engine turned off, but no one got out.

He rubbed the back of his neck. This van wasn't here to move anything from the boat. Surveillance? Did someone know he was inside? No, he'd made sure no one saw him. Piper's car was parked under the house. Maybe they were spying on her.

Whatever the reason, with Silva in the boat on one side of the house and a surveillance van on the other, as of now he was trapped.

Mandy and I made our loop and sped toward Joyce's home. Just as she had said, the rain stopped and an exquisite rainbow appeared in the sky. The water was still choppy, however, so we kept the speed relatively slow.

I explained all that had happened. She listened without asking any questions until we pulled up at Joyce's landing.

"There's a lot of holes in your theories." She stopped the engine and let us drift to the dock. I jumped out and tied up.

"I know."

"And this whole thing about Hannah being Dove . . . well, it kinda smacks of bein' somethin' ya desperately want to be true."

"You were the one who talked about 'having a feeling.'"

"The feelin' I was talking about is a nudge from the Holy Spirit, not a gut-wrenchin' desire to have your little girl back again."

I blinked and stared at her.

She sighed. "I'll tell ya what, as long as I'm not doing somethin' immoral or illegal, I'll go along with your feelin'. Who knows? Maybe the Holy Spirit is tryin' to get your attention."

After stumbling up the now-muddy hill, we reached Joyce's porch. No one seemed to be around. We circled the house, then rapped on the back door. "Hannah?" I called out. I could see into the living room and kitchen through a tiny slit where the curtains met.

The faux wall swung open, and Hannah uncoiled from her position on top of the dryer. She ran to the door and opened it. "It's you! I was so frightened."

I so wanted to hold her and hug her! My beautiful Dove had finally come home. For the first time in fifteen years, tears burned my cheeks.

"Piper, what's wrong?" Hannah asked.

"Noth . . . nothing. I'm . . . happy to see you." I swallowed hard, then headed to the bathroom to find tissues. After blowing my nose, I returned and avoided looking at Mandy. I knew she'd be giving me a look of pity. "Hannah, were you hiding just now?"

"Yes. Someone was walking around the house last night. I'd locked the doors, but someone tried to get in. I hid under the bed." She looked at Mandy. "Hi. I'm Hannah."

"Mandy Chou. How ya doin'?"

"I'm an idiot. Forgive me for not introducing you two." My brain seemed full of cotton.

"That's okay." Hannah gave a slight smile with the undamaged side of her face. "Do you think I could go back to the house on the mainland? I don't mean to be a fraidy-cat, but I don't like it here."

"I was going to suggest the same thing," I said.

Hannah didn't have to be told twice. She immediately charged off to pack.

Mandy moved closer to me. "Is your family's house on the mainland a good idea? If someone is after her, they'd look there next."

"That's true."

"And, not to be cruel, but she's pretty recognizable. Why don't you let her come home with me? I've got a guest room, and my place is pretty remote. No one would think to look for her there."

"I couldn't ask you to do that—"

"You're not askin'. I'm offerin'."

"Then I'm accepting. Let me pay you something . . ." *Pay!* What had Tucker said? *"Your father's life insurance, carried by the company, bailed out Boone Industries. The insurance on the yacht brought in a much-needed boost, which it needed to cover payroll for expansion and new hires."* Boone Industries hadn't done any expanding in the last fifteen years. In fact, the last few stockholders' meetings had revealed a steady reduction in payroll and staffing due to not replacing retiring employees. The company had mechanized several positions as well. Could that "expansion" have been hush money for keeping Hannah? Making Joyce an "employee"?

"What's going on, Piper?" Mandy asked. "All of a sudden you sort of zoned out."

Glancing around to be sure Hannah was still packing, I said, "It just occurred to me that I hadn't really thought of Joyce as someone involved in all that's going on. She should have been the first person I suspected. What was she doing with my daughter? In fact, Joyce and Silva could have been tangled up in this together. They were each other's alibi."

"Piper, about this whole idea that Hannah is—"

Hannah walked into the room, suitcase in hand. "I'm ready."

"Let's go then." I didn't want, or need, anyone else to doubt me about Hannah. I moved to the front door, peered around to see if anyone was watching, then trotted as fast as I could down the path to the boat. Mandy and Hannah followed just as quickly. I didn't share our destination with Hannah until we were safely on our way.

"Why do you think someone might be after *me*?" Hannah asked.

I wanted to tell her everything and to start to make up for the fifteen years we'd been apart, but Tucker's words of caution held me back. "I'm not really sure just yet. I hope I'm being overly cautious."

"My car's at the harbor marina," Mandy said to me. "I'll dock there, then drive you to your car. Where are you going next?"

"I thought I'd find that woman at the condo and talk to her some more, then try to locate Tucker. He could have gone back to work or checked in with the folks at the *Hunley*."

We reached the public docks at the marina. I jumped off the boat and tied it up while Hannah and Mandy collected their things. As we walked toward the parking area, Mandy said, "Didn't ya say your brother would be watchin' to see if ya contacted Tucker?"

"Yes, but—"

"And I'd bet *Senator* Boone has some investigators on staff, or he wouldn't have found out about Tucker's past, right? It would take a lot of diggin' to come up with Tucker's old identity."

"I guess," I said reluctantly. The parking lot was practically empty because of the heavy rains, with only a Camry and an older pickup. Mandy headed for the Camry.

"So I'd suggest we not get your car, but instead let me drive you around in case you're being followed."

"That sounds like a great idea, Mandy." I couldn't help smiling. I wanted to spend more time with Hannah—make that Dove. In fact, I didn't want her to go with Mandy; I wanted her to stay with me. Maybe I could simply run away with her. It wouldn't be kidnapping. I couldn't abduct my own daughter.

As long as I could *prove* she was my daughter.

If necessary, Tucker could call the police and complain about the van. He could sneak out of the house while the police were talking to the occupants.

He still felt trapped.

In the dining room was a well-stocked wet bar. He hadn't touched a drop of alcohol since he'd been taken in by Clan Firinn, but that didn't mean the desire wasn't in the back of his mind every minute of every day. He stuck his hand in his pocket and squeezed the rocks until it hurt, then closed his eyes.

The Night had been stormy. Monsoon rains sent sheets of water over the windshield of the car. His wipers couldn't keep up. The headlights of the car barely split the darkness. He'd injured his arm somehow and was driving with one hand on the wheel. The deer appeared in the middle of the road, frozen motionless. He'd swerved . . .

Who am I kidding?

The Night was clear, lit by a full moon. They'd been to a party and he was drunk. Again. And driving.

"Darling, please pull over and let me drive." His wife had her hand on his arm, clutching it. Tears streamed down her face. *No injury. No rain*. Just her frightened grip on his arm and her tears.

She glanced ahead and screamed.

He returned his attention to the road.

A truck barreled down on them, horn blaring.

Adrenaline shot through his veins. He was in the wrong lane. He spun the wheel.

Too late.

A screeching of tortured metal, the sting of flying glass, the world spinning out of control, a flash of black river, freezing wet, cold.

He woke up in the hospital.

A man was sitting beside the bed, reading a book. He looked up. "Ah, you're awake. I'm Scott Thomas of Clan Firinn."

The enormity of his situation landed on his chest like an anvil. They were gone. His wife. His child. He killed them. Tears burned his cheeks.

The man seemed not to notice. "I'm here to talk to you about your future."

Tucker blinked. Future?

Scott leaned forward. "Have you ever read anything by Corrie ten Boom?" Tucker barely heard the words. Only blackness lay before him.

"She wrote, 'Never be afraid to trust an unknown future to a known God.'" He closed the book. "I figure it's time you got to know us, that unknown future, and Him."

Tucker opened his eyes and turned his back on the wet bar. He resolutely sat in front of his computer and pulled up the link analysis chart he'd started. He added in all he'd learned from Boone Industries' financial records. He wanted to follow the funds transferred from the company's coffers, then hack into the police department's records on Montgomery, Sparrow, and Dove. What he *didn't* want to do was think about Piper's delusion about her daughter. Or the booze in the other room. That would be a known future.

It didn't take us long to reach Mount Pleasant. Now that the island was behind us, or maybe because being at Joyce's house alone had made her lonely, Hannah was on a roll.

"Did you know I can speak German? *Ich werde Murstard auf meinem Bratworst haben*. That means 'I'll have mustard on my bratwurst.' A lot of people speak German in Wisconsin. And eat cheese curds. I like curds when they're deep fried or really fresh and they squeak. How about you, Piper?"

"Do I speak German, or do I like cheese curds?"

"Right."

"Um—"

"I miss Wisconsin, but I like it here. Well, sort of, because I was afraid last night, but when I get really scared, I sing. I know a lot of songs. I thought I'd try out for *The Voice* someday. They judge your singing without seeing you, at least not at first. It's not like *America's Got Talent*. There you're judged on how you look before you even open your mouth. Right now I sing in the church choir. Did you ever sing in a choir?"

"No—"

"That's too bad, 'cause singing makes you happy. So do dogs. And puppies. I'm going to have a whole bunch of dogs when I have my own place. I get an apartment when I go off to college. That's what Grandma said . . ."

At the mention of her grandmother, she frowned, then pulled out her phone and began scrolling. A fat tear rolled down her cheek. I wanted to hug her. And hear her voice. "Maybe you could sing for me."

"Okay, but not right now."

Once in town, I directed Mandy to the condos. We pulled around and parked in front of Raven's old unit.

"Tell me again. Why are we here?" Mandy asked.

I turned to face her. "I've gone through everyone in my family or connected to the family to see if anything was reasonable to explain the . . ." I couldn't think of a word to cover the accidents, deaths, missing people, and events that had been going on.

"Curse?" Mandy offered.

"I guess. I tried to picture different people with their motives and possible alibis. The only person who was a blank spot was Raven. The police wouldn't say who they interviewed or what was said—just that everyone was in the suspect pool. This is Raven's last known address, and her neighbor mentioned a man, a husband. I wanted to follow up on that and maybe, um, go inside the condo." I indicated with my eyes that Hannah was listening.

Mandy took the hint. "If ya decide to look around, maybe Hannah and I could go get some ice cream or somethin'. I *am* a sworn officer and all."

"That's a plan. If you want to stay in the car, I'll see if I can find the lady." They agreed. Leaving my purse, I got out and moved toward the building. I had no idea which unit belonged to the woman, but maybe she'd see me and come out. If not, I was willing to knock on a few doors.

A dog barked frantically somewhere nearby. That was promising. I followed the sound. It came from Raven's empty apartment.

My stomach tightened. I glanced over at Mandy, sitting in the car. In an instant she'd shot from the driver's seat and was beside me. "What's wrong?" she asked. "Your face is all wanky."

I put my face to one of the windows but couldn't see the barking canine. "There's a dog in there."

"So?"

"This is an empty condo."

"Did ya try openin' the door? Maybe the dog just got locked in somehow." She turned the knob and the door opened a crack. The dog was silent for a moment, then renewed its agitated yapping.

Mandy nudged the door with her foot, took a step forward, then a quick step back. "Pew. Okay, that's not a good smell."

I caught a whiff, turned, and immediately threw up on the steps.

"I can't say that helped with the stench much," Mandy said dryly. "Maybe ya should wait in the car."

"I'll be fine."

"We should call the police."

"Not to split hairs or anything, but aren't *you* the police? I'd say we're almost legal." I took a deep breath, pinched my nose, and entered.

"Wait! Piper, this could be a crime scene."

I ignored her and reached a short hallway with a door on my left. The barking came from that direction. I opened the door and the strange-looking three-legged dog bounded out, then leaped into my arms.

I almost dropped him. His hairless skin felt warm under my hands, and he shook with anxiety. I started to leave, but the dog gave a sharp bark at something on my right. I turned.

I caught a glimpse of a bare foot streaked in rusty-brown blood and covered with flies.

CHAPTER 20

Tucker rubbed his eyes, burning from staring at the computer screen.

Sparrow had been an interesting read. Two years younger than Tern, she had been five years older than Piper. As a young child she'd appeared in a number of photographs with her family, usually sitting slightly apart from them. Tucker hadn't found any photographs of her after she'd become a teen. Her obituary offered little information about her life, but a bit of digging produced the news that she'd been diagnosed with autism. He also found a reference to her in the local police records. She'd been arrested for making a public disturbance. No charges were filed.

Then she was dead.

The police report on her death stated that she was found lying next to an overturned golf cart on the island. Her head had struck a rock. No autopsy was performed.

If her death was more than an accident, what motive would there be? The most common reasons for murder were robbery, jealousy, and vengeance. None seemed to fit. Money? She wasn't rich, but she held shares in Boone Industries. Maybe someone wanted a bigger slice of the pie by removing her as a shareholder.

So much for having the perfect home for the perfect family on the perfect island as Piper had mentioned.

Stumbling from the condo, I didn't stop racing until I'd reached the car. The dog struggled in my shaking arms. My stomach threatened to upchuck again.

"Let me have him." Hannah was standing beside me, reaching for the canine. I hadn't even heard her get out of the car. As soon as I relaxed my grip, the dog bounded into her arms.

Mandy had apparently gone inside. She emerged, closed the door, wiped the knob, and joined us by the car. "Get in."

"What happened?" Hannah asked.

"A dog got locked in the bathroom," Mandy said smoothly. "I need to stop and run into the store for a moment. Hannah, could ya stay in the car with the dog?"

"Sure. What's his name?"

"Fluffer," I said.

"Gunn," Mandy said.

"FlufferGunn? Okay."

Mandy pulled into the first convenience store we came to. The rain had started again with gusty winds. A few people were outside. She parked close to an old pay phone. We both got out, went inside, and walked to the refrigerated drinks section. "Well? What did you see?" I grabbed two waters.

"A lot of blood. It was an older woman. Someone murdered her. I'm thinkin' she's been dead for a day or less." She picked up a Coke.

"It has to be the woman I spoke to when Tucker and I came

here yesterday. That's her dog. Why'd you hustle out of there? Aren't you going to call the police?"

"I am. But I'm going to call in an anonymous tip. I found this in the corner of the kitchen." She held out her cell phone. She'd taken a photograph of a piece of paper on the cream-colored tile floor. It was a preliminary sketch of the men who'd died in the *Hunley*. Signed by Tucker.

Tucker searched for Joyce Mueller in Wisconsin. No luck. There were 2,321 Joyce Muellers in the state and surrounding states. He didn't even know what kind of doctor she was. Medical? Veterinarian? PhD? Psychologist? Dentist? Even that didn't help. No Dr. Joyce Muellers in Wisconsin, period.

Returning to the financial records of Boone Industries, he focused on the time period when the company started having cash-flow problems. Montgomery Boone, according to Silva, used the expensive yacht to entertain clients and transport guests. He pulled up the list of entertainment expenses. Montgomery had used the yacht on average eight times a year for entertainment that ranged from one to seven days. The list showed dates, clients, and expenses. The clients, primarily for the plumbing side of the business, were cross-referenced with their revenue statistics. It appeared that the strategy was successful, as sales jumped after each wine-dine cruise. The longer trips, however, didn't include as much information. The clients were listed by initials. *H.D.* Home Depot? *L.J.*? If the *L* was for Lowe's, what was the *J* for?

Tucker went back to the photos of the Boone family.

Montgomery had been a strikingly handsome man. In most of the images, Caroline rested an arm or a hand on him. Tucker leaned backward in his chair and stared at the computer screen. "Tell me, Caroline Boone, what were your organic, conservation-minded thoughts on taking a huge yacht out to entertain clients? Isn't that a rather large carbon footprint?"

Did she ever go with him?

It took some searching, but he finally located a few expenses that had her name connected to them. Cash draws for birding tours. The first one was Brazil, the Atlantic Forest. Five days. At the same time, Montgomery had gone on a four-day cruise with H.D.

Each of Caroline's birding trips corresponded to Montgomery's longer cruises.

"Montgomery, you dirty dog. No wonder you named your love boat *Faire Taire*. 'Be silent.'" He hobbled into the kitchen and found a can of soda in the refrigerator. What he really wanted to do was take a shower.

A quick search of emails showed little activity, but a deeper probe indicated a lot of deleted material. Interesting for a house used primarily by guests. He'd come back to that.

He turned to the case file on Dove's disappearance. He was searching for the report on the recovery of Dove's body. He found it along with her autopsy report. Under the date it read,

> I, Stan Gragg, at 0828 hours received a call to Curlew Island in reference to a body. My investigation revealed the following information.
>
> At 0730 hours, JOEL CHRISTIANSON, an employee of the BOONE FAMILY, was repairing the road near the

home of JOYCE MUELLER, located at the north end of the island. Joel Christianson stated he heard a dog barking and identified it as the black Newfoundland dog owned by the Boones. He said Dr. Mueller wasn't home and he believed she had returned to Wisconsin sometime earlier in the week.

He left the road and walked to the leeward (west) side of the island to investigate.

He found the dog standing over the remains of a body.

The dog was weak and appeared in distress. He picked up the dog and carried it to the cart he used to hold his tools.

He drove the dog to the Boone residence and called the police.

He requested the responding personnel to use the dock at the north end.

His wife, MILDRED CHRISTIANSON, was present in the Boone home and took possession of the dog.

He informed CAROLINE BOONE, TERN BOONE, and ASHLEE YATES, all present in the family home, of the discovery of the body. Ashlee said he'd inform his wife, SANDPIPER BOONE YATES, as she wasn't feeling well.

Along with Tern Boone, Ashlee Yates returned to the Mueller dock to wait for police.

At approximately 0850, I arrived on the island with EMS personnel JAY ROSE, CARA BERGER, and JACK HOLLOWAY.

We met with Tern Boone and Joel Christianson, who

took us to the body, which had washed up on a narrow piece of land extending into the ocean. The body, obviously a child, was in an advanced stage of decomposition.

- Supplemental reports attached:
- Evidence collected
- Pictures
- Witness statements

Officer Stan Gragg had also been the first on the scene when the call came in on Ashlee's attack and the missing boat. Marion Inlet was a small department, so Gragg's frequent involvement wasn't that significant.

Tucker looked at the photos, then wished he hadn't.

"Obviously planted and obviously false." I handed Mandy back her phone. "Tucker has a clear alibi. And you and I both know Tucker didn't kill that woman."

"The problem is the police don't know it, at least not yet, and Tucker will be blamed." Mandy and I headed for the counter to pay for the drinks. "Someone is tryin' to frame him to get him out of the picture."

"Why?"

"I don't know. Maybe to be able to get at you."

We stopped talking until I'd paid and we were back outside. The rain had started up again. We stood for a moment under the overhang of the building, waiting for a slight break.

Mandy's statement sent my thoughts churning. "If the murderer's goal was to separate Tucker and me, or get him off Curlew, or get him in trouble, all they needed to do was wait. Tucker's snooping and Tern's discovering him effectively did all that. That poor woman died for no reason."

"Maybe. Didn't ya say she saw a man she called Raven's husband hangin' around? She was a witness. Killin' her was silencin' her, and tossin' the blame on Tucker was just whipped cream on their plan." Mandy checked around her, then ran to the pay phone. Using some napkins she'd grabbed from the counter, she picked up the receiver and dialed. She spoke for a moment, then hung up and nodded toward the car.

I ran and jumped in. "Aren't you afraid the surveillance cameras will record you making that call?" I whispered.

"Nope," she whispered back. "I know the owner. He's too cheap to fix his cameras. Last one broke two weeks ago." She grinned and pulled out into traffic.

"I hate to be a bother, but I need to use a restroom," Hannah said. "And I think FlufferGunn does too."

I crossed my eyes at Mandy. "Um, Hannah, you don't have to call her FlufferGunn. You can call her any name you want."

"Good. I'll call her Piggy."

A blast of rain hit the window, and the small red light on the television went out. Tucker's computer screen dimmed, and the house became silent as the air conditioner stopped. The power outage was brief, but the rain intensified. Tucker returned to his hacking, this time investigating the hidden deleted emails. They originated here, signed by "Raven," and were addressed to Caroline's or Tern's addresses.

The emails themselves were vague and generally contained excuses for why she wouldn't be in touch. They mentioned her traveling to remote places. Someone in Piper's family, maybe Raven herself, wanted everyone to believe Raven was out of the country—a perfect alibi.

Tucker found the local weather website. A hurricane watch had been issued. "What does that mean?" he muttered.

He found a site that explained a hurricane watch meant hurricane conditions were a possibility within the next forty-eight hours. It went on to describe preparations, including bringing in outdoor furniture, making sure there was an emergency kit, and reviewing evacuation routes. Finally, homeowners were advised to board up windows and doors.

The hairs on his neck stood up. He had to get out or he'd be imprisoned inside a house in the path of a hurricane.

What about Piper? He needed to get her away from her murderous family. That would mean getting Silva to take him back over.

He stood and moved to the window overlooking the dock.

The *Taire* was gone.

Time slowed down. I felt a tightness in my chest. "Wh-wh-why would you name the dog Piggy?"

"I just like the name." She hugged the dog. "I really do need to go . . ."

I scrambled to organize my thoughts. "Mandy, you know the farmer's market in town? The one on the way to our mainland house?"

"Hard to miss, but I think they're closed today."

"They have porta potties."

"Right. Good idea. And they're private," Mandy whispered.

On the ride over to Marion Inlet, I tried to figure out a scenario that would explain all of the seemingly impossible facts about Hannah/Dove. I drew a blank. The only thing I knew to be true was that Hannah was my daughter.

My cell rang as we pulled into the spacious parking lot of the farmer's market. Only two cars were evident. "Hello?"

"Hi, Piper. This is Four Paws Rescue. We have to evacuate all the critters. I know I just called on the goose, but I was wondering if you could help us?"

"Of course. Just . . . just do what you have to do and let me know the damages."

"Bless you, Piper!"

"Thank you. Good luck." I hung up. "When this whole hurricane passes," I said to Hannah, "I'm going to introduce you to a two-hundred-dollar goose."

"Huh?"

"Never mind."

The pop-up tents were gone and the permanent booths empty, but the blue porta potties remained. The rain was steady, and Mandy turned on the heat to offset the dampness.

Hannah opened the door and Piggy did the world's fastest business, then leaped back inside and snuggled in Hannah's arms. "I'm sorry, Piggy, but I gotta go too." She placed the dog on the seat and made a dash for the nearest restroom.

"What's the significance of the name Piggy?" Mandy asked.

Before I could answer, her phone rang. She fished it from her purse. "Hello . . . Hello? I can't hear ya. Call me back in a minute.

I'll get somewhere so I can hear." She hung up. "I think that was my brother. Let me try someplace else."

Leaving the car running, she dashed for the nearest booth, an open-sided covered space with built-in tables to display wares. She held her phone in front of her like a divining rod.

Taking my purse with me, I got out and scurried after her. I had absolutely no memory of telling Joyce that Dove had a stuffed rabbit named Piggy.

Mandy's phone rang again. "Yeah, that's better." She listened. Slowly her gaze moved to me. "When do you think that could be?" Pause. "What if it moves? Okay. Yeah, I'll tell 'em."

She disconnected, stared at her phone, then at me. "That was my brother, the fisherman. Remember when I said I'd ask him to take a detour and check out a specific area?"

I gasped. "He found Joyce?"

"No. At least I don't think so. He went out fishin' this morning where I'd told him to go—basically where I figured the boat might have drifted from. He said the wind and a nasty current moved him over a bit, and the storm has churned things up. His anchor caught on something, and he hauled up a hunk of rusty welded metal attached to a chunk of fiberglass."

My hands became damp. I dumped my heavy purse on a nearby bench and wiped my palms on my slacks. "So what are you saying?"

"Well, he couldn't be certain, so he suited up and took a quick look. There's a boat down there, all right, badly damaged. He took a picture." She held up her phone so I could see the photo. "He said it looked like an explosion sank it."

I could just barely read the name painted across the stern. *Faire Taire.*

CHAPTER 21

The van at the front of the house was still parked in the same place. To get over to Curlew he'd need to distract the occupants and pilot a boat over himself. He was bathed in sweat.

"Come on, Tucker, buck up. You've had plenty of time to get over your paranoia." The talking didn't help.

The heavy rains brought an early darkness that made it difficult to see around the room. He shut down the computer so the lighted screen wouldn't show through the sheer panels. There would be no way to navigate an open ocean in the dark, but there was a good chance Silva was picking up the family to evacuate them from the island. Tucker refined his plans. He'd watch for the Boones' return and somehow try and get Piper away from them. He trusted that Piper would have figured out how to get Hannah.

His stomach grumbled. Did he dare risk opening the refrigerator again to check for food? Just as he stood, an engine started up outside. The lights on the van came on and it drove away. "Thank You, Lord," he breathed.

The refrigerator yielded Hannah's pepperoni pizza missing two slices. Perfect.

The *Faire Taire* sank? An explosion? I thought my knees would buckle. I groped for something to sit on, ending up on a display table soaked in rain.

Sinking the ship would explain why it was never located and how the body everyone called Dove washed up on the island. If it was an explosion, it probably killed the thief as well. All the parts fit, down to the last detail.

Could I be wrong that Hannah is Dove?

No. I wouldn't believe it, couldn't believe it. I had no place for such doubts. *Think about something else.* The thief.

A thief missing for fifteen years. Just like Raven.

I felt like someone had just dumped a second box of puzzle pieces into my partially finished jigsaw.

Hannah spotted us from the porta potty and ran through the rain to join us. "How come you're over here?"

"Better cell reception. Are you ready to go?"

A movement out of the corner of my eye made me glance in that direction. Someone in a hooded raincoat stood by one of the cars parked in the lot, taking photographs. Of us. "Mandy!"

Mandy knew what to do. I snatched up my purse and both of us dashed toward the figure, who attempted to get the car door open and leap inside before we got there. I slammed against the person while Mandy shoved the door shut, blocking escape. Dropping my purse, I yanked the hood down.

Bailey Norton shoved me away. "I should charge you with assault."

"And I should charge you with invasion of privacy."

"I'm a reporter. I'm doing my job. Speaking of which"—she pulled the hood back up over her now-dripping hair—"you might want to identify the girl with the burned face over there." She nodded toward Hannah.

"None of your business." I stuck out my hand. "Give me your camera."

"Not on your life."

I looked over at Mandy. "Isn't she breaking some law or something?"

"Not yet."

Bailey raised the camera to take a photograph of Hannah. I put my hand in front of the lens.

"Move your grubby hand."

"Put down your camera."

She lowered it.

I moved to block her view. "Listen—"

"No, you listen. You and your entire family are news. You're entertainment. You're like the Kennedys, but your compound is in Marion Inlet, not Hyannis Port. Your family has money, good looks, and political pull. Best of all, just like the Kennedys, you have a curse."

"That's not true—"

"Of course it's not." She smirked at my expression. "I read that journal about the shipwreck. I also managed to take a sample of the paper and ink, and I found out both are recent. The journal's a fake, but only I and the forger know that."

"What—"

"It won't matter because I won't reveal that. Oh, Piper, the kind of juicy tabloid news your family will supply me with will make my career."

My mouth finally started to work. "You won't be able to get within ten feet of us—"

"Au contraire, my little naive stray." She held up her hand. An impressive diamond solitaire sparkled from her ring finger. "I'm practically family myself. I'm engaged to Ashlee. We'll be married at Christmas."

My mind went blank.

She glanced down. "Your stuff's getting wet."

My oversized purse had dropped to the pavement, spilling the contents out into the rain. I bent to pick it up.

Bailey beat me to it and snatched up my key ring. "Did Raven give this to you?"

I grabbed it from her grasp. "That's none of your business."

"The last time I was on Curlew . . ."

She must have enjoyed watching my face react. "Oh yes, I've visited the island. No one was around except Ashlee, of course, and that boat captain, who keeps his mouth shut for a price. I got a chance to check out all the *bed*rooms."

I wasn't going to listen anymore. I savagely stuffed the contents back into my purse.

"Anyway, that exact bird on your key chain was on Ashlee's wall. As you know, Ashlee now has Raven's room."

"I know. It's a robin. All the bedroom walls have bird prints. So?"

"So you know there's a locked safe behind it, right?"

I wasn't going to give her the satisfaction of knowing she'd scored a point. "So? Why are you telling *me*?"

"Quid pro quo. I told you. You'll tell me what's in it."

"Fat chance."

"If you do, I'll share a juicy piece of family history with you.

If you don't, you can read it in print." Without another word, she got into her car and drove off.

I became aware of someone shoving me. Mandy gave one last push and I was at the passenger side of her Camry. The rain had intensified to monsoon level and I was soaked.

"Get in."

I obeyed. The car had been running the whole time and the warmth enveloped me. I started shaking. "D-d-did you hear what she said?"

"I was standin' right there. Hard to miss. Ya turned into a statue."

Hannah was already in the rear seat. "Who was that?"

We started forward. Mandy turned on the headlights.

"The queen of villains. Cruella de Vil, Nurse Ratched, Joan Crawford, Annie Wilkes." I took a deep, shuddering breath. "Almira Gulch—"

"She's a newspaper reporter," Mandy said.

"The Wicked Witch of the West—"

"Who's Annie Wilkes?" Mandy turned toward downtown.

"*Misery*, 1990. Maleficent—"

"We get your drift," Mandy said.

I turned up the heat. "Where are we going?"

"I was hopin' ya'd tell me. I've gone around this block twice."

"Where do you live?"

"About ten miles—"

"Too far. I need to find Tucker. Hannah, you stay with Mandy. For now, take me to the family house."

Tucker was eyeing the third slice of pizza when the phone rang. After a few rings, it stopped, then started again. This repeated several times before stopping. In the silence that followed, a car engine sounded. A Camry had parked by the front door. No one got out for a few minutes, then Piper jumped out and ran up the stairs as the car pulled away.

He was at the door and pulled her inside before she could check the chimes.

"Tucker!" She gave him a hug.

His heart raced. He felt her trembling, her own rushing heartbeat. She let go and stepped awkwardly away, her face flushed. "I'm . . . I'm happy to see you. Um . . . Tern—"

"I'm sorry," he said at the same time.

"He shouldn't have—"

"I should have—"

"You first," he said.

"I had no idea you'd be here. Did Tern change his mind?"

"Hardly. Who drove you here?"

"Mandy Chou. I told you about her. She's with marine patrol. Hannah is staying with her."

Her trembling didn't stop, and he realized she was soaking wet. He went into the living room, now almost completely dark, grabbed a beige cashmere throw blanket, returned, and wrapped it around her. "Come in and get warm and dry."

Once they were both seated on the sofa, she reached for his hand. "Listen, we just got a phone alert. Hurricane Marco has turned. We're under a hurricane warning. The phone here's probably been ringing off the hook. Automatic warning system to every phone in the region."

His shoulders tightened. "It has. What's the difference between a watch and a warning?"

"It's basically saying there's a chance the hurricane may hit within the next twenty-four to thirty-six hours."

"We need to get out of here." He stood.

"Wait. Hurricanes are erratic. It could change course again. Several times in the past we've evacuated and were never in danger. And Hurricane Marco is moving very slowly, so there's plenty of time to get out of its path. Here's the thing you need to know."

He could barely see her face in the dim light.

"By now, Tern, Ashlee, and Joel would have closed all the hurricane shutters and prepared the house on Curlew. In the morning they'll evacuate the island, get this house shut down, and move inland."

"Which is what we should do."

"We will, but I have irreplaceable mementos that could be lost should a storm surge wipe out the house. I'm sure no one will think to grab up my journals, Dove's bunny, or her christening gown."

She'd never mentioned a christening gown. Maybe the seeds he'd planted were taking root. "You didn't mention that you christened Dove."

She shifted. "There are a lot of things I've . . . boxed up or deliberately not thought about. Her gown, bonnet, and favorite pacifier are in Mother's room."

"Then just call up Mildred and have her collect those things."

"I will. But if I wait until everyone is gone, I'll have this one window of opportunity to search the house and collect the proof I need that Hannah is Dove and that she was concealed from me."

"Piper, all you have to do is get a DNA test for Hannah."

Piper was silent, but he could feel the slight trembling in her hand. "But what . . . what . . ."

"What if the DNA comes back and she's not Dove?" he said quietly. "Is that what you wanted to say?"

"I would be losing her all over again," she whispered.

"You'll have to take that chance."

A hot tear struck his hand. He reached for her face, but she stood and dropped the blanket. "There's a safe in Raven's room. I need to look in there. It could contain something my sister Raven wanted to tell me, at least I think she did." Piper pulled a key ring out of her pocket. "Raven gave me this key ring and a blank key."

"A key blank will open nothing—"

"But it has the potential to open anything. One way or the other, the silence in the family has got to be broken." Her voice grew stronger. "I'll learn to live with the truth, no matter how hard. Are you with me?"

"Of course. But the hurricane . . ."

"We have time. Have you seen if Mother and the others have evacuated?"

"Silva came over earlier with a load of boxes and suitcases. They were picked up by a U-Haul."

"Standard procedure for a hurricane. The kennel should have picked up Nana—"

"Nana wasn't on board."

She sucked in a breath. "Of course he was. You just missed him."

"No. Nana's hard to miss. Sometime later I noticed the boat had left."

"He'd be heading back to help Joel and Tern finish the lockdown, then get everybody off first thing in the morning. The heavy bands of rain will start hitting then. But Nana should have come over first."

"Don't worry. I'm sure Nana will arrive with the rest of the family—"

"No. That's what I'm trying to say. Mother won't ride over with Nana. She always sends him first. I wonder if they're thinking about leaving him on the island."

"Ask about him when you call Mildred."

"I will. And if they've decided to leave him, I'll need to get him to safety."

"How are we going to get over?"

"Not we. Me. You have to stay here. I'll have a few hours between the time they leave and the time I need to evacuate, but I need to know if anyone turns around and heads back out. I'll have no way of knowing short of watching both docks, which is impossible. You'd call the satellite phone. I'll get what I need, then head back."

The rain spattered against the window with renewed force.

"I see a couple of problems with that. One is I'll be trapped inside here when they close up the house."

"I'll show you the way out."

"Aren't all the boats going to be pulled from the water?"

"Tucker, don't worry. I can work the winch and get the boat into the water."

"What about the rough water?"

"We have one very good, deep V–hulled boat. I'm going over tonight—"

"Tonight! You can't go out in this weather."

"Tucker, I have to."

"Stay here tonight and go in the morning."

"Why, Tucker"—her voice took on a deep Southern drawl—"spendin' the night here with you wouldn't be proper now, would it?" He could hear the humor in her voice, then she grew serious. "I'll tie up at Joyce's dock and use the rest of the night to check out her place for anything that sheds light on Dove and Hannah. In the morning I'll watch for everyone to leave, then check out Raven's room."

"How safe is that?"

"In theory, perfectly safe."

"In theory?"

"All of our boats are equipped with GPS, which is accessible by computer or phone. I suppose, should anyone check, they could see one of the boats leaving the boathouse. But what are they going to do about it? Don't worry. My family thinks I'm with Mandy Chou and know enough to get out of harm's way. They won't expect me to head back to the island. And remember, I'll be calling Mildred, so they'll believe I've left and will meet up with them."

"If I can't talk you out of going out tonight, let me at least fill you in on what I found out. Sit down. Some of this may come as an unpleasant surprise."

She sat down beside him. "I have updates for you as well, but you go first."

He told her about his theory that someone might have killed Sparrow to secure her shares in Boone Industries.

"That thought had occurred to me as well."

He went on to inform her about Montgomery's affairs.

"It's hard to think of your own father that way. He always presented himself as someone . . . honest. Upright. He always went along with Mother's belief that we had the perfect home on the perfect island for the perfect family. Yet if he was so morally corrupt . . ."

"Piper, there isn't any such thing as a perfect person. All of us are sinners in one way or another. I should know. I've spent the last eight years atoning for what I did and finding forgiveness."

She stiffened beside him. "You're sounding religious."

"I like to call it a relationship. Sometime soon we'll talk about this, but I do want to say the aching desire for your lost daughter is the same that your Father in heaven feels for you."

She let out a small gasp.

"When you're ready," he continued, "we'll have that conversation. In the meantime, what did you need to tell me?"

She gave him the news about the fate of the *Faire Taire*. Then she told him about the dead woman at the condo and the attempt to frame him for the murder.

An unpleasant tingling shot up his spine. It took him a moment to speak. "So yet another murder, and this time the killer didn't take the time to make it look like an accident. I think the murderer is getting bolder. Certainly he's getting more violent. You need to take this all to the police. Let them deal with it."

"What would I take? My father's or Sparrow's accidents? Already investigated. Old news. The woman at the condo? We anonymously called that in. How am I going to explain how I knew she was dead? By now the police may be looking for Joyce, but I don't see them making much progress with this hurricane threat. And even *you* don't believe me about Dove being Hannah."

"Piper, you've already had two attempts on your life."

"Two?"

"Someone gave that shooter at the café the money to buy the gun. And his victims were women who looked a lot like you."

"I don't—"

"BettyJo wasn't an accident. At dinner you told everyone you were going for a walk. But it was BettyJo who walked out on the deck and was shoved into the empty pool."

In the silence that followed, a clock ticked somewhere nearby, and the refrigerator kicked on with a hum. Piper found her purse and pulled out the small game-score notepad she'd used for brainstorming.

"This is my analysis of alibis and motives. I can't trust anyone in my family or on the island. I'm assuming the worst—that someone I love is a cold-blooded killer."

CHAPTER 22

In the dim illumination of a night-light, I found clean, dry clothes in Mother's bedroom—waterproof cotton trousers, camp shirt, vest, and raincoat. The vest had numerous pockets where I could store anything I found in the safe. I'd talked tough to Tucker about going to Curlew, but that's all it was. Tough talk. I'd taken the different boats out, but never in these conditions. And his point about the attempts on my life had sunk in.

This was the stupidest thing I could ever do.

No. The stupidest thing was to attempt to take my own life. This was second on the list. I moved to the mirror. I whispered, "'You've got to ask yourself one question: "Do I feel lucky?" Well, do ya, punk?'" I tried to grin, but it came out a grimace. "*Dirty Harry*. The year was . . . was . . . I can't remember."

Working my way through the house, I found a small flashlight and fresh batteries in a kitchen drawer. I put them in one of the vest pockets. Then I picked up the phone and dialed the island.

Mildred answered. "Boone residence."

"Hi, Mildred. Listen, I'm heading inland at this point. I'll meet up with everyone at the usual place. Could you pack up my journals, Dove's rabbit, and her christening gown?"

"Of course. Where are you now?"

"On my way. Oh, and what kennel is Nana going to?"

"Silva would know. Did you want me to see if he's back and have him call you?"

"So he's already left with the dog?"

"I assume so. I've been busy packing up and preparing the house. I could find Tern or your mother—"

"Never mind. Thank you." I hung up. I had no choice now. I couldn't leave Nana on the island.

Tucker was by the front door. "So you're not going to change your mind."

"No. The family will arrive in the morning, lock up this house, then head inland. Silva will take the *Taire* to a marina we use that's safer than here. Pay attention to which direction he turns. Right means he's heading for the marina. Left, he's heading back to the island. In the hall closet you'll find a trapdoor leading to a ladder that will take you to the ground. The trapdoor is only secured by the inside latch. Even if the rest of the house is closed down and boarded up, you'll be able to get out that way."

"Piper—"

"Dial the island number and let it ring twice. Hang up and dial again, this time one ring. That means not everyone—Mother, Tern, Ashlee, Joel, and Mildred—came over with Silva and someone's still on the island. I'll get off as fast as I can. If anyone heads back over, if Silva turns left with the boat, do the same thing."

"But—"

"Once it's daylight, if I'm not back in four hours, take my car.

The keys are with my notes. You need to get clear of here before they shut down the roads."

"What if you're stuck on the island and can't get off?" He seemed determined to talk me out of it. I was determined that he wouldn't.

"Let's hope that doesn't happen. If the north end of the hurricane comes at high tide, we could have a storm surge."

"Has that happened around here before?"

"I suppose."

He waited.

"Hurricane Hugo in 1989 had an estimated storm surge of over nineteen feet."

He caught his breath. "What's the island's elevation?"

"Fourteen feet at the highest," I said reluctantly. "Stop worrying. I'll get on and get off." I drew in a deep breath. "After what you told me about Father, I'll check out his office in the studio. I'm sure he had a satellite phone installed, so I'll be able to hear you. I'll look in Tern's and Mother's rooms for evidence that they concealed Dove's survival, and finally Raven's room for that safe. I'll also rescue Nana." I reached for the door. "I wrote all this down, along with Mandy's cell."

"Piper . . ."

"Yes?"

"Just . . . be safe. Don't take any chances."

I tugged up my hood, then jerked the door open and charged out into the rain before I could change my mind.

The steady slap of rain on my hood was loud. If someone were to run up behind me, I wouldn't hear them. Angling toward the second boathouse, I stopped and turned every so often to check for movement. Unfortunately, everything moved. The steady downpour sent the palms and palmettos tossing and grasses swaying.

Headlights came into view at the end of the street. I'd made it to the second boathouse by then and ducked behind it. The car drew closer. Suddenly a spotlight lit up the yard and raked across to the house. I risked a peek. Police. Maybe someone noticed the slight glow of Tucker's computer screen and called it in. Or Tern made good on his threat to have Tucker arrested and they were searching for him. Or they'd found the old woman's body at the condo and were following up on the planted clue that Tucker was the killer.

They could also be looking for me. Whoever was trying to kill me could have told the police some lie so they'd notify my family where I was. Then the killer could make one final attempt on my life.

If they got out of their car and did a more thorough search, they'd find me. The only place I could retreat was to the water. Snakes and alligators lived in those waters.

I could just walk over and talk to them. I *did* own the house, or at least the corporation did. I had a right to be here. They'd just place a call to Tern or Mother to confirm I could be here.

Right.

The light went off. A second peek showed they'd completed their search and were driving away. Wasting no more time, I unlocked the boathouse by flashlight and went inside. The automatic garage door squealed as it opened, and I held my breath, hoping the police hadn't hung around the neighborhood. A quick check showed the key to the boat was in the ignition. I engaged the winch, grabbed the remote and bow line, then walked with the boat as it slowly backed down the rails. Once afloat, I stopped the winch, unhooked the cable, and reversed the winch. I tied the line to a ring at the bottom of the rails and returned the remote to the boathouse.

The water was tossing even in our little inlet. I had to use a light to see where I was going, but I caught a break in the rain. While clearing the mainland, I put on a life jacket. The boat had a built-in computer system with navigational software. I set my destination to Joyce's dock, then adjusted my speed so the bow would lift with the waves. I aimed for a 45-degree angle on the waves to be sure my propeller stayed in the water and I had control.

The black night, even inkier water, and chilly air caused my shaking to return. I should have looked for gloves and a sweater. I should have listened to Tucker.

Admit the real reason you wanted to go tonight. If all we'd discovered about my family was true, we, or at least I, had lived a massive lie. People had been systematically murdered by someone I knew and loved. I didn't want anyone around if, or more likely when, my world came crashing down.

The rogue wave came from nowhere, crashing over the stern of the boat and dragging it down. I held on to the steering wheel and braced myself against the seat. The boat struggled against the extra weight of the water, slugging up and down the waves. *Just a little farther, hold on, almost there.* My chattering teeth added to the shaking of my hands.

Joyce's dock came into view. I wouldn't be able to do an elegant docking. I'd be lucky if I didn't crash into it.

I made it, though I nearly ended up in the churning water when I jumped from the boat. Hopefully the pumps would have all the water cleared by the time I returned.

Using the flashlight, I crawled and slipped up the muddy path to Joyce's house. Someone, probably Joel, had closed all the hurricane shutters and moved everything off the porch. Inside the house, the air was stale and smelled of old garbage. I decided to keep the lights off and use only the flashlight, just in case Joel was taking his caretaking duties further than usual.

Even though I'd gone through the house with Mandy, and Hannah had searched for evidence of what had happened to Joyce, neither investigation had really been meticulous. Starting in the kitchen, I pulled out each drawer, emptied it on the counter, then felt around and underneath for anything taped in place. Cupboards received the same treatment. I inspected all the appliances as well as the kitchen table and chairs. There had to be something that would show Joyce had taken custody of my daughter fifteen years ago. It wasn't logical. It didn't fit the facts, but it was the only hope I could cling to.

But all I confirmed was that Joyce was an impeccable housekeeper and did very little cooking. I moved to the living room. Joel had moved the outdoor furniture into this room, crowding the small space. She had a bookshelf of bird identification books with her birding journals below. Each journal was leather bound with her name and the year it covered engraved on the front. I opened the one dated the year of Dove's disappearance. The entries stopped in October. A four-year hiatus came next, then partial birding journals. Circumstantial evidence that something other than birding occupied Joyce starting around the time of Dove's disappearance.

Before tackling her bedroom, I checked the hidden room with the washer and dryer. The shelves held only laundry detergent and the box of dog cookies. An electrical circuit-breaker panel was on the wall on the left, and an ironing board with an iron hung on the right. Nothing but dust bunnies lurked behind the washer or dryer.

I gave her bedroom the same treatment. I pulled out drawers, removed clothing from the closet, and stripped the bed. Once again I found nothing. I found myself staring at the now-empty closet with just the clothing rod and breaker panel. I was tired and had little to show for all the searching. Except . . .

Breaker panel? Why would a house this small have two? I opened the cover. It looked like the standard issue. The one in the laundry closet looked identical. The bedroom was part of the original cement building, whereas the rest of the house was newer. There wouldn't have been electricity available for the original structure.

Joyce had a small tool bag in the kitchen. I found a Phillips screwdriver and raced to the bedroom closet. After opening the gray metal door, I went to work on the screws.

The panel came off. Instead of wires, I found a space with a dusty box.

My vision narrowed to just that box, illuminated by my flashlight. I licked my suddenly dry lips and reached for the box, lifted it out, and moved to the living room. The only clear space was a corner of the coffee table. I placed it there and removed the lid.

My breath caught. Inside was an amber teething necklace. I lifted my own necklace from my shirt, took it off, and placed it beside the other necklace.

They were identical.

CHAPTER 23

Two necklaces. Two little girls? One who lived. One who washed up nearby. One taken home by Joyce and raised like a granddaughter. One left to be found by the family dog.

Be rational. Two girls drowned at the same time. The same place. The same age.

I put my hands over my ears. The thoughts continued.

And the one who died had Dove's DNA.

I didn't believe it. I wouldn't accept it.

"God," I whispered. "If You're up there, if You have even the tiniest bit of love in You, if You have the slightest mercy, You will make this right. You will give me back my daughter. Do that and I will believe in You, worship You, and spend the rest of my life thanking You."

I waited, hoping for a sign that God heard me and was willing to hold up His side of the bargain. All I heard was the wind whooshing through the nearby palmettos.

Maybe I should have asked on my knees. Or prone, arms outstretched. Did God want my life in exchange for hers? I would offer that as well.

Still no answer. The house creaked and moaned, and the wind whistled around the windows.

Negotiation? *If what Tucker said is true and You want me like I want my daughter, I'll come to You. Would that be fair? Do You really understand my pain?*

What if God needed something from me first? Money. Some good deeds. Talking to a priest or rabbi. Joining a church. All that would take time. I didn't want to wait anymore. Fifteen years had been an eternity.

I didn't know any answers. And the ache in my chest was unbearable.

His cell phone rang. "Landry."

"Tucker, this is Scott from Clan Firinn. After your emails, I wanted to follow up."

He clenched the phone. "Thank you."

"What's going on, Tucker?"

"I guess you could say I hit a few more bumps in the road."

Scott was silent for a moment. "How are *you* doing?"

Tucker tried to think of an answer.

"That's what I thought," Scott said. "You know, fears, doubts, worries, indecision, blame are all part of the human condition. We all make mistakes, but mistakes aren't failure. Clan Firinn's given you the tools to cope, but we'll always be here to brush you off and set you back on your feet if you do fumble. Are you hearing me, Tucker?"

"I hear you."

"How's it going with the rocks I left you?"

Tucker touched them. "Still safely in my pocket. What am I supposed to do with them?"

"You'll know. Stay safe and keep in touch."

After disconnecting, he shoved the black thoughts of his future out of his mind. He'd move to the attic. The window overlooking the dock had the best view.

I didn't dare move to the family compound until I could be reasonably assured the island was empty. If I showed up too early, Nana would find me in a heartbeat and proudly announce my presence. Moving into the bedroom, I curled up on the bed, wiggling around until the various outfits I'd strewn across the surface became a somewhat comfortable mattress.

I didn't think I could sleep, but it seemed that I'd barely closed my eyes when the blackness beyond the windows turned gray. I checked my watch. Eight a.m. How had it gotten so late?

Knowing Tern and Ashlee, they'd want to get to Marion Inlet well ahead of the storm and have the mainland house locked up tight. They'd probably be boarding the *Taire* right now.

The rain was a steady drizzle and the wind gusty as I jogged down the cart trail. As I got close to the house I took a diagonal footpath, one that would let me see what was going on at the dock.

I crept through the last few feet of underbrush, then settled where I could watch the action. Silva was busy loading several plastic tubs into the boat. Soon Tern appeared, holding a suitcase in one hand and Mother's arm in the other. They walked onto the dock. Behind them was Mildred, holding a small bag, then

Ashlee with several suitcases. Joel followed at the rear with a handcart of additional luggage.

Nana was nowhere to be seen.

They finished loading and Silva pushed off.

My face grew hot. I backed away. So it was true. They were leaving Nana to die. Stomping on stiff legs, I moved to the house. As expected, the hurricane shutters were fastened down and nothing of value remained outside.

The wind had picked up slightly. The outer bands of the storm would bring intermittent torrential downpours. I could check on the hurricane's path on the radio once I'd checked out my father's office. *How strange that I haven't gone into my father's studio in years, yet for the second time in less than a week, I'm back.* I hadn't really even thought of my father for a long time. He'd died when I was sixteen and had been distant and uninvolved with my life, much like my mother—not surprisingly, as I'd spent much of my school years at an exclusive, and terribly expensive, boarding school in Massachusetts.

Before I reached the studio, Nana barked someplace up ahead. I hurried toward the sound. I found the frantic dog locked inside the pool area behind the six-foot wrought-iron fence. He greeted my appearance with more barking and leaping at the fence.

"Poor Nana. Did you accidentally get locked—"

Someone had wrapped a chain around the gate and fastened it shut with a lock.

I'd never find the key.

A blast of wind reminded me of the hurricane's ticking clock. I raced to the studio and quickly entered. Hoping the generator, working on a timer, was still operating, I flipped on the fluorescent lights. The room lit up with a jaundiced light. I swiftly scanned around for a pair of bolt cutters. The hydraulic table had been moved from the center of the room and was now next to the door. The studio space was filled with the golf carts and lawn furniture.

I threaded through the jumble of furniture to the far side, where the few tools were kept. No bolt cutters. Sledgehammer? Could I bash a hole in the wrought-iron fence? Hammer and chisel? Iron rods? A six-foot ladder . . .

I grabbed the ladder, fought my way past the carts and furniture, then charged through the murky drizzle to the pool fence. The top of each picket extended above the top rail. Grunting with the effort, I lofted the bottom of the ladder over the fence, lowered it until it touched the ground, then wedged the top over two pickets. Nana would have to climb up the rungs, then jump down from the top. Not hard for a border collie, but could I get an untrained Newfie to do it? He was iffy with "sit."

"Come on, Nana. Here, boy. I've got a cookie—"

Nana launched himself up the rungs and leaped from the top as if he'd always been a champion at agility. Once on the ground beside me, he opened his mouth wide, scooped up my arm, and gave me an enthusiastic sliming before tearing up the steps to the house for his cookie. I followed him.

An aluminum roll-down shutter protected the door leading from the deck to the house. I raised it with a switch. The door was locked.

"You have got to be kidding me!" Who would lock a door on an island with a hurricane coming?

Who would be stupid enough to go to a barrier island with a hurricane coming?

I didn't have any keys for this door or any door in the house. I'd never needed any. Someone was always here.

Nana pawed at the door.

"I know I promised you a cookie, but you'll have to wait."

The dog perked up his ears at the word *cookie*, then looked expectantly between me and the door. I didn't bother to elaborate. I'd exhausted his vocabulary.

Rain began to come down harder. I didn't have enough time to find a way into the house, search Father's office, then get both Nana and me off the island before it was too late.

Nana dashed down the path toward the ocean.

After lowering the shutter, I started for the studio. Before I got there, Nana had returned with a gift for me. It appeared to be a piece of driftwood. As the dog grew closer, the treasure in his mouth took shape. Fingers. A watch. An arm.

Adrenaline flooded my system. I opened my mouth to shriek, then clapped my hand over it.

Nana drew closer. I recognized the watch—a Jaeger-LeCoultre Reverso. Mother had given Joyce the watch a few years ago for Christmas. "No! Nana, no! Drop it!"

Nana clearly didn't want to drop his gift. He sat and stared at me.

I tried not to vomit. "Nana, drop it. Now. Pretty please?"

The softer voice worked. The dog placed the arm on the wooden path.

I couldn't leave the only evidence of Joyce's fate to get washed away. Stomach churning, I called him over, then walked to the studio.

The room was quiet compared to the storm outside, with only the buzzing of the overhead lights and Nana's panting.

After a few moments I found what I was looking for—a shovel.

Where was I going to put it?

The only place I could think of was on top of the workbench. I'd need to be sure Nana didn't have access to this area.

Carrying the shovel, I reluctantly trekked to the arm. The closer I got, the more the stench grew. I picked it up with the shovel, then vomited. *No one should be found like this.*

I brought the remains into the studio, making a point of not looking at it, and placed it on the highest shelf.

The stench filled the room.

After opening the nearest window, I raced outside and pulled off the shutter. Flying debris would probably break the glass, but at least I could enter the studio.

Poor Hannah. I didn't want to be the one to tell her Joyce wouldn't be returning.

After crossing to the office door, I wasn't surprised to find it locked. I put on a work glove, picked up a hammer, and positioned myself in front of the glass window in the door. I turned my head and swung the hammer. *Crash.*

I jerked my hand back. The shattering of glass was shockingly loud.

Nana had calmly watched everything I'd done so far, but the crashing glass had him pawing at the door. Angling across the room, I let him out into the storm.

I had no idea what Father's office looked like, nor if there was anything I could use there to get into the main house. I'd never been inside.

Tucker had no intention of falling asleep, but he must have drifted off. He woke to a blast of rain against the window. His watch told him it was early. He should have time for coffee. While waiting for the coffee to brew, he turned on the television. The news was all about Hurricane Marco with information on voluntary evacuations, evacuation routes, emergency numbers and locations, and other equally frightening information. The station went to commercial break. He filled his coffee cup and was about to turn off the television when his own photograph appeared.

"Early this morning," the newscaster said, "Mount Pleasant police discovered the body of a woman in an unoccupied condominium. An anonymous caller reported the body, though the address originally given was incorrect. Officials said the body hadn't been dead more than a day, though cause of death was pending autopsy. The woman's identity has been withheld until family has been notified. This man"—the newscaster paused for effect—"has been identified as a person of interest. His name is Tucker Landry. If you have any information on Landry's whereabouts, please call the number on your screen."

He staggered against the counter. If the police found and arrested him now, Piper and her family could provide him with an alibi, but it would take some time for all that to come together. In the meantime, no one could provide Piper with a warning should any member of her family decide to return to the island.

In any case, he couldn't flee now even if he wanted to. Returning to the attic, he resumed his lookout.

I turned on the light to my father's office and came to an abrupt halt. Of all the things I'd expected to find, this wasn't even on my radar. The room was empty—not just free of furniture, but someone had ripped into the walls and suspended ceiling. The panels and wallboard had been removed. Rusted nails protruded from the studs, and the framework of the ceiling was exposed. A thin layer of dust lay on the floor.

Whatever might have been hidden here was long since removed, including an extension on the satellite phone. Tucker could have called me and I wouldn't have heard it. I'd need to call him as soon as I got into the house.

In the corner of the room was a narrow door that could lead to a bathroom. I crossed the room, leaving footprints in the dirt, and opened the door. Beyond lay steps going upward. Dusty cobwebs draped the walls and ceiling. Whatever light originally illuminated the stairwell had long since burned out.

A tremor went through me. The space was narrow, tight, dark, confined.

But I believed it would lead to Mildred and Joel's apartment. From there I could get into the house—and to the phone.

I closed my eyes and put my foot on the first step. "Abbott and Costello. 'Yes, now, on the St. Louis team, we have Who's on first, What's on second, I Don't Know's on third . . . That's what I want to find out. I want you to tell me the names of the fellas on the St. Louis team.'" The next step. "'I'm telling ya. Who's on first, What's on second, I Don't Know's on third.'" Third step. "'You don't know the fella's name? Yes. Well then, who's playing first?'" A gauzy piece of cobweb draped across my face. I snatched it off, then climbed more steps. "'Yes. I mean, the fella's name on first base.'" My voice shook. "'Who. The fella playing first base for St. Louis?'" *How much farther?* "'Who. The guy on first base. Who is on first!'" Four more steps. "'Well, what are ya asking me for? I'm not asking you. I'm telling you. Who is on first.'" My outstretched hand touched a door. I frantically groped for the knob. *Please don't let it be locked!* The knob turned.

Resistance, something on the other side. Opening my eyes, I pushed harder. A stack of plastic boxes had been shoved against the door. I pushed them aside and leaped into the apartment. "Thank you, thankyouthankyou!" I shut the door with far more force than necessary. "*The Naughty Nineties*, 1945," I announced to the empty apartment.

I felt like a sleazy burglar invading Mildred and Joel's home. The stair door opened to a laundry area with a stacked washer and dryer. The kitchen and living area were open to each other and separated by a granite-topped island. The gas fireplace had framed images across the mantel—recent photos of Mother, Tern, me, and several older photographs. I didn't want to snoop, but I moved closer. In the dim light coming through the shutters, I could make out a very young Mother and Mildred on the beach in front of the house. It had to have been taken when the island was just purchased and before the house was built. They'd just staked out a sea turtle nest site.

The second photo was of my father and Joel, both in uniform. I'd forgotten that the two men served together and that my parents had introduced Joel and Mildred. The third photograph was of my grandparents, Mother's parents, seated on wicker chairs on a well-tended lawn, with a nurse holding baby Caroline, who was wearing the family christening gown—the same one I'd used for Dove. Someone had incorrectly hand-dated it 1955, probably assuming the frown on Grandma's face reflected the time they'd gone broke.

I'd already gone this far. I couldn't exclude anyone in my investigation. I swiftly checked closets, drawers, cabinets, under the bed. After knocking on walls, looking for extra breaker panels, and stomping on the floors, I was ready to move on. If Mildred and Joel were killers, they kept no souvenirs. I checked my watch. Too much time had elapsed. When I left the apartment and entered the enclosed walkway between buildings, the banging of the rain told me the hurricane wasn't veering from its path.

Tucker had just settled in when he spotted the *Taire.* It docked and Joel hopped off, then helped Caroline and Mildred to disembark. Tern followed, then Ashlee, and finally Silva. The men grabbed luggage and followed the two women toward the house, then passed from view. From this angle, he wouldn't be able to see who got into the cars and left.

He raced down the stairs as fast as he could manage with his crutches, then sped into the kitchen. He was in time to hear car doors slam and see one car leave. He couldn't tell who was in it.

The coffee felt like acid in his stomach. *Fat lot of good I'm doing Piper!*

Banging from the living room told him they were lowering the hurricane shutters. So probably Mildred and Caroline had left in the car with Joel.

In the distance, an engine turned over.

Oh no! He returned to the attic as fast as he could manage. The *Taire* was gone and he didn't know which way it had turned.

CHAPTER 24

The elevated walkway from the apartment opened to the north wing. I ran to the kitchen, then slammed to a stop. Both the handset to the satellite phone and the two-way radio microphone were missing. If anyone was still on the island, Tucker wouldn't be able to notify me. And I couldn't call him to check.

A swift look in Mother's and Tern's rooms yielded no proof that either knew of Dove's survival—or had helped to conceal her from me.

Heading to Raven's old room, a thought struck me. *What about the DVD?*

The memory jerked me to a stop. "Which DVD?"

You know. With Raven.

The clarity of the thought made me gasp. I raced to my bedroom, pulled out the movie *Signs*, and retrieved the hidden DVD.

Watch it now.

Was this what Mandy called hearing the Holy Spirit? Or did my own imagination combined with all I'd learned about my family contribute to this urging?

The generator would stop at any time. The television wasn't

even hooked up to it, but my computer had a DVD player and battery. I paced while the laptop booted up, then fast-forwarded the recording to the end. What was I supposed to see? Raven and I again played in the surf with Nana. Again the camera followed Raven. We waved at the camera and a hand waved back. I stopped the video and studied the hand. The glint of a ring showed between two fingers. I knew the ring, and the hand. Ashlee had been filming us that day.

I shoved down ugly thoughts as I ran to Raven's room. Ashlee couldn't stop filming Raven that summer. *Stop thinking about it.* He claimed he was always busy, that work was keeping him late. *No more!* I reached her room and shoved open the door. It hit the wall and bounced off.

Clearly Ashlee had left in a hurry. His bed was rumpled where he'd probably packed his suitcase.

The overhead light flickered, then went out. The generator had gone off. It was housed outside under the house. I'd planned on leaving through the back door, which I could open from the inside. But without thinking I'd lowered the electrical shutter. I'd have to get out the same way I got in—through the apartment. Down the tiny, narrow stairs.

Metal roll-down doors came down over Tucker's view from the attic. The banging ceased and the house was dim from the lowered shutters and rain. He crossed the attic and made it down the stairs. As he made his way through the living room, the tiny red, green, and blue lights that indicated the DVD player, television, and speakers were powered went dark. They'd turned off the electricity. He picked up the phone and dialed the island number. Nothing. He hung up and tried again. Then again. The only sound was the harsh hissing of static.

His heart jerked. How could he get word to Piper that someone could be heading to the island?

I switched on the flashlight and found my way to the robin print hanging on the wall. Lifting it off, I found the recessed safe with a combination lock.

The air left my lungs like a deflated balloon. I'd thought the key blank would somehow work. I had no idea what the combination was. Whatever Raven had meant for me to find, she'd put it out of reach.

Wait! Raven did like to do sleight-of-hand tricks. Misdirection. So if it wasn't the safe . . . I picked up the print and examined it carefully. The print itself was a classic Audubon work, framed, with a small sleeve in the back for the certificate of authenticity. Nothing was in the sleeve.

What was Raven's message? The key ring pointed to the print. Behind the print was a safe. The key on the ring wouldn't open a combination safe. Maybe the message had been in the sleeve and someone had found it?

I ripped open the glued edges of the sleeve. In the bottom corner was a torn piece of parchment, as if it got caught when someone quickly pulled out the paper. It had an inked impression along one edge.

No time to figure out what it was. I had to leave. Quickly.

I raced to the top of the stairs before pausing. I didn't have time to close my eyes and grope my way down. I'd just have to run. Turning on the flashlight, I yelled, "Bogart and Bergman! 'But what about us? We'll always have Paris. We didn't have . . . we . . . we lost it until you came to Casablaaaaaanca!'" I tore down the stairs. "'Where I'm gooooing, you can't follow. What I've got to do, you can't be any paaaart of.'"

I reached the studio somehow and gasped out, "*Casablanca*, 1942." The sound of the wind was constant and loud. Stopping at the cart nearest the sliding garage door, I checked for a key to the ignition. Gone. None of the carts had a key.

Nana had waited for me in the relative safety of the space under the house. He bounded out. I gave him a hug, then the two of us aimed for Joyce's place. Half running, half walking, we plowed through the wind and rain. My raincoat had soaked through, and my shoes squished with each step. Downed palmetto fronds and branches littered the path.

We circled Joyce's house to get down to the landing and my boat.

The boat was lying on its side, smashing against the dock with every wave.

My stomach clenched and a bolt of adrenaline shot through me. I was stuck on the island.

Wait. Joyce's satellite phone. I hadn't paid any attention when searching the house earlier. I entered the house, wincing at the mess I'd made. The phone was missing. Only a cut wire showed where it had rested.

Nana had followed me into the house and moved toward the hidden cookies. Suddenly he stopped, raised his head with ears alert, then spun and darted to the door.

"Nana, no! Come back here!"

The big dog pushed through the door and disappeared.

Rats! Why hadn't I put him on a leash? If I had to find the dog and drag him back here . . . I didn't even want to think about it. There was no way I'd leave him loose in this storm.

I followed him.

Tucker played through his choices. If he could get in touch with her on a two-way radio . . . He had no idea how to do that.

Maybe it was time to talk to someone who knew about what was going on. He picked up the phone and dialed Mandy Chou.

I hurried through the rain after Nana. "When I catch up with you, I'm renaming you. You're no Nana. You're like Hooch. Or that Saint Bernard . . . what was his name? Mozart. No. Beethoven. You're Beethoven." I could easily follow his tracks in the mud beside the path. I came to a fork where one direction led to the house, the other to the dock. His tracks headed to the dock.

Slowing down, I approached with caution. The *Taire* was tied up to the dock, engine running. In the dim light of the cabin, I could see Silva waiting at the helm. Nana was already on board, cheerfully settled into the rear cockpit settee.

No one else was around.

Silva could get me off this island. The *Taire* was large enough to handle the waves—assuming we left right away—and Silva was an excellent captain.

But what was he doing here? Had someone noticed that Nana wasn't on board when they evacuated? Someone had deliberately locked the dog into the pool area. An opportunity to return, like I did, when the island was supposed to be empty? Was someone searching for something like I'd been? Searching for me?

Regardless, I needed to get on that boat and get away from here.

The settee gave me an idea. The curved seating surrounded a table with electric legs. The legs allowed the table to be raised for meals or lowered to provide a large flat surface with space below for storage. It was lowered at the moment, allowing the giant Newfoundland to sprawl across it. I could slip under the table and get across to the mainland. It was dark enough that no one would be able to see me. There was only one problem. My claustrophobia.

Mandy answered immediately. "Piper?"

"No, it's me, Tucker. We haven't met. I'm—"

"Piper's hero. I know who ya are. How can I help ya, Tucker?"

He explained what had transpired and the problem with the phone. After he finished, he waited for Mandy to comment.

"Well, that sounds like one big ol' goat rodeo," she finally said. "Listen, I've only known Piper for a few days, but she's impressed me as being smart, tough, and resourceful. She'll get to safety somehow. Speakin' of which, you'll need to get out of here pretty quick. I saw on the news that the police are lookin' for ya. What do ya say if Hannah and I come pick you up and we get on out of Marion Inlet?"

"I think I should stay and wait for Piper."

"Then I think we'll come on over anyway." She disconnected.

What was he doing here? He hadn't helped Piper, couldn't help her now. He was holed up in a house on stilts with a hurricane on the way. The police were after him. He was about to be picked up by a stranger. Rescued by a woman. Wasn't he supposed to be the one helping women? All he'd ever done was let them down . . . or let them drown.

Tucker made it as far as the dining room, where the well-stocked wet bar was located. The desire to drink was overwhelming. Just one. Something for the road. He could control it.

He could almost taste the burn of the whiskey on his tongue, feel the liquid heat rushing down his throat, enjoy the rush of the alcohol as it hit his stomach.

He reached for a bottle.

Crouching, I hurried onto the dock and onto the boat's transom. I didn't worry that the boat would bobble under my weight and be noticed by Silva. The boat was already tossing in the rough seas. Dropping to my hands and knees, I crawled next to the lowered table, closed my eyes, and slipped under. I started reciting "Who's on First." I'd gotten as far as, "Have you got a first baseman on first? Certainly. Then who's playing first? Absolutely," when the engine revved and the boat moved away from the dock.

The first big wave rolled me from under the settee. I doubted Silva would pay any attention to anything going on outside of the helm. I stood. The ocean roiled around us in shades of angry brown and green. The boat rocked and bucked like a bronco under my feet.

A storage compartment inside the nearest seat held life jackets. I pulled one on.

The rain had increased and the wind sent sideways sheets of water off each wave. A second breaker almost sent us over. I grabbed the gunwale and held on. What was wrong with Silva? He wasn't even trying to hit the waves correctly.

Nana had jumped off the lowered table and was standing straddle-legged on the deck.

After the boat righted, I wiped the water from my eyes and looked frantically around. It was almost dark, but we had no running lights on. A glass door and large glass windows looked into the saloon, a plush room with a galley, leather seating around built-in cherry tables, and a flat-screened television. In the dim light I could see Silva seated at the helm.

His hands weren't even on the wheel. The autopilot light was on.

"Silva!" Another wave hit and splashed over the side and into the cockpit, sending the boat into a corkscrew. The propellers lifted from the water and briefly spun wildly. I grabbed one of the bolted-down stools in front of the wet bar. I was shaking so hard from the cold wind, rain, ocean, and, most of all, fear that I could barely hang on.

Nana slid across the deck, his nails extended as he tried to grip the smooth surface.

The boat steadied briefly.

Slowly I moved toward the saloon. This boat needed a pilot, not autopilot, and Silva seemed intent on going down.

The man was no longer even upright. He'd toppled sideways

in his seat, both arms dangling to the floor. His back was stained deep crimson.

I reached for the sliding door and opened it slightly. The stench of gas hit me.

I shut it quickly and leaned my face against the glass to see better. In the light of the instrument panel I could see a clock duct-taped to the dashboard.

The second hand was about to click on 12:00.

I spun and lunged away. "Nana!"

The boat exploded.

CHAPTER 25

Tucker opened the trapdoor, then climbed down the ladder beneath the house. Only the streetlights gave illumination. The few homes around him were shuttered and dark. Piper's car was still parked where she'd left it. The wind was constant and strong, the rain at times flying sideways. Even though he was in the center of the house, a fine mist dampened his face. In one hand he clutched a bottle of whiskey.

A car drove up and parked.

He ducked behind a support column. A small woman got out of the car and looked around, then raced up the stairs and pounded on the door. "Tucker? Tucker! It's me, Mandy Chou."

Tucker left his hiding post and walked to the base of the stairs. "Mandy?"

She rushed down to him. "Tucker! Quick. On the way over here we saw an explosion. It was in the direction of Curlew Island."

Tucker's heart leaped to his throat. "*On* the island?"

"No. A boat. I called the coast guard, but they said they didn't have anyone close. A container ship off Charleston Harbor is in distress and has everyone tied up."

"What—"

"How long ago did the *Taire* leave?" she asked.

He told her. She looked at her watch, chewed her lip, then said, "The boat had time to reach the island, wait for a short time, then be headin' back for the mainland. No one has gone out from the harbor since the hurricane warning. I think we might consider that the explosion was the *Taire*."

"Then I have to get out there."

"Tucker, ya don't understand—"

"No. *You* don't understand. I've let down too many people in my life. I told Piper I'd help her, be there for her. She's out there. I know it, I feel it in my gut. If I don't help her, her family sure won't. They want her dead." He'd been squeezing the bottle of whiskey in his hand so tight it hurt. He made a deliberate attempt to loosen his grip.

Mandy's gaze went to his hand. She stiffened. "I don't think you're in any condition—"

He shook his head. "Don't worry. I haven't touched a drop." He held it up so she could see the unbroken seal, then threw it under the house. *That felt good.* He pulled a rock out of his pocket and threw it at the bottle. It hit with a satisfying *clink*. *That felt even better.*

"Good aim."

"I'll have to go after Piper. The Boones have other boats—"

"No! You'd go down in these seas unless you're an extremely competent sailor. Are you?"

He didn't answer.

She began to pace. "Okay, okay, okay, okay. I am supposed to render aid to boaters in distress. If I called it in after we were already out there . . . I'll still get fired . . . but what else can I do?" She stopped pacing. "What I need ya to do—"

"I'm going with you." Despite the cool gusts, he broke out in a sweat.

She leaned close and stared at his face. Then she gave a short nod. "Let's get going then."

I couldn't see, couldn't breathe. My ears rang. I flailed, surrounded by water, not sure which way was up or down. My head hurt. My face hurt. I opened my eyes to watery blackness. Kicking my legs, I opened my mouth to scream, then the life jacket pushed me up and my head cleared. I sucked in a deep breath, only to have a wave splash water in my mouth. I started coughing. Water everywhere. No light. The boat must have already sunk.

Where was land? Where was I? The water tossed me like a cork, alternately crashing over my head, then sending me into a trough.

I was going to drown, to wash up like that tiny body did fifteen years ago. No one would even know for several days I was gone.

No one except the person who'd set the bomb.

The cold water leached the heat from my body. I didn't know how much longer I could keep going.

Something bumped into me.

I screamed.

My body was jerked around, then started cutting the water. My arm brushed against swirling fur, muscles tensing, a leg driving forward. *Nana.* The giant dog had the tether line on my life vest in his jaws and was towing me backward through the waves.

Thank You, God! I began to kick to help him. I just prayed that Nana knew which way was land.

Mandy drove like a race-car driver, tearing through the empty streets. Halfway to the marina, Tucker noticed Hannah in the back seat. "What are we going to do with Hannah?"

"Hello? I'm right here. You can talk to me directly," Hannah said to Tucker. "But to answer you, wherever you go, I'm tagging along. So is Piggy. In the words of Ruth, 'Don't urge me to leave you or to turn back from you.'"

"'Where you go I will go,'" Mandy added.

"'And where you stay I will stay,'" Tucker said. "I get the drift."

Mandy gave a half shrug. "I can't leave her at my house or the Boone place with a hurricane on the way. I'd hoped she could stay with you and the two of you would get out of danger, or that I could drive her to a shelter."

"And I told her," Hannah said, "that I'd tell everyone what Mandy was going to do and then invent a whole bunch of stuff to tell the police. Besides . . ."

Tucker turned to look at her.

"Grandma wanted me to fly out to meet someone." Hannah cleared her throat. "She said it was time I knew. I don't know what she meant, but I think she wanted me to meet Piper."

Marion Inlet was a ghost town. The downtown stoplight bounced on its wires. They pulled into the harbor lot and parked. Hannah got out first. "Tucker," Mandy said quickly, "I don't expect to find much, if anything. You realize that?"

"Yes, but we have to try."

They hurried across the lot to the docks. Most of the slips were empty, with a few of the larger boats tendered in the protected harbor. Mandy led the way to the official marine patrol boat. "Get in and put on life jackets, then hang on. We're in for a bumpy ride."

Tucker didn't have to be told twice, though tying the life jacket on with his slick hands was difficult. He kept the image of Piper in the front of his mind. *I can do this, but I have to face my other demon. Water.*

I'd been in the ocean forever. My arms and legs ached. The salt burned my throat and nose. I couldn't take a deep breath or more water would get into my lungs. The waves were getting larger, the troughs deeper. Still the dog plowed on.

Nana doesn't have a life vest. How much longer could he go on? Maybe I could get him to release my life jacket. Then he, at least, would have a chance to survive. He would die trying to save me.

I tried to find the release on the life jacket. I could slip out and go down to the depths. Like my daughter. *There's no way she could have survived. The DNA proved . . . proved . . .* My brain couldn't form the thought. My fingers were numb. I couldn't feel anything.

Tucker wanted Mandy to go faster, but he figured she knew what she was doing. The ocean tossed them around, stinging them with wind-whipped pellets of water. He had one arm around Hannah, bracing her, while his other clung to the boat. He had no idea what she could see through the driving rain and ocean spray. The spotlight she'd turned on showed small mountains of black sea. He closed his eyes. His stomach clenched so hard he thought he'd vomit.

Eventually she slowed. "Now, Tucker, ya need to make yourself useful. I'm gonna run a grid as best I can, so you'll need to work this spotlight." She handed him a large flashlight. "I'd say call out her name, but with this wind, it wouldn't carry five feet. Hannah, you come over here and hang on real tight."

"What am I looking for?" Tucker asked.

"Hopefully debris, maybe a life jacket." She didn't look at him.

Holding tightly to the handrail, Tucker edged toward the water. Dark water. Murky, brown-black, crashing, closing in. *Stop it!* He turned on the light. The rain was a curtain of silver, sucking in the beam. He gritted his teeth and moved the light around, searching for something, anything.

His jacket was soaked and adhered to his back with a clammy embrace. Water dripped into his eyes and down his face.

In the distance, a light flashed.

Nana was straining, his legs pumping harder, faster. He whined and jerked on the tether.

The crashing water thundered around us.

"Nana." I knew he couldn't hear me. I couldn't hear my own voice. "Sweet Nana, let me go. Save yourself. You did your best."

Something hovered in my mind, but I couldn't grasp it. Was

it something I still had to do? Something I should know? Was it important?

Whatever it was, I wouldn't cause Nana to die.

Again my brain nagged me. *You know.* I knew what? About Dove? Or the island? Sea turtles? Bailey Norton? I couldn't make any sense of it.

A large wave picked us up and hurtled us. It crested, flinging water over our heads. I made one last attempt to unsnap the life jacket. It opened. I was flung forward, rolling, tumbling, then falling.

The boat dipped and Tucker lost sight of the light, then another wave lifted them. He saw it again. "Over there!" he called to Mandy. "Two o'clock. A light."

She looked, then eased the boat in that direction. "It's comin' from the island. Maybe Piper made it ashore and spotted our searchlight."

Tucker prayed. *Please, Lord, let Piper be safe.*

Mandy, face stiff with concentration, frantically worked on keeping the boat from capsizing, but water kept rolling in. The deck was awash, and anything not fastened down rolled with the seesaw movement. She gave Tucker a quick glance, then nodded to Hannah. Tucker moved closer so he could hear her without Hannah overhearing.

"We'll be lucky if we make it," she said. "If we do get to the island, we'll have to hunker down and wait out the hurricane. It's only going to get worse out here."

He touched her shoulder to indicate he'd heard her, then

stepped over to Hannah. "Tuck Piggy into your life jacket and hang on." He made sure she had hold of a rail with both hands, then did the same.

The light grew closer, but the water in the boat grew deeper.

CHAPTER 26

I hit something with a bone-jarring crunch and rolled in the crashing surf. Smashing my hand against something hard, I then flipped over and landed on my back. Water was everywhere and it tumbled me like a washing machine. A final rush forward in the swell and the water receded. I could breathe. *Land! He did it!* I wanted to kiss the ground, but something had grabbed my leg and was dragging me backward. Nana. He didn't let go until I was out of the sea. I was afraid he'd yank my pants off. "Nana, good boy! I've got it from here."

Nana released his grip on my clothing and lay down beside me, panting from his exertion. I wrapped my arms around his neck and hugged him. "You'll have cookies the rest of your life," I whispered. His wet warmth felt good.

A blast of wind wildly tossed the bushes around us and the rain came in sheets. Onyx blackness surrounded us. The hurricane was almost here, and I had no idea where we were.

"Nana, go find a cookie."

The Newfie jumped to his feet and dashed off.

The light came from two floodlights at either end of the dock. A third light illuminated the beachfront, now pounded by waves. Mandy worked the wheel and engine, trying to get close enough. They didn't so much dock the boat as ram onto it. A wave lifted them above the dock, then dropped them, smashing the bow and lodging it in the splintered surface. The next wave submerged the aft.

"Get off! Get off now!" Mandy yanked Hannah, clutching Piggy, to the side, waited for the water to recede slightly, then pushed her onto the dock. "Run!"

Tucker didn't wait. He grabbed Mandy's hand and leaped for the dock. The next surge caught them both and hurtled them sideways. He caught the nearest piling, jerking Mandy backward to safety as she was about to be swept away. Before the next surge, he let go of the piling and charged up the dock to the beach, half dragging Mandy behind him.

Mandy's boat endured one more assault before firmly embedding into the dock.

Mandy turned and watched the boat merge with the dock. "Well, that just creams my corn."

"'I think next time we're gonna need a bigger boat.'"

She looked at him blankly.

"Er, *Jaws*. Never mind. Where's Hannah?"

"I saw her on the beach. She must have gone looking for Piper." Mandy continued toward the path leading to the house.

I'd figured Nana would lead me to civilization, not go in search of cookies by himself. I could barely see my hand in front of my face. Wherever I was, sitting this close to the Atlantic with a probable storm surge was a very bad idea. I got to my feet. My left knee must have hit a rock. It throbbed with a deep ache and felt swollen. My hand felt the same. Touching my face, I explored several raw areas from the explosion.

I was lucky to be alive.

If I kept the thunder and crash of the angry seas behind me, I'd at least be moving away from that danger.

Placing both hands in front of me, I moved forward.

Tucker's injured leg hurt like crazy. His crutches were long gone. All the carts had been moved from their shed and undoubtedly stored for the storm.

He trailed after Mandy the best he could up the slight incline. He had to lean into the wind, and the rain at times blew sideways. Mandy, much smaller and more slightly built than he, struggled even more against the gale.

He finally reached the house, stopped, and stared at the front door. The aluminum roll-down shutter was raised, and lights glinted from inside the foyer. "Piper?"

His voice was lost in the wind. Neither Mandy nor Hannah was waiting for him outside. After surveying the area, he entered the house.

Moving slowly, too slowly, I pushed through dense underbrush. Larger branches slapped me despite my hands being up. I finally folded my arms in front of my face and pushed through. A particularly dense tangle of foliage caught my foot and I fell, landing on my already-bruised knee. I let out a howl of pain that the wind snatched away. *Doggone dirty rat fink Nana!* Where was my faithful dog now?

You're the one who mentioned cookies to a treat-obsessed Newfoundland.

Pushing to my feet, I hobbled forward, this time even slower. My anxiety spiked. If the north end of the storm hit at high tide, which would be around six something in the morning, the storm surge could be extremely dangerous. And if Nana had towed me to the island rather than the mainland, the surge would wipe out everything, including one gimpy woman.

I fell again, landing hard on some sharp rocks. The jolt of pain brought tears to my eyes. I was about to think up more things to call Nana, but something about the rocks was different. I touched them, then picked up a few. Not rocks. Crushed shells. Like the surface we used on the island paths. Nana had brought me home to Curlew Island.

Tucker found Hannah and Mandy in the foyer. Both women were shivering slightly and rubbing their arms. With the foyer open to the rain, there was little protection from the elements. He was about to ask why they hadn't gone upstairs to the main floor, but he answered his own question by glancing up. The glass wall and door that Piper had referred to were both closed.

The intercom on the wall squealed.

He jumped.

"Sorry about that." The voice was loud and echoed around the room. "This is Piper. I'm glad you found me. I'm hurt. I may have broken my leg. I can't get to the controls for the glass doors at the top of the stairs. Can you help me?"

It didn't sound like Piper. The voice barely sounded human.

Tucker stepped over to the intercom and pushed the button on the microphone. "How did you hurt your leg?"

"I docked at Joyce's, then came here. The phones weren't working, so I turned on all the lights, hoping someone would see them. Then I came up here to wait, but I tripped and hurt my leg. Please hurry."

"What do you think, Tucker?" Mandy came up beside him. "That doesn't sound like Piper. It doesn't even sound female."

"I think that's the system, but let me try something." He pushed the microphone button. "Piper, do you remember when we were in the study and I told you I had certain skills?"

She didn't say anything for a moment, then said, "You told me you had hacking skills. Why are you asking me that now?"

"Just being cautious. We'll be right up." He looked at both Hannah and Mandy. "We were alone when I told Piper that."

"If she can't open the doors up there, how are we supposed to get up?"

"Follow me." He limped across the foyer and opened the door to the elevator. "You two can go up first—"

"No way," Hannah said. "I'm staying with both of you."

The three of them got into the elevator and pushed the up button. "Wait," Hannah said. "Let me get Piggy." She stuck her arm out to stop the doors, but they continued to shut.

Mandy yanked Hannah's arm clear just in time. The door closed and the elevator moved. Then stopped.

The crushed-shell path stretched left and right of me. One way would lead to Joyce's place, the other to the family house. When we'd taken off in the *Taire*, we would have been on the western side of the island. Nana swam to that side. If west was behind me, north would be on my left and the family home on my right.

Slowly, wincing in pain, I stood. Joyce's place was the highest on the island, but the family home was raised.

Where would Nana go? Dogs knew nothing about storm surges. He wouldn't be able to get into the house. He *could* have headed to Joyce's place, but chances were he'd try to get into the house—into his cave.

I turned right. As long as I felt the shells crunching under my feet, I'd be on the path and not likely to run into something.

The back of Tucker's throat burned with bile. He jammed his finger into the up button. Nothing happened. He jabbed again.

Hannah grabbed his arm. "Wha . . . what's going on? Why aren't we moving?"

Mandy's face was a frozen mask.

The intercom next to the control panel let out a small squeak, then the eerie voice whispered, "It didn't occur to you that this could be used as a two-way system? I've been able to hear every word you've said."

To take my mind off my aching knee, hand, and face, not to mention the deluge of rain, I ran through a litany of movie dialogues. Maybe something from *Forrest Gump*? "'Lieutenant Dan got me invested in some kind of fruit company,'" I whispered. A colander full of apples flashed through my mind. Joyce's apples. But Joyce was dead. No longer lost. *Really most sincerely dead.* And someone had tried very hard to kill me. Why?

My thoughts wouldn't settle. *Focus.* Back to *Forrest Gump.* Next line. "'So then I got a call from him, saying we don't have to worry about money no more . . .'"

Money. Follow the money, that's what Tucker told me. Where was money? Expensive. Joyce's furniture was expensive. But she was a doctor, made lots of money. So I assumed. But she'd have even more money if the funds Tucker found were going to an "employee"—Joyce. And look at her watch. But she didn't buy that watch—Mother did. Why would Mother buy someone a six- or seven-thousand-dollar watch? Like a payout. Payoff?

What if . . . what if . . . ? I reached up and touched my face. One side injured, like Hannah. Hannah wasn't in a fire. A fire would have burned both sides of her face. She was in an explosion. Like me.

"State it as a series of facts, Piper. Organize it."

Seventeen or eighteen years ago, Raven gave me a key ring with a blank key. No explanation. Dove went missing fifteen years ago. She was last seen on the *Faire Taire*. The *Faire Taire* didn't just sink. It exploded.

Joyce left the island around the time of Dove's disappearance. Joyce faithfully kept birding journals until the October of Dove's "death." For the next four years, she stopped. She had a necklace in her possession that was identical to mine. My necklace was recovered from the body that had washed ashore.

I circled back around to the thought of two little girls. One who lived. One who washed up nearby.

Stay with facts. Okay, just before Joyce disappeared and her boat was discovered by marine patrol, she called and said she wanted to talk to me. That message was posted in the kitchen where anyone and everyone could read it. Joyce had already arranged to fly Hannah out to the island. Before I could talk to Joyce, she was gone.

And someone tried to shoot me. Someone with a grudge against the company and who'd been given a rifle to do so.

"Conclusion," I whispered. Joyce was going to break her silence and tell me my daughter washed up . . . Wait. Joyce had a birding scope. Maybe she saw the explosion of the *Faire Taire*. Maybe she went out to investigate in her boat and found my badly injured daughter, rescued her. Decided to keep her and let everyone think she'd disappeared with the stolen yacht.

That still didn't fit all the facts. A body did wash up, a body with my daughter's DNA.

A light twinkled ahead through the madly dancing trees. I stopped. There shouldn't be any lights on anywhere.

Continuing forward, I moved from the center of the path to the edge, keeping the tossing foliage between the light source and me.

Someone had opened the storm shutters and turned on every light in the house.

CHAPTER 27

I had no doubt that whoever had rigged the *Taire* with a bomb was now in the house. He, or she, or they, must have come over on the boat with Silva driving, probably using the excuse that Nana was still out here. How had Bailey referred to Silva? *"That boat captain, who keeps his mouth shut for a price."*

The price Silva was paid was his life.

It seemed someone *had* checked the GPS and seen that one of the family boats had been used to go to Curlew. They lit up the *Taire*, knowing I'd try to escape the island on the larger boat. They waited on the shoreline until I boarded, then engaged the autopilot from a remote.

But why turn on the house lights?

I knew the answer even before I'd finished asking myself the question. Another trap.

The murderer, or murderers, would believe the explosion killed me, but then they'd be stuck on the island until the hurricane passed. Why not turn on all the lights as a beacon to attract any would-be rescuers? Staying in the shadows, I crept around the house, then headed for the dock. If someone was here for rescue, I should see a boat.

Like the house, the landing was lit up. A good-sized boat was embedded into the dock, a hole in its side getting larger as the waves rocked it back and forth. It said Marion Inlet Police Department Marine Patrol on the side.

Mandy? Did she get off the boat successfully? Where would she be?

The house. She would be inside, probably with the killer.

Would I now need to rescue my rescuer?

If Mandy was in uniform, she should be armed. The problem was, whoever was behind the murders was extremely skilled at appearing like a good person. My protective big brother, the state senator? My ex-husband, the outgoing sports jock? My mother, the gentle bird-watcher? Joel, my father's right-hand man? Mildred, the elderly housekeeper? Raven, my invisible sister? Or even someone not directly connected to the family?

I couldn't go in there with guns blazing. There were no guns on the island unless Mandy had brought one. No bows and arrows or even slingshots. I didn't know self-defense. Nana had already proven he'd give his life for me—if it was a water rescue. The only thing he ever guarded was his food dish, and that was from birds.

I did have one weapon: surprise. I was supposed to be dead.

Tucker wanted to scream, to pound the walls, to curse the one who had so cleverly trapped them, but both Hannah and Mandy were holding in their feelings. The elevator space was tight—at most one of them could sit at a time. At least the light was on.

He took off his soaked jacket and pressed it against the

intercom. "Do you think we can negotiate out of here?" he whispered.

"Hard sayin'," Mandy whispered back. "That's one sick individual."

"What's he, or she, gonna do with us?" Hannah asked quietly.

Mandy looked at her watch, then glanced at Tucker.

"Mandy"—Hannah folded her arms—"you don't have to candy-coat anything for me. Looking like this . . . well, I'm pretty tough."

Mandy patted Hannah on the shoulder. "I can see that. I won't pull any punches. We haven't had an update on the storm. When we left, it was a category four. It could have changed since then, either upgraded or downgraded. It could have changed direction. All that being said, if it stayed the same, this house will take a pretty direct hit. The damage could be extensive. We are also stuck pretty much at ground level, so a storm surge is a real threat."

Tucker leaned against the wall to stay upright.

"So we could be either crushed or drowned?" Hannah asked.

"Ya really *don't* like sugar-coatin'," Mandy said. "That about sums it up."

Drowned. Just like his wife and unborn baby. Fitting ending for his life. *Stop it! I may be deserving of that end, but Mandy and Hannah aren't.* "Well then, let's get to work." He reached up and felt the ceiling for any panels. It appeared to be one piece of steel.

Mandy fished a coin from her pocket. She edged to the control panel, handed Tucker the soggy jacket he'd used to muffle their conversation, then used the coin as a makeshift screwdriver.

Hannah looked from Mandy to Tucker, then, in a clear,

sweet voice, began to sing "Amazing Grace" softly. She sang a second, then a third song he didn't know.

"Stop singing in there!" the voice crackled from the intercom.

"Open the door," Tucker said.

An eerie sound came through the speaker. It took Tucker a moment to figure it out. Laughter.

The house had no video surveillance equipment, and the rain made it difficult to see, but I still approached with caution. The shutter over the front door was raised, and lights came from the foyer. I moved to where I could peer inside. The glass wall separating the foyer from the upstairs landing was moving, rolling back.

Only people who lived here knew where those controls were located.

I'd bet my Jimmy Stewart collection that this *was* a trap. Jogging to the studio, I figured I'd come up with a plan while sneaking into the house by way of the apartment. Once inside, I could flank the enemy.

Tucker again muffled the PA system. "How are you doing?" he whispered to Mandy.

"Not good. There's no reason we can't move, so whatever was done to the mechanism, it's on the outside. What about you? Any luck on the ceilin'?"

"No. Welded shut. Everyone needs to shift so I can work on the doors."

Mandy moved away from the control panel, allowing Tucker a better angle to pry the doors open. He slid his fingers along the seam, feeling for enough space to get leverage. The two doors were flush. He checked the top and bottom of the doors as well. Standing, he tried shoving against the door with his hands pressed against the surface. They slipped with the sweat on his palms.

His chest felt tight. Blood pounded in his ears. He didn't want to, but he looked at the two women. They could see the answer in his face. "The door seems to be sealed tight."

"How tight?" Hannah asked.

He didn't answer. He didn't have to.

Once more I faced the narrow stairs going up to Mildred and Joel's apartment. I couldn't shout, or even speak out loud, any movie dialogue to help me get to the top. I'd have to move as quietly as possible.

The force of the wind whistled through the eaves of the building and drummed branches against the walls and shutters. The open window rattled with the gusts and stirred the dust from the surfaces. I sneezed, then pinched my nose to stop further sounds.

Give God another try. The words rose unbidden from my brain. He hadn't exactly answered my last prayer, but He hadn't said no either. I couldn't remember much from the required chapel sessions at the boarding school. "Okay, God, I really need Your help," I whispered and started up the stairs. "The Lord is my shepherd, I shall not want . . . Something about green pastures . . . Oh, help my soul." I shut my mouth but continued to try to remember. Why was it I could remember complex movie dialogue but not this? Wasn't this important? *No.* I'd created a world to live in without God, family, friends. I didn't think twice about giving money to a homeless man or injured animals or some kind of women's march, but I gave nothing to anyone *of me*. Because I was empty inside.

I was at the top of the stairs.

Waiting until my heart rate slowed, I held on to the doorjamb. *Thank You, God.* I made it.

Moving carefully in the dim light, I crept through the apartment, then down the short, enclosed walkway to the foyer of the north wing of the house.

The effects of the storm were muted here. Footsteps tapped in my direction. I slipped into the media room, leaving the door open a crack.

I'd left a trail of water on the light bamboo wood floor from the walkway to the media room. Anyone walking this way would be sure to see it.

I held my breath and listened.

The footsteps retreated.

I exhaled with a *whoosh*. I couldn't stay in the media room all night. I needed to get up the courage to confront the person causing the "curse" of the Boone family.

How strange that I should be hiding in here. I'd probably entered the media room less than a dozen times in the past fifteen years, preferring to watch movies in my room. Yet I'd been here twice in as many days. Media room, sewing room, Sparrow's room. Sparrow, the first to fall victim to the curse. Just like . . .

At once everything became clear. Sparrow. Father. Dove. Joyce. The photograph of my grandparents. A movie. The scrap of paper. Mother. The attempts on my life. I knew who I had to face.

CHAPTER 28

I edged from the media room toward the front of the house. As I expected, a lone figure waited, back to me, next to the railing overlooking the front door and foyer.

"Hello, Mildred," I said.

She turned. I'd been wrong. There was a gun on the island. It was now pointed at me. "Hello, Piper." She didn't seem particularly surprised at my appearance. "So, you survived the explosion."

"Yes." I touched the side of my face where debris had cut me. "So did Dove, didn't she? You used the same MO on both the *Faire Taire* and the *Taire*. You put them on autopilot and blew them up. They found the *Faire Taire*, by the way."

"What made you think of me?"

She seemed so casual, so untroubled by a hurricane racing toward us, so relaxed with the pistol in her hand pointing at me. I was younger, stronger, and faster than she was, but not faster than the bullet in her gun. If I could get close enough, I could wrestle the pistol from her.

My mouth was parched, my body cold. "Many things, starting with something you said that lodged in the back of my mind. 'Both your brother and your mother want everything to be perfect, and my job is to keep it that way.'"

She nodded like a proud schoolteacher. "That's right. Keep the perfect home on the perfect island for the perfect family."

I edged closer to her. "And Sparrow wasn't perfect."

A deep furrow appeared between her brows. "No. She wasn't, and she was getting worse. The Kennedy family gave me the idea. They lobotomized their daughter Rosemary when she was twenty-three to keep her from embarrassing the family. I couldn't do that, of course. But it gave me an idea."

I felt sick to my stomach but had to go on. "You arranged for Father's accident."

"He was a womanizer. It was only a matter of time before it became public."

"You tried to kill me."

She shrugged. "You were pretty pathetic with your half-packed suitcase and journals. Your mother and brother talked about how he got a boost in the polls with a sympathy vote after the shooting. You know how much it means to them to get that wildlife bill passed."

My stomach lurched. I blinked rapidly to clear my vision. "You planned that mass shooting. Ami died. And two other women."

She shrugged. "I wasn't sure he'd go through with it."

"You killed Joyce."

"I couldn't be sure what she would tell you."

I couldn't move for a moment. I felt like someone had dropped a brick on my heart. "Tell me about what?"

"You've put that together."

"Dove." I didn't want to connect all the clues, to think the unthinkable, to face the monstrous evil that Mildred had done. The house rattled and shook with the wind, as if angry with me for my hesitation. "That day, fifteen years ago, Ashlee was nervous, sweating. He wanted to go to the mainland without anyone along, like Silva or, heaven forbid, his daughter. He was meeting with his lover, my sister Raven." I stopped for a moment to make sure my voice wouldn't shake.

Mildred nodded. "Raven called Ashlee, said she was going to come clean. Demand that Ashlee divorce you and marry her."

"You overheard." My head buzzed. "Went to the mainland first. Came up behind Ashlee and knocked him out. Somehow dragged him out of sight. Then waited on the boat for Raven. Did you know Dove was on board?" My lips were numb, the words difficult to form.

"Of course not! I'm not a beast."

I blinked.

"I honestly didn't see her, Piper. I loved her. She was beautiful. No, I lured Raven on board, took care of her, and sent the boat off with her body." She glanced down at the pistol, then raised it slightly so it pointed at my heart.

The wind rattled the house again, banging doors in the apartment, bringing with it the stench of human remains. Joyce. "Didn't Ashlee wonder what happened to Raven?"

"Ashlee didn't care. He was happy Raven was gone and his problem was solved. I sent him some emails, supposedly from her. He never bothered to question them. He was devastated about what happened to his daughter."

I moved closer. "I assume Joyce saw the explosion, got in her boat, and pulled my daughter out of the water, but she was terribly hurt." Another step. I had covered over half the distance between us. "And you—"

"Piper, Dove is gone. You know about the body, the DNA. She's never coming back."

Before I could stop it, I moaned. I covered my mouth to stifle any more sounds.

A dog started to bark in the foyer below. I glanced over the railing. A bald, three-legged canine was digging at the elevator door.

"Piggy?"

Mildred's eyes widened, then she inclined her head to the left. "That snoopy marine lady, your boyfriend, and a girl with a deformed face are in the elevator, just waiting for the storm surge."

I stared at her, the blood rushing from my head. Hannah's words came to me. *When you see something you like, your eyes grow wider, your mouth opens slightly, and then the corners of your lips tighten into a tiny smile.*

I glanced toward the stairs, widened my eyes, and let my mouth drop.

Mildred swung around, pointing the pistol in that direction.

I flung myself at her, grabbing the gun in both my hands, and smashed my body into hers. She flew backward. We hit the railing. With a *craack!* it broke. We plummeted to the floor below.

CHAPTER 29

We smashed against the marble floor with Mildred on the bottom.

Searing pain shot up my leg from my ankle. I couldn't breathe, the wind knocked out of me. My left arm went numb. I rolled onto my back, tears from the pain springing to my eyes. *Air will return. Don't panic.* I sucked in tiny breaths until my lungs could fill again.

I glanced at Mildred. Her eyes were closed, but she was still breathing. I kicked the gun away from her hand. With her shattered legs, she'd never reach it even if she did regain consciousness.

Rain poured down my face. The deluge had overwhelmed the drainage in the room, leaving several inches of water on the marble floor. Only near the walls was there any protection from the rain.

The front door had been wedged open. The wind blew through, forcing the door to slam backward, then forward, shattering the wood.

A drenched Piggy yelped in fear and cowered in the corner.

Something banged near me. The elevator. Hannah, Mandy, and Tucker were inside.

Rolling onto my side, I then pushed to a seated position. My ankle throbbed and my arm was useless.

The front door burst open. Nana raced over to me and stuck his face in mine. "Good Nana, good dog. Help me." The dog stood motionless as I used his body to get to my feet. I could barely put any weight on my leg. Hobbling over to the elevator, I pushed the down button. Nothing happened. I tried the up. Still no response. I thumbed the intercom. "Mandy? Hannah? Tucker? It's me, Piper."

"Stop playing with us," a strange voice responded.

The crash came from the other side of the door, followed by a second bang. Tucker placed his ear on the metal panel.

"Is the house coming down?" Hannah asked, her lower lip trembling.

"I don't think so." Tucker straightened.

"Mandy? Hannah? Tucker? It's me, Piper." The voice sounded a little different but still distorted.

Could it be? Mandy mouthed.

"Maybe. But maybe someone wants to toy with us some more. We have to find out," he answered. "Stop playing with us," he shouted through the door. He tried to think of a conversation he'd had with Piper that couldn't have been overheard. His mind went blank.

Mandy watched him, signaled for them to trade places, then pushed the intercom. "Piper, it's Mandy. What did I order for lunch when ya met me at the Fish Grill?"

A pause, then, "Are you serious?"

"I need an answer. I don't know if it's really you."

"It was Buddy's Diner, not the Fish Grill. You had she-crab soup, roasted beet salad, and blackened grouper. And you had dessert."

Mandy grinned. "It's Piper."

Tucker whispered, "Yes!"

Mandy leaned into the PA. "We're stuck and gettin' a bit low on air."

Piper didn't speak for a moment, then said, "I'm working on it."

I looked around the foyer for something to pry the front off the control panel. I spotted Joel's toolbox near the planter in the center of the room. My heart sank. The only reason a toolbox would be so convenient was if Mildred had brought it to disable the elevator. She'd set a trap for people like she set traps on the island for snakes.

I limped over, opened it, and grabbed a screwdriver. The screws were loose and came off quickly. One of the wires had been cut. I peeled the plastic coating away and twisted the two ends back together, then pushed the down button.

Sparks flew out of the panel, then a small fire started. It was quickly extinguished by the rain. The controls were now a charred lump. Worse, the intercom was now severed. I could speak to them if I went upstairs to another room, but that would take time.

I drove the screwdriver into the seam where the elevator doors met. I wasn't strong enough to do more than chip the paint.

I'd need tools, a sledgehammer, something large enough to penetrate.

A quick glance at Mildred showed me she was still breathing. Her legs were bent at unnatural angles. I looked away quickly. Nana had been watching me from a safe distance. "Come here, Nana." The dog came to me. I put my hand on his back. "You need to help me walk."

Somehow he understood. The only place that I knew where a sledgehammer might be was the studio. I'd have to face the fury of the hurricane to get there.

"I smell smoke," Hannah said in a high-pitched voice.

"Me too." Tucker sniffed near the panel. "It's coming from here. I bet Piper tried to get the controls working, but they fried instead."

"Try the intercom," Mandy said.

He pushed the button. "Hello? Piper? Hello?" Not even static. "Let's hope she can help us soon," he finally whispered. Tar-black despair washed over him. He could barely draw a breath. If he didn't suffocate first, he was going to drown in an iron coffin just as surely as his wife had.

In addition to the rain, the wind whipped up debris. Fronds, branches, leaves buffeted Nana and me. We crossed under the house, which provided some protection, but the ground between the house and studio was exposed. My arm was still slightly numb and provided minimal defense. Twice branches smacked into me.

The studio, even with wind whistling through the now-broken window, was quieter than the crashing outside. Quickly I inventoried what I had available. Sledgehammer, hammer, wrench, metal wedge, short iron rod, and rope.

With only one working arm, it would take me several trips to take the tools to the house. I needed wheels—a cart, wheelbarrow, something. I didn't know where the golf carts' keys were stashed, and the carts probably would blow over in the wind anyway. My gaze finally fell on Father's old hydraulic table. It had a flat surface, about two square feet, that would hold the tools and, more importantly, was on wheels. One by one I stacked everything on the table, then I called Nana over. I tied one end of the rope around his collar and the other around the table. "Okay, Nana." I opened the door. If the dog took off . . . I'd just have to hope he'd stay with me and pull.

We couldn't take the shortcut under the house but had to stay on the paved path. More branches slammed into me and the rain was almost a physical force. I limped, pulled, tugged, steadied, and shoved the table, with Nana jerking ahead at random moments. By the time we made it to the foyer, sensation—mostly pain—had returned to my arm. I didn't care. They were going to die if I didn't succeed.

After untying the dog, I pushed the table close to the elevator. I placed the metal wedge on the floor next to the elevator doors' seam, hefted the sledgehammer, and struck the wedge. Pain shot up my arm, but I ignored it. The door didn't move. A second strike jammed the metal farther into the seam, forcing the door to open a tiny crack.

"Thank the Lord," Mandy shouted through the small gap. "Air!"

Her voice gave me renewed strength. I hammered the wedge half a dozen more times, mostly using one arm, until it was flush with the doors. They wouldn't budge any farther.

My head pounded with my racing heart. The sledgehammer was slick in my hands, and now both arms ached. The opening was about three inches. Through the crack I could see Tucker.

I pressed my face against the cleft. "I can't get it to move any farther. I need a wider wedge, or . . . something."

Mandy peered at me. "What about . . . whoever trapped us in here? Are you safe?"

"Mildred." I glanced over my shoulder. "She's . . . Her legs . . . She's unconscious."

Tucker appeared next. "If you can't get us out, you need to get to safety."

The lump in my throat kept me from speaking for a few moments. "I won't leave you."

Hannah's hand slipped through the doors and I grabbed it. After a moment she let go.

I turned and looked around me through blurred vision. *Great pep talk, but how are you getting that door open?* I pivoted back. "Is there any way I can get to you from the top?"

"No," Tucker answered. "It's welded."

A bigger wedge? A two-by-four jammed into the opening? No, the wood would just break, assuming I could exert enough pressure on it. The metal rod? Same problem. I wasn't strong enough.

Nana bumped a nose against my hand. "I don't think you're powerful enough either." I stroked his wet head. Something strong. Pushing, pulling . . . the hydraulic table? If I put it on its side and pushed the edge of the table surface through the opening? Did the hydraulics still work? No matter, it was all I could think of.

Somehow I had to tip the table over, jam it so the edge of the table was inside the opening and the wheels rested against the wall, then engage the hydraulics. Hopefully as the table opened, it would force the door, not tear out the wall.

If it didn't work, I had no plan B. Except to stay with them.

My strength was all but gone, my arms aching, my leg swelling to melon size.

Tucker stuck his hand out. "Piper, listen, you need to get out of here. The hurricane will be here in full force very soon—"

"I'm not leaving. I have a plan."

"What do you want us to do?"

I hobbled over and took hold. His fingers stroked my hand. "I . . . I don't know. Maybe pray. I tried, but it didn't work."

"Who knows, Piper, maybe it did. We'll pray." He let go. I could hear murmurings, but I didn't wait to listen. Somehow his words had given me a boost.

I forced the table close to the wall, to the right of the elevator, locked the wheels, then removed a large edging stone from the planter in the center of the room. Placing the stone like a fulcrum next to the bottom of the table, I jammed the rod under the table, across the top of the stone, then put all my weight on the far end of the rod. The table tilted sideways, then flipped on its side with a tooth-rattling *crash*. The wet marble floor was slippery, but it took agonizing minutes to force the table, inch by inch, near the elevator. When I finally lined up the edge of the table with the gap, I again picked up the sledgehammer.

Nana, who'd been watching me from the side of the room, cocked his head.

"This one is for Ashlee, for having an affair." *Wham!* I smashed the sledgehammer against the table, shoving it closer to the opening. "And this is for Raven, for betraying her own sister." *Wham!* I broke out in a sweat. The blows radiated up my arms. "And this is for Father, who claimed we were the perfect family while sleeping with other women." *Wham!* My strength was almost gone and I still had several inches to go. "And." *Wham!* "This." *Wham!* "Is." *Wham!* "For." *Wham!* "Mildred!" *Wham!* The last blow jammed the tabletop firmly into the opening. I sank to the floor, breathing heavily, my arms too weak to even lift the electrical cord and plug it into the wall.

A gust of wind whipped through the door and rattled the palmetto behind me.

"Piper?" Tucker called. "Are you okay?"

I nodded. *I don't have time to rest.* I crawled to the table, shoved the rocks and metal rod out of the way, then grabbed the cord and plugged it into the wall. *Now for the real test.* I pushed the on button.

Nothing happened.

"No!" I flipped it off, then on again. Nothing.

"God, You can't do this to me." Tears mixed with the rain drenching my face. I tried again. Then again. I wanted to scream, to kick the table, to pound on the door. "Please, please, please." I moved to the wall, unplugged the cord, and tried the lower outlet. Still nothing.

My brain was a fog. I couldn't come up with another plan. They were going to die horribly, and I was too stupid to figure out how to save them.

CHAPTER 30

Rain streamed down around me. Wind whipped through the smashed door and flung the plantings around, and all I could do was stare at my father's broken hydraulic table. I grabbed and held on to the amber necklace at my neck. I should tell Tucker, Mandy, and Hannah I couldn't help . . . because the table . . . the table . . . I squeezed the necklace until it hurt. *I found a necklace at Joyce's place.* Behind the fake electrical breaker box. Sparks. Plug in, outlet. *What?* I'd fried the electrical circuit on the elevator. Did I throw a breaker? Maybe. But I had no idea where the breaker box was. This house was huge.

Could it be . . . ? Was there a chance that not all the outlets were connected to the same breaker? I hunted a different wall and found an outlet. Grabbing the cord, I stretched it to its full length. It just barely reached. Plugging it in, I reached for the on and up buttons. *Please, Lord.*

The table started to move. Shrieks of joy came from the elevator.

The tabletop, jammed into the elevator opening, remained stationary. Slowly the legs extended, moving toward the wall.

Once the legs touched the wall, something would have to give. Hopefully it would be the door, not the wall.

I moved closer so they could hear me. "I don't know how this will work, but the second this door is open enough to get through, you'll need to get out. I don't know how well the wall is going to do with all the pressure on it."

"Got it," Mandy said.

The legs touched the wall and continued to open. With a *crack!* the wheels punched through the plasterboard, opening jagged holes.

I held my breath.

The table stopped. The engine squealed, grew higher pitched. With a wrenching screech, the door moved an inch. Then another.

Another inch. The wall sprouted cracks radiating outward from the holes.

More screeching, another inch. Hannah shoved her body through, and I pulled. She flew outward, stumbling over the prone table. I shoved her free and reached for Mandy.

The wall started to give way.

"Mandy, quick!" I grabbed her hand and pulled. The woman cleared the opening and leaped over the table.

"Tucker!"

A large *crack!* and the legs shot outward two inches. The wall was collapsing.

Tucker shoved his upper body through the opening and reached out both arms. Mandy and I each grabbed one and pulled. If he got stuck and the wall broke through, he'd be cut in half. I put one foot on the table and leaned my weight away from it, pulling the man as hard as I could.

"Now!" he shouted.

Another shriek from the hydraulics, a *boom!* from the wall, and the table legs straightened, smashing the wallboard and framing outward, revealing a metal piling.

We yanked Tucker's body clear just as the elevator doors clanked shut.

The momentum sent Mandy, Tucker, and me backward, landing hard on the wet marble.

"Ump!" I landed at Hannah's feet. I looked up with a grin.

She was sheet white, staring at something to my right. I looked.

Mildred was leaning her upper body against the edging stones, her shattered legs in front of her. "I suppose you're going to leave me."

"No." I stood. "We'll be taking you to higher ground with us."

"What?" Tucker said. "She tried to kill us, kill you!"

"Yes. And she'll stand trial for all she's done. But I'm not leaving my aunt here to die."

"What?!" This time Tucker, Mandy, and Hannah all spoke together.

"I don't have time to explain. We have to—"

Piggy let out a sharp bark. I turned.

Mildred's lips were pulled back into a snarl, her eyes narrowed in hate. She'd somehow reached the pistol and now held it in shaking hands, aimed at Hannah.

I leaped in front of Mildred, blocking her target.

She pulled the trigger.

I launched myself at her, smashing the pistol away.

Her eyes widened, mouth opened in a scream. One last breath came out before her head dropped and body went limp. Her eyes remained open but now empty of rage. Empty of life.

I landed next to her and tried not to cry out. The bullet had missed Hannah, but a million stinging scorpions in my side said the slug had still connected.

"Piper!" Tucker was beside me, lifting me, pushing my hair out of my face. He looked at his hand, now covered in blood. "She shot you!"

I attempted to smile. "'It's just a scratch. I've had worse.' *Monty Python*—"

"Piper, stop it. We have to get moving. Just tell me how badly you're hurt."

"1975."

"You're delirious."

"I'm not delirious. In pain, yes. Help me up."

His mouth dropped. "But—"

I reached up and closed his mouth. "Tucker, I'm not Superwoman. I'd love to stay here and have you hold me, but we have to move."

"Can you make it upstairs?" He carefully lifted me to my feet. The scorpions renewed their stinging.

Burning tears streamed down my face, hidden by the rain. "This house won't make it through a direct hit. All it would take is for one piling to weaken and it will go down. We have to make it to the highest point of the island."

As if to emphasize my last statement, a blast of wind shook the house and a crashing sound came from somewhere.

"Let me see." Before I could stop him, Tucker had lifted my shirt and checked my injury. "The bullet looks like it passed through your side. Hopefully it didn't nick anything important." He slipped off his shirt, ripped it in half, folded it, and pressed it to my side. Bees joined the scorpions. I hissed under my breath.

"How are we goin' to make it?" Mandy asked. "Y'all are injured—"

"We'll make it, I promise," I said as firmly as I could. "We'll go outside, then I'll go in front because I know the way. I'll lean on Nana here. Mandy, you put your hand on my shoulder and your arm around Tucker to help him. Hannah, you get on the other side of Nana and hold on to him. You can put Piggy inside your jacket."

Before they could come up with any arguments, I moved toward the door. "Watch for blowing branches and debris. Hopefully we won't have to deal with falling trees, palms, or palmettos. Let's go." I called Nana over and took hold of his collar. The others followed.

Outside, the wind was a solid wall of force driving the rain sideways. Walking was torture. I cradled my side and clung to Nana. Mandy gripped my shoulder, and Hannah's hand slipped through Nana's collar next to mine.

The lights in the house went out, leaving us in a swirling blackness.

"Nana, take me to Joyce!" I shouted over the wind. The dog started walking.

CHAPTER 31

Tucker rested his arm over the diminutive Mandy's shoulder and leaned on her to walk. She may have been small, but she was strong and tough. Just like Piper.

All the lights went out, plunging them into darkness. The wind and rain, combined with flying branches, leaves, and sand, pelted them. Even standing upright was difficult. He didn't see how they'd possibly maneuver across the island in pitch blackness before the full brunt of the storm hit. He'd never prayed so hard in all his life.

They awkwardly navigated the path, him limping and Mandy trying to provide support and keep up with Piper. Nana's furry rump was slightly in front of him. Talking was out of the question, the words snatched from his mouth before they'd been formed.

He resumed praying.

I'd sounded so brave and wise when I told the others the house wasn't safe. I'd somehow assumed I could feel the crunch of the crushed-shell path under my feet and know when we were walking in an area free of foliage. I hadn't thought of the organic rubble blown onto the trail, nor the projectiles that felt like we were fending off a volley of enemy arrows. At least I could tell the ground was rising slightly. I was physically drained, and every step sent a burning knife into my side. But I had to keep my promise to get everyone to safety.

I tried to bargain with God again. I'd offered to spend the rest of my life worshiping Him in exchange for Dove. His answer had been no. "God," I whispered, "this isn't for me this time. Just help me get Hannah, Tucker, and Mandy to safety. Oh, and Nana and Piggy. I can't do this alone. And right now I need help . . ." My throat felt raw.

I stumbled and let go of Nana, then immediately grabbed for his collar. He had stopped. When he felt my hand, he started walking again. Again I stumbled and fell forward, catching myself before my face planted into the ground. The earth was rock hard under my hands. Hard like . . . cement. *Could it be?* Joyce's porch. I groped around until I found the wall of the house. *Yes!* I turned so the house was behind me, then crawled back to the edge of the porch. Mandy should be straight ahead. I found her legs. She flinched, then touched my hair.

I stood, put my face near where I thought her ear might be, and yelled, "We're here! Straight ahead." Locating Nana, who rewarded me with a soggy lick, I again grabbed his collar and let him show me the door. I banged my hand on the hurricane panel. The porch afforded us some slight protection from the rain, and we huddled next to the building. "There's a drawbar holding this shut."

Tucker moved next to me and felt around until he found the

bar, then lifted it and set it aside. His arm slipped around me and he held me close for a moment before opening the panel, then the door. I could feel his warmth even as he moved away.

"Can we turn on the lights?" Hannah sounded as exhausted as I felt.

I felt for the wall, found the light switch, and flipped it a few times. "Looks like the electricity is out. I think there's an oil lamp on the desk . . ." Hands out in front of me, I felt for the desk. My leg found it first. "Ump. Found it." The oil lamp was where I remembered it. Opening the desk drawer, I felt for matches. Unsuccessfully. "Hannah, did you find matches when you spent the night here?"

"No. But there's a flashlight in the kitchen. Ouch!"

"The living room is full of outdoor furniture," I said. "Watch your step. As for the kitchen, I searched it earlier. Everything's on the counter."

"I'll check out the bedroom," Mandy said.

"I'm staying put until you find some kind of light," Tucker said. "I have no idea where anything is."

I nodded, then realized he couldn't see me. "Good idea."

The gale outside shook and whistled around the house while the endless rain thundered on the metal roof. We created our own din thumping and banging around for a light. Shortly a pale yellow beam cut through the darkness. "Found it, but the batteries look low," Hannah said.

A loud *bang!* came from the porch.

"We don't have time to look for more batteries." I pointed. "That sounded like a tree coming down. We need to move into the concrete bedroom."

I didn't have to repeat myself. Tucker and Hannah spurted

to the room. "Nana, come on." The dog cheerfully trotted after me.

Crash!

I shrieked and spun. The kitchen had disintegrated under the thick trunk of a palm tree. Wind slammed into the room, bringing torrents of rain.

Tucker yanked me into the bedroom and slammed the door. "How strong are these walls?"

"Hopefully strong enough." He hadn't let go of me but was studying me in the dim light. "What? Do I have something on my face?" I reached up to check, but he shook his head and let go.

The ground shook.

Both Nana and Piggy started barking. "What was that?" Hannah's voice was high pitched.

The door rattled and shook. The dogs increased their baying.

"I'd venture to say we made it just in time," Mandy yelled over the clamoring canines. "Sounds like Hurricane Marco just hit Curlew Island."

CHAPTER 32

Tucker and Mandy shoved the dresser in front of the door along with the chair and nightstand. I leaned against the wall and tried to think of something besides my throbbing side. The hurricane sounded like a locomotive train rushing past. The metal shutters over the windows rattled and grated against each other, adding to the cacophony.

I'd stripped the bed earlier and covered it with Joyce's clothing. Mandy and I gathered the clothes and tossed them onto the chair. Hannah corralled Piggy and took refuge on the bed. Mandy and I joined her. Tucker was the last to crawl on the bed and prop himself against the headboard. Hannah wiggled next to him and he put his arm around her. I thought about snuggling up on the other side of him. I ended up at the foot of the bed, my swollen leg stretched out in front of me.

"How long will this go on?" Hannah asked.

"It will seem like forever." Mandy grabbed a pillow and wrapped her arms around it. "But I expect it'll move on in a couple of hours. High tide will be somewhere between five forty-five and six in the morning. Don't have my chart so I can't be exact. That's when things can get dicey. Why don't ya turn off the light for a bit. Save what little battery we have."

Hannah complied.

"How are you doing, Piper?" Tucker asked.

"About how you'd expect. I don't suppose any of you have an aspirin?"

"No." Mandy cleared her throat. "I have to ask. Why'd you say Mildred was your aunt?"

"A whole bunch of things came together in my brain." I shifted, trying to find a comfortable angle. "I found a piece of paper that had an impression on it that Raven had hidden. Then there was the movie *Giant*, a photograph of my grandparents, and a christening gown."

"You're not okay, Piper," Mandy said. "You're ramblin'."

"No." I gave up on comfortable. "I found a photograph of my grandparents dated 1955. They were with a nurse holding a baby in the family's heirloom christening gown. I thought the baby was my mother."

"Okay," Tucker said.

"But when I mentioned the movie *Giant* to Mildred the other day, she reminded me that 1956 was the year of Mother's birth. The only reason the family's heirloom gown would be on another baby is that it was another member of the family. I do remember Joel saying that Mildred's mother worked for my mother's family and that Caroline was like a sister to Mildred. I just didn't think that was literal. I think my grandfather and my father both had an eye for other women. With Grandfather, it was the housekeeper. The torn paper from the print looked like the edge of a birth certificate.

Maybe Raven found it and was trying to decide what to do about it."

"Why didn't your family just acknowledge that Mildred was an illegitimate child?" Mandy asked.

"Pride, I suppose. Both of my grandparents died very young. I'm sure they didn't confide in Mother about an older half sister. Mildred must have found out and decided to get even—and very rich."

"How?" Hannah asked.

"Tucker, both you and I came to the same theory—that the last surviving member of the family would own Boone Industries. But everyone had to die first in such a way as to not leave any loose ends."

"That awful woman was aiming at me," Hannah said. "You saved my life."

Lord, does that count for anything? I almost gave my life for Hannah's. Can You change Your mind and give me back my daughter? "I don't really know who she was aiming at."

"Did y'all know she was crazier than a pet coon?" Mandy asked.

"No. I knew she would give her life for my family. I didn't know she'd be willing to take lives."

"Do you think she murdered the old lady at the condo?" Tucker asked.

"I don't know. Maybe. The old lady saw a man she assumed was Raven's husband around the condo. She could have identified him later. I believe Mildred killed both of my sisters, my father, Silva, and . . . Dove." I wouldn't mention Joyce just yet. Hannah had enough to deal with.

"Hannah, you're shaking," Tucker said. "Are you cold?"

"No. Just . . . scared."

"Maybe you could sing for us. I don't think Piper's heard your voice."

"That would be lovely," I said.

Hannah started to sing in a clear, silvery voice. Mandy and Tucker joined in on "Amazing Grace." Several more hymns followed, then she got us all singing a slightly off-key version of "California Dreaming."

"That was fun," Mandy said. "Do ya know 'Drop Kick Me, Jesus, Through the Goalposts of Life'?"

"That's not even a song!" Hannah said.

"Is too," Mandy said.

"Not!"

"I'm afraid Mandy's correct," Tucker said. "Written by Bobby Bare, who also brought us 'Redneck Hippie Romance.'"

Hannah giggled. "Okay, I have one. I don't know what the words mean." She cleared her throat.

"You are my anja, my so-may, my fend.
I'll be right wid-jou tee-da n.
N wen-jou fee the somy-gay,
I'll keep you safee on the tay
Our see-son to-gay
Will be fo-ee,
My anja."

All the hairs on my neck stood on end. I couldn't breathe. An ice pick rammed into my heart. "H-Hannah . . . where did you learn that song?"

"I think my mother sang it to me."

In a trembling voice, I sang,

"You are my angel, my soul mate, my friend.
I'll be right with you till the end.
And when you fear the stormy gale,
I'll keep you safely on the trail.
Our season together
Will be forever,
My angel."

"You know the song!" Hannah said.

"I wrote that song. For my daughter, Dove."

Tucker felt his mouth drop open. "I would guess that Joyce—"

"Joyce never heard me sing it." Piper's voice was breathless. "No one but Dove ever did."

"We found out," Mandy said, "that Mildred could overhear and listen in on everything going on in the house. She must have heard you sing and—"

"No, no, no! Hannah sang the song with the words she understood, the words a toddler would use."

The identification of the song was chilling, but Tucker needed to bring Piper back to reality. "What about the body of the child, the DNA, the hairbrush?"

The bed bounced slightly as Piper shifted her weight. "That was Raven's key."

"I don't understand any of this." Hannah's voice was high pitched.

"Let me try to explain." Piper was silent for a few moments.

Tucker imagined the storm raging around them was as tumultuous as the tempest within Piper. He didn't know if he could bear her trying to resurrect her daughter.

"Tucker, you saw the home movie taken by Ashlee of Raven and me on the beach. Mildred confirmed they had an affair."

"I'm sorry to hear that," Tucker said.

"I'm sure it wasn't his first or last affair. He liked . . . admiration. Raven stopped coming to the family gatherings after that. If Raven became pregnant that summer, her daughter would be only a few months younger than Dove. And it could be that the birth certificate I thought was Mildred's was actually for Raven's daughter. As they had the same father, and Raven and I were sisters, Raven's daughter would look a lot like Dove."

"That's a pretty big *if*, Piper," Mandy said.

Piper shifted again. "Turn the light on for a moment."

Hannah complied, shining it in Piper's face.

Piper held up two identical amber necklaces. "Mother bought this for Dove"—she lofted one—"and this one for her other granddaughter." She held up the other.

"You're saying your mother *knew* about the affair? And the baby?" Tucker shook his head.

The flashlight flickered and Hannah quickly shut it off.

"Mildred said Raven was going to tell me about the affair and demand a divorce. She left out that Raven brought her daughter with her to show me. Mildred murdered Raven and sent her body off in the boat with a bomb set, just like she tried to do to me today. But there were two little girls on the boat—and one survived."

"But the DNA showed the body was Dove." Tucker had to get this through her head. "You saw the chain-of-custody form, the brush—"

"Once the body washed up, Mildred knew they'd need DNA. She knew Joyce had found Dove and taken her away, so the dead child had to be Raven's daughter. She knew where Raven lived, where she could find hair to put in Dove's brush."

Tucker let out a frustrated sigh. "But—"

"You saw a photo of the body." Piper's voice was hard.

"Yes."

"Was she wearing a life jacket?"

"No."

"Right. Dove would have had on a life jacket. Joyce rescued her, took her in, raised her. That Boone Industries money we believed went to Joyce was a good guess. Probably for Dove's care."

"Grandma loved me."

"Yes, she did, Hannah. But in the end, she decided to tell me who you really were."

"She's dead, isn't she?" Hannah's voice was muffled.

"I'm afraid so."

Hannah buried her face in Tucker's shoulder, silently sobbing.

"Piper," Mandy said. "Do ya really believe your mother and Mildred worked together? That Mildred did all that killing?"

She was silent, then took a deep breath. "No. Not working together." She didn't speak for a few minutes. The sound of the storm filled the room. "Mildred didn't say she killed Sparrow. She said Sparrow was the start, and the Kennedys' handling of their daughter Rosemary was the inspiration . . ."

"What are you thinking about?" Tucker asked.

"Mother's comments about the perfect family, home, and island were known to everyone. What if Mildred acted on these wishes, either directly or indirectly, so that Mother would ultimately be the prime suspect? When Mother was the final surviving family member, she'd have a terrible accident, and Mildred would produce her birth certificate and claim everything."

"When ya say acted indirectly, you mean—?" Mandy asked.

A large *crash!* overhead made Tucker duck and Hannah let out a squeak. "I have an idea on that," he said. "Silva said he wanted to retire on a boat like the *Taire*. I doubt he made enough money to buy such a boat—"

"But Mildred could have brought him in on the scheme, maybe even promising him that boat," Piper finished. "He was an expert on boat repairs and machinery. Probably could figure out how to cause a welding accident. When he was no longer useful to her, she took care of him."

"And Joel was in the military," Tucker said. "He'd know about rifles and ghost guns. Who knows what Mildred promised him or held over his head."

"But that's—" Mandy said.

"Sick? Twisted? Fanatical?" Piper shifted again.

Her injuries must be causing her a lot of pain. Tucker wanted to hold her, comfort her. He stayed at his end of the bed.

"I wonder what's happened to Tern." Piper's voice shook slightly. "He'd be with Joel right now."

Tucker realized he could hear Piper much more clearly, along with the panting of Nana lying beside the bed. "I think the hurricane is moving away."

"Thank the Lord!" Mandy said.

They listened for a bit. The rumbling was decidedly less. Now an intermittent *boom!* and *crash!* could be heard.

"What's that?" Piper asked.

"I don't know. Hannah, could ya hand me the flashlight?" Mandy flipped it on, slid to the edge of the bed, and stood. She immediately put the flashlight on her feet. "I think we got a problem here."

Tucker scooted over and looked. Mandy was standing in several inches of water.

CHAPTER 33

I slid both of my feet over the side of the bed into the cold water. "Storm surge. We need to get higher."

"I thought we were at the highest place on the island." Tucker stood.

"We are, but we can't get trapped in here. We need to get onto the roof." I slogged to the night table blocking the door and tried to move it aside. The throbbing in my side increased to a fiery lance.

Hannah stayed on the bed and held the light while Mandy and Tucker removed the barriers. Tucker reached over to open the door.

"Wait!" Mandy stepped in front of him. "The ocean out there is swirlin' and full of rip tides, waves, and crazy currents. Y'all could get sucked out and be gone before we could stop it. We have to stay together. See if there's any rope or belts or somethin' we can hang on to."

A fast search of the room yielded nothing. "How about we rip up the sheets and blankets?" I asked. The water had grown noticeably deeper, now reaching to my knees.

No one had to be encouraged to work faster. We quickly ripped sheets and tied them together. By the time we'd finished, the water was to our thighs. Nana had jumped on the bed and watched us work.

"There's a ladder, or steps, or some way to get up to the roof, right?" Tucker tied the sheet and blanket strips together.

"Yes. On the north side." I pointed. "A metal ladder attached to the building."

"We'll create a tag line, attaching this to a fixed point." Tucker gave each knot an extra tug, then opened the door. A hip-deep wave swept through the opening, knocking Hannah off her feet.

Mandy helped her up. I turned and looked out. Gray light filtered through the massive debris pile in front of the door.

I leaned against the dresser, my mind a blank. We'd never get through the beams, fallen palms, and tree trunks blocking us. The water rose to my waist.

Tucker swore, then started yanking at the beams, then the palm trunk. Nothing budged. His face had gone chalk white.

Of course. His wife and unborn baby drowned.

Nana swam past me to the opening, then attempted to climb up. One of the beams shifted slightly.

Tucker grabbed my shoulders. "Piper, think! Is there any way out of here?"

"The shutters on the windows are electric. I don't think we can smash through them." I tried to picture playing on the roof as a child. We'd always climbed up using the outside ladder.

The water rose again, covering my wound. The salt stung like fire ants. I couldn't think. The pain filled my brain. I had to use my hands to stay upright as the waves tried to sweep my legs out from under me.

Roof. I'm walking on the flat roof. All over . . . No, watch it, Sparrow! There's a hole, an opening.

"Piper!" Hannah had climbed onto the bed. The water was to her knees.

"There!" I pointed. "About halfway, maybe two feet from the outside wall. There used to be an opening—"

Tucker didn't wait. "Mandy, help." He grabbed the dresser, now completely submerged, and the two of them manhandled it to under where I'd pointed. He jumped on the top and started hammering on the ceiling with his fist.

The water rose again. I was swimming.

Mandy swam onto the dresser next to Tucker. "Look. The wood's wet here. The roof is probably gone and rain's been soaking through."

I rapped my foot against something hard. The metal floor lamp with the mica shade was lying on its side. It had a heavy round base. Holding my breath, I dove down, grabbed the lamp, and surfaced. "Here." I thrust the lamp onto the dresser.

Tucker hefted the metal base and smashed it into the wooden ceiling. Chunks of beadboard dropped down.

I swam to the bed and stood next to Hannah. Even standing on the bed, I was chest-deep in water. Nana was swimming around, pawing at the walls and whining. Hannah had buried her face in shivering Piggy's side.

Wham! Another blow. More wood. Tucker was having trouble getting a good swing.

Did I remember correctly? Was the opening on the other side? There wouldn't be time to try another spot. Did I lead them here only for them to die?

Wham! Wham! Wham!

I couldn't look. Would we run out of air before the water filled the room?

Wham!

Mandy screamed. I looked.

Gray light came from a small opening. With renewed strength, Tucker slammed the lamp base into the wood, making a larger hole. Without pausing, he grabbed Mandy and shoved her through. "Quick, Hannah—"

"I can't swim."

He dove into the water and swam to her. "Give Piggy to Piper, then wrap your arms around my neck."

"I'm scared."

"I've got you."

She reluctantly handed me the dog, then jumped on his back. He swam to the opening, swung her around, and lifted her.

Nana paddled over to him and he boosted the big dog out. Now it was just Tucker and me. I started swimming, but Piggy wiggled from my arms.

The dog sank from sight.

CHAPTER 34

I dove after him, groping around, trying to find him in the swirling, dark ocean water. I felt rather than saw Tucker join me. Just as I touched a warm body, Tucker grabbed me and pulled me to the surface. I held up Piggy. The poor dog shook like a leaf and was coughing up water.

The ceiling was less than a foot from my head. My claustrophobia took over. I sucked in air and water, tried to scream, pounded the ceiling. *Get out, get me out!*

Stop it! A still, quiet voice whispered in my ear. I stopped thrashing. Turning in a circle, I looked for the opening. There. Holding Piggy aloft, I swam toward it and shoved the dog through.

I didn't have enough energy to reach through myself. I started to sink.

Hands locked around my sides and I flew upward. Someone grabbed me, pulled up, out. I was on the roof.

Mandy and Hannah were staring at me. "Where's Tucker?" Hannah asked.

I looked back into the hole he'd made. Black water lapped at the edges.

"Oh no!" Mandy dropped to her knees and stuck her arm into the water.

Falling to my knees beside her, I did the same. How long had he been without air? I found myself chanting a mindless, "No, no, no, no."

I continued to search the cold water, then looked at Mandy. "I'm going back down."

"No, Piper—"

A hand grabbed mine and I pulled with all my might. Tucker's head, followed by his arms and shoulders, flew through the opening. He lifted himself clear. His skin was white, lips purple, and eyes bloodshot. He was the most beautiful sight I'd ever seen.

"Tucker." It was all I could say.

The three of us slowly pushed to our feet. The metal roof Joyce had built over the cement building had been ripped off by the hurricane, which was lucky for us. Just the original flat roof remained. From our viewpoint, all we could see was water and the tops of a few shredded palm trees. Nothing remained of any other structures on Curlew Island, all swept out into the ocean.

Mandy helped Piggy cough up the last of the water, though like us, he was shivering from the cold. After handing the dog to Hannah, Mandy peeked over the side of the building. "Water's goin' down. Coast guard should be here soon enough."

Hannah sat on a corner of the roof and stared out at the slate-gray sky and sea. I started to go to her, but Tucker put a restraining hand on my shoulder. "Let her be. Give her some time and space."

I nodded.

Tucker turned away, staring at the restless gray-green waves surrounding us. Slowly he reached into his pocket, pulled out a stone, then threw it into the water.

EPILOGUE

WADMALAW ISLAND, SOUTH CAROLINA
SIX MONTHS LATER

The piercing scream ripped up my spine. I dropped the spoon and ran to the door.

Hannah pointed at Piggy. "He just ate some cat poop."

"He'll live. Can you go check on the pygmy goat?"

Hannah nodded and took off running with Piggy following, cat-poop dinner not slowing him down in the least.

I returned to making banana pudding.

With the scouring of Curlew Island, Tern decided to go public with Boone Industries. He also stepped away from political office.

Joel was arrested for his role in providing the rifle in the café shooting and in teaching Mildred how to set explosive devices. He claimed he had no knowledge of what she'd been planning. His trial was set for June.

Silva's body was never recovered, but his hefty bank account pointed to his motivation.

The previous week Dove's—make that Hannah's—DNA test results had come back. God had indeed given me back my daughter.

I'd started attending a women's Bible study. After all, I promised. I was learning a lot about forgiveness. Hannah went with me.

With the money from the business, I decided to open my own small shelter for animals no one wanted. In addition to the goat, we had a one-eared cat, two chickens who refused to lay eggs, an orphaned litter of puppies, and of course Nana. We placed the goose with Mandy. They seemed to get along just fine.

Tern and I had had dinner here several times, though so far he had been resistant to adopting a chicken. I figured he would eventually relent.

Ashlee married Bailey Norton four months ago and I was present at the wedding. Bailey left her job with the newspaper when she compared her lifestyle as Ashlee's wealthy wife to her meager reporter's salary. Ashlee initially called Dove often, though not so much recently as he and Bailey were already expecting their first child.

Tucker pulled up and parked in front of the house. I knew my face would give away my thoughts, and I didn't care. I flew into his arms. "How did it go?"

"I have a new assignment working with the Doe Network on unknown remains."

"That sounds . . . um . . . interesting?"

"It will be, and I can work anywhere."

"That's great news! What else did they say?"

"They asked me about the three stones."

"What—"

A small electric car drove up and parked. My mother stepped out, then stood hesitantly by the open door as if ready to bolt.

For a moment I was rooted to the ground. I'd pictured this moment for the last six months, imagining what I would say. I took a deep breath. "Hello, Mother."

"Sandpiper."

In the months since the hurricane, she'd aged, her face now a network of tiny wrinkles.

Dove slowly walked over to the other side of the car holding Piggy. I signaled to her. "Come here, sweetheart."

Dove trotted over and stood beside me. I put my arm around her. "Mother, I'd like you to meet your granddaughter Dove."

Mother didn't speak for a few moments, then said, "Will you ever forgive me? Either of you?"

"Mom, I already have." As I said it, I found I meant it. I felt the huge brick on my heart lift.

Her face crumpled and she pulled a tissue out of her pocket. "What about you, Dove?"

"Yeah. But I'm not gonna call you Grandma."

"Okay," she managed to squeak out, then opened her arms. "Come and give me a hug."

Dove slowly walked over to Mother and held out her hand.

Mother shook Dove's hand, touched her hair, then looked at me. "I've set up a trust fund in Dove's name. She'll never have to worry about money. And I've consulted with the best plastic surgeon about her face—"

"Dove will make her own decision about her face. I think she's beautiful."

"Yes, of course—"

"As for the trust fund, I think the amount you paid Joyce to care for her over the years would be a suitable sum."

Mother looked down and nodded, then quietly said, "I didn't know about Raven. I believed *her*."

Mother couldn't bring herself to say Mildred's name. After a few moments, she cleared her throat. "Her name was Robin."

"What?"

"Your niece, Raven's daughter. Her name was Robin. I looked it up. Afterward."

So Raven had reached out to me, to tell me the truth.

"I-I had no idea. She manipulated us all . . . I didn't . . . I didn't . . ." Mother waved a hand in the air.

"I know."

Two chickens strolled by, clucking and pecking at the ground every few steps.

"Meet Megan and Kate." I grinned at my mother. "As you can see, I've become a bird-watcher."

"Oh." She stepped backward slightly.

"Do you want to help me feed the puppies?" Dove asked Mother.

"Puppies," Mother said faintly. "Of . . . course. I'd love to." She glanced down at her immaculately pressed white linen slacks.

Dove grabbed Mother's hand and headed toward the shelter. "After you feed them you have to rub their tummies so they'll poop."

"I can't wait . . . ," Mother weakly replied.

Tucker came up beside me. "You got through it."

"Yes." I turned to him. "You were about to tell me about your trip to Clan Firinn. About the three stones."

He reached in his pocket, took out the last rock, and studied it. "*Jerry Maguire*, 1996."

I shrugged. "I don't know what you mean."

He looked up, grinned, and tossed the rock over his shoulder. "'You had me at *hello*.'"

AUTHOR NOTE

My dear readers, yay! You made it to the end of Piper and Tucker's story. Although I live in the wild west, my husband, Rick, and I have taught forensic art at the Mount Pleasant Police Department for many years. We have grown to love this beautiful low country area with its friendly people, wonderful food, and breathtaking beaches. I hope you've caught a brief glimpse through these pages of the depth of history, culture, and beauty of the area. As always, if you feel so inclined, I'd love to hear from you. I answer all my emails, which should be directed to carrie@stuartparks.com. You'll find my schedule on my website www.CarrieStuartParks.com. God bless.

ACKNOWLEDGMENTS

I have so many folks to thank, and I do so with heartfelt gratitude. In no particular order, I'll start with the folks at the Mount Pleasant Police Department. I can't even start to express how kind these folks are. In 2005 my dear mother passed away while I was teaching there, and the compassion the officers and staff shared forever touched my heart. A special note of thanks to Stan Gragg, Deputy Chief of Police. Yes, there really is a Stan Gragg, AKA Stan the Man. Over a bowl of creamy shrimp and grits, he went over how he'd conduct an investigation on a mass shooting. Lovely lunch . . .

Rick's aunt, uncle, and cousins reside in the Charleston area and have welcomed us with open arms, good food, and a place to crash for a night or two every year. Thank you for the hurricane insight to Danny, Kathy, and the entire Marcey family of South Carolina. A special thanks to Angelo. I'm not sure for what, but I haven't had time to kill you in one of my stories, so that will have to do until such a time as I arrange your demise.

I had several brainstorming groups for this book, the first being the Phoenix session with Colleen Coble, Robin Carroll, and Lindsay Harrel. We have more fun throwing out story ideas with each other than you'd believe. That and chocolate makes for a perfect weekend.

The second brainstorming session was with my forensic art class here on the ranch with Joyce Nagy, Michelle Hawn, Kali Bellman, Priscilla Patterson, and Val Copeland. They always inspire me with their law enforcement insight. I just wish Heidi would have been there.

To my dear friend Lynette Eason, I just wish our week in Isle of Palms had worked out for you. I know we would have created The Great American Novel together.

My agent, Karen Solem, is and has been a guiding and inspired friend. Thank you again for your suggestions and advice. Love ya, m'friend.

HarperCollins Christian Publishing team is a dream come true. They are the best in the industry and I am so grateful for all you've taught me and all you've done for me. My dear editor and publisher, Amanda Bostic, continues to have faith in my stories and writing. She's teamed me up with the fantastic, award-winning author and editor, Erin Healy. The two of them polish my writing to the highest. Jodi Hughes keeps polishing through the final edits. My marketing and publicity team is fabulous—thank you, Paul Fisher, Kerri Potts, and Margaret Kercher. I'm truly blessed by all your hard work.

Thank you, FrankNBarb. Always.

Rick, you drive me nuts, but you do have some great ideas. Now go watch hockey. And don't tell me about the Sharks. I'm writing.

Finally, eternal gratitude to my Lord and Savior, Jesus Christ, in whom all things are possible.

DISCUSSION QUESTIONS

1. Tucker was given three stones by his counselor, Scott Thomas. He threw each stone away. What did the stones represent in his life?
2. The Boone family seemed obsessed by perfection, and in particular other people's impressions of them, yet they were total hypocrites. How did they show this?
3. Piper held on to different gifts from members of her family: Raven's keychain with a blank key, Sparrow's sewn pencil case that didn't hold pencils, Ashlee's expensive Coach purse, Tern's studded bracelet hiding her scars. What did each gift represent? How did it reflect on the person who gave it to her?
4. Piper wrote to her daughter every day. In her heart, she believed Dove would always be the perfect little girl she lost. How did she respond when she found out the truth?
5. If you were to find a Bible verse for Piper, what would you choose? Why?

6. Piper had an M. Night Shyamalan *Signs* movie poster on her wall, a movie that she really enjoyed. In the movie, the character Graham Hess said the following. What do you think? "People break down into two groups. When they experience something lucky, group number one sees it as more than luck, more than coincidence. They see it as a sign, evidence, that there is someone up there, watching out for them. Group number two sees it as just pure luck. Just a happy turn of chance . . . (Group number one) deep down, they feel that whatever's going to happen, there will be someone there to help them. And that fills them with hope. See what you have to ask yourself is what kind of person are you? Are you the kind that sees signs, that sees miracles? Or do you believe that people just get lucky? Or, look at the question this way: Is it possible that there are no coincidences?"
7. Have you ever visited (or do you live) in the low country of South Carolina? What is unique about this region?
8. Have you ever experienced a hurricane or massive storm? Share the experience. Did it change you or affect you in any way?

An artist hiding from an escaped killer uncovers one of World War II's most dangerous secrets—a secret that desperate men will do anything to keep hidden.

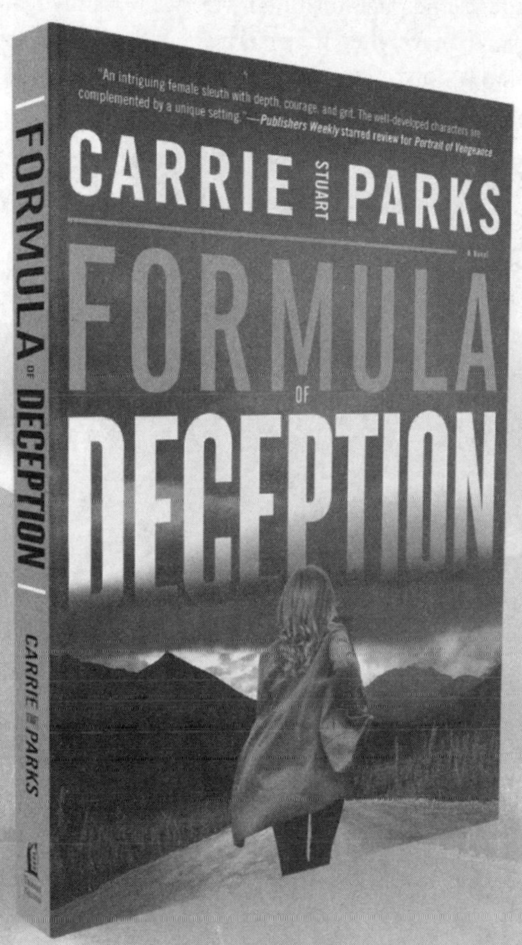

"The sinister tone of this fast-paced story line creates an almost unbearable tension that will keep readers glued to the page."

—*Library Journal* for *Formula of Deception*

AVAILABLE IN PRINT, E-BOOK, AND AUDIO!

9780785226130-B

LOOKING FOR YOUR NEXT GREAT NOVEL?

"I love Carrie Stuart Parks's skill in writing characters with hysterical humor, unwitting courage, and page-turning mystery. I hope my readers won't abandon me completely when they learn about her!"

—Terri Blackstock, *USA TODAY* bestselling author of the If I Run series

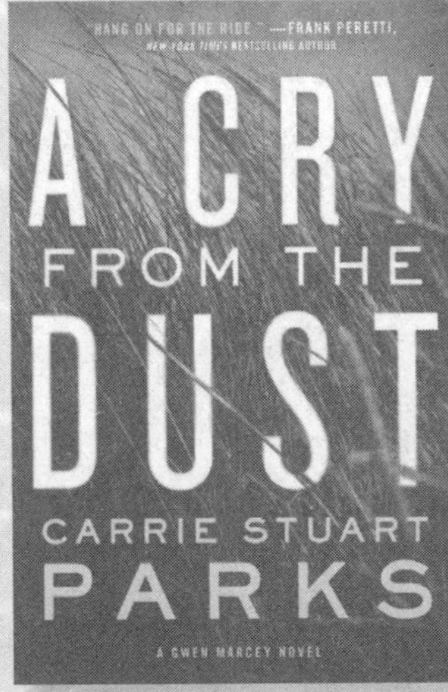

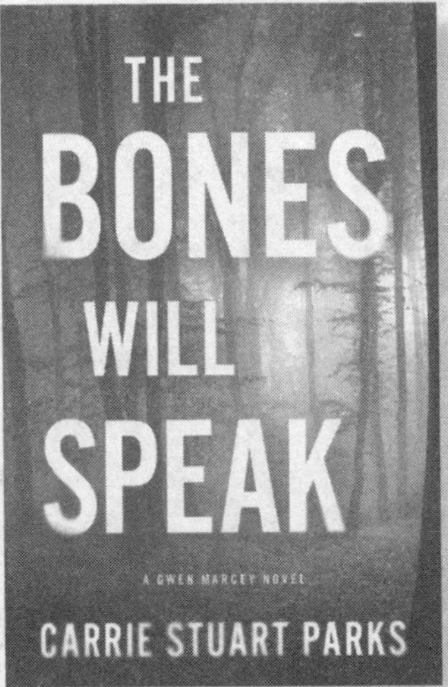

9780785226130-A

AVAILABLE IN PRINT AND E-BOOK

ABOUT THE AUTHOR

Andrea Kramer, Kramer Photography

Carrie Stuart Parks is a Christy, multiple Carol, and INSPY Award–winning author. She was a 2019 finalist in the Daphne du Maurier Award for excellence in mainstream mystery/suspense and has won numerous awards for her fine art as well. An internationally known forensic artist, she travels with her husband, Rick, across the US and Canada teaching courses in forensic art to law-enforcement professionals. The author/illustrator of numerous books on drawing and painting, Carrie continues to create dramatic watercolors from her studio in the mountains of Idaho.

Visit her website at CarrieStuartParks.com
Facebook: CarrieStuartParksAuthor
Twitter: @CarrieParks